The Plague Hunter

(2nd edition)

Bob Sanderson

DEDICATION

This book is dedicated to my wife Menna, my son Jon, and my daughter Nicola.

ACKNOWLEDGMENTS

A special thank you to my wife Menna, who has had to listen page by page to my developing story, then read it, and finally collaborate with me in battling our way through the jungle that is the rules and pitfalls of punctuation. We have arrived somewhere; it may only be a clearing rather than a final destination, but, as we sit exhausted, it is a happy place.

I would also like to thank Sonia Dixon at Walsall libraries for inspiring myself, and others, to find the writer within us and Sue Clark for her expert advice on grammar and green pen on the final proofing.

1 SURVIVAL

London – August 1665

The filthy rags wrapped and tied around his hands prevented his skin from coming into contact with the rotting flesh of the corpse as he lifted it by the armpits. He looked across into the tired eyes of William and nodded as, between them, they swung the naked body unceremoniously up onto the cart, where with a dull slapping thud, it landed onto the grisly collection of the day's unfortunate dead.

Pushing his knuckles into the small of his back he arched it to relieve his aching muscles, before pulling up higher over his nose the coarse woollen scarf that was covering the lower half of his face. It was now moist and uncomfortable, dampened by his exhaled breath, but it helped a little in masking the putrid stench of the dead, and he hoped to God that it would prevent him from joining them.

Thaddeus Cleaver had witnessed many horrors in his thirty-six years. Whilst fighting for the parliamentarians as a thirteen year old during the civil war he had seen countless broken and dismembered bodies. Yet none of his previous experiences had prepared him for the daily spectre of the limp and lifeless pallid grey corpses of men, women and children, disfigured by gangrene, and displaying the telltale buboes in the regions of their neck, armpits and groin, confirmation, as if it were necessary, of their death from the plague.

At times, Thaddeus would be required to take away not only the dead, but also the dying, and he found sleep an infrequent visitor as he couldn't banish from his mind the faces of the damned who looked at him through misting eyes set deep in already decaying flesh.

Thaddeus turned at the sound of tapping behind him to see the old woman leaning heavily on her obligatory white walking stick, which denoted her as the local searcher, hired by the parish to diagnose and report back cause of death, for which she would take a fee from the family of the deceased.

'One groat or two for this one, Mary?'

The old woman's gnarled face transformed into a toothless grin, as looking above the man's scarf, directly at his warm brown eyes, she gave him a knowing wink.

'Two groats, Mr Cleaver. He died from a nasty case of consumption, so no need to paint the door or arrange quarantine on this occasion. Unfortunately the family can't afford a funeral so that's why I wanted him up on the cart.'

Thaddeus despised corruption but he knew that the old woman had been plucked from destitution to carry out this dangerous and unenviable work, and deserved suitable compensation for her shortened expectation of life. He was amazed that any cases of the plague were actually recorded at all in the bills of mortality, as diagnosis meant that whole families would be shut up inside their homes after the victim was taken, awaiting certain death as a watchman guarded the paint daubed door to prevent any of them from leaving. An extra groat as a bribe to say that they had died from something other than the plague was a small price for the relatives to pay for a chance for them to leave and survive.

4

'I hear that St Bride's has now stopped individual burial except for the well to do, and that they've dug a pit for the poor bleedin' masses. Is that true, Mr Cleaver?'

Thaddeus began throwing a sackcloth cover over the corpses in the cart and nodded his head as he spoke in muffled tones through his scarf.

'Sadly, it is, Mary, they started using it yesterday. They say that over two thousand were put to rest last month and the count gets higher every day.'

Running his fingers through his brown fringe he gave her a final nod before climbing up onto the driver's seat of the cart next to William. He picked up the reins, and with a flick of his whip encouraged the tired old skeletal horse to strain in its harness as the iron hooped wooden wheels started to slowly gain momentum and noisily clatter along the filthy cobbles of Lower Thames Street.

It had been a very long night, and they had still yet to deposit their grisly load into the St Bride's Pit before they could feed themselves. After this they would try to get some sleep in the hovel that had been assigned to them in the churchyard, isolating them from the panic-stricken citizens of the parish. As the cart trundled towards Ludgate they saw in the distance two rakers shovelling human excrement up onto a cart for them to later deposit onto existing foul smelling heaps piled up against the outside of the city wall. When they saw Thaddeus and William the two men instinctively ducked into an alleyway, distancing themselves from the carriers of death, where they watched disdainfully from their perceived safe sanctuary as Thaddeus encouraged the horse to negotiate the narrow space between the raker's cart and a house wall. Once they had safely passed through the narrow gap Thaddeus let out a gentle laugh as he turned to William.

'You really know your worth when you get looked down upon by shit shovellers.'

The cart trundled on towards Ludgate. The gatekeepers knew Thaddeus and William now by sight and their macabre load gave confirmation as to their mission, meaning that they did not have to challenge them for passes to exit the city, and for that they were thankful. Soon they reached the open gates of St Bride's churchyard. Thaddeus urged the old horse through and onto the main pathway towards the church itself. Dawn was just starting to break which gave an eerie highlight to the mist which, thickened by smoke from the randomly placed fumigating braziers, slowly rose from between the gravestones like a thousand ghosts on resurrection day. The pathway continued around the church to a graveyard at the rear, before gently sloping away into the mist from which could be heard the sound of spades cutting rhythmically into gravely soil which, once displaced and tossed aside, fell like distant sporadic bursts of hailstones onto the growing mounds surrounding the pit.

Now being close enough to see it clearly, Thaddeus jumped down from the cart, and taking the bridle in his hand led the horse in a small circle before forcing it to take a few steps backwards, so that the rear of the cart now stood above the open pit. William stood beside him as they pulled back the sack cloth cover and pulled the corpses one by one into the freshly dug chasm where the gravediggers stood, roughly manhandling the bodies into rows before shovelling on a layer of lime, followed by a shallow covering of soil. Over the coming weeks this would continue, layer upon layer of the anonymous dead until the pit was full and work would then begin on digging another. Only God knew when it would stop.

William ladled more of the hot pottage into his bowl. Hunger had made both him and Thaddeus devoid of scruples when it came to filling their bellies, and he had managed to forage a few withering vegetables for the pot that evening from the homes of the victims. He was an affable youth of about eighteen with unruly fair hair and a round grinning face. Although Thaddeus would not call him a close friend, he could not but help like this young man with whom he spent each night engaged in ghoulish hard labour and each day cooped up in a stifling dirty hovel praying for sleep, that pray to God would be free from hellish nightmares.

'Do you ever get scared, Mr Cleaver? I mean do you think about dying, like them?'

Thaddeus sipped the thin liquid from his spoon, thought for a moment, then turned his head towards William.

'There are many kinds of death, William. Some of us die many times before they cover us up in our grave. At times I have thought that it's better to pass painfully into oblivion like the poor souls we have brought here tonight than to die quietly inside yourself. I think that scares me most of all.'

The young man looked confused. 'I don't

understand, Mister Cleaver.'

'As you get older, William, you will. Each time that life strips you of things that you hold dear, of people that you love, you die inside, and the pain isn't brief, not just a few days of agony then merciful release, but sometimes years and years of torment that eats you from within and destroys your very soul.'

'You've had bad times then, Mr Cleaver?' Thaddeus started to quietly laugh to himself.

'You could say that, William. I'm not saying that nights like tonight are good in comparison, but let's say that the life I have lived so far has prepared me well for the misery of the plague cart. And what about you? As young as you are, I'm sure you have seen things before that have made you fearful; what brought you here knowing that it could lead to a short life?'

'A short life but a rich one, that is if I survive and have a chance to spend it. Apprenticed to a butcher I was until the plague took him and his Missus. I managed to get out of the shop before the searcher came and had a red cross painted on the door, so I had my freedom, but nowhere to live. I was on the streets for about a week then I heard that they needed a new bearer due to one of them dying, and when they told me the pay, it was like I'd been blessed, Mr Cleaver, truly blessed. I know this dirty shack is no palace, but this summer well... I like dozing in the heat during the day, and then we're kept warm enough at night by working ain't we? So its better than living in the stinking gutters.' Thaddeus admired the boy's spirit but had concerns for his naivety.

'What about your parents?'

'My father died fighting for Cromwell, and my mother and sister sodded off years ago, up north I think. She took up with a pedlar and thought I would get in the way. You ask me what I have seen to make me fearful, well then, Mr Cleaver, it's poverty. After my mother left I had to fend for myself, living off my wits most days; at times beating the dogs in the street with a stick so that I could eat the scraps of food that they had found. She deserted me, Mr Cleaver, left me by the roadside with only the clothes I stood up in. I was on my own and that made me afraid, it was like I was invisible, people in the street would walk by and look right through me. It was coming on winter and I'll never forget the cold, it hurt. At night I thought I was going to go to sleep and never ever wake up. I think that's why seeing the plague dead every day makes me fearful now; they just went to sleep didn't they, and they will never wake up.'

William was no longer looking at Thaddeus but sat staring blankly, cupping his bowl in his hands as he spoke. Thaddeus poured him a mug of ale and handed it to him.

'But it all turned out alright for you, William, you got off the streets in the end.'

'Thanks to the butcher's wife. She found me with the dogs, fighting for bones in the alley at the back of the shop. She was a good soul and took me in, cleaned me up, fed me and convinced her husband eventually to take me on. I thought I'd found a great life until the plague took them; then there I was back on the streets again, but not for long eh; got money in my pocket now, Mr Cleaver. Maybe if I can save enough I can rent my own butchers shop when this is all over, I think I know enough to get started.'

'I'm sure you do, William, I'm sure you do.'

It was now daylight and the silence of the churchyard was being broken by the faint sounds of life floating across from within the city walls. Thaddeus gulped the remains of his ale and lay full stretch on the lumpy straw mattress that was his bed. He would try to sleep before the day got too hot, then, as on previous days when the sun was at its height, he would go and sit outside the tarred canvas shack and doze alongside William until, once again, night would fall, and they would both re-enter the city gates to collect the bodies of those that would never again see the sun rise.

2 MORE PRECIOUS THAN GOLD

London - August 1665

Adam Thackery lay on his side in bed, cradling in his crooked arm the head of his dying wife Emma as he tried to encourage her to take a sip of water from a stemmed wine glass. She looked much older than her 39 years as the last few pain-racked days had taken their toll and ravaged her once good looks, leaving her gaunt and waxen. As a man of some means he had sent a servant for the plague doctor a few hours earlier, and Emma now screamed in fear as the bedroom door opened to reveal the sinister figure, wearing a floor length waxed leather coat, gauntlets and a beaked hood reminiscent of a giant crow.

The nightmare vision crossed the threshold, his wide brimmed leather hat accentuating his physical presence, which seemed to dominate the room. Adam was almost overwhelmed by the mixture of aromatic smells emanating from this strange looking creature, a mixture of camphor, incense and oil. He could also detect the smell of garlic as the doctor breathed rhythmically through two holes below the eye sockets on the bronze beak, which was stuffed along its length with a mixture of herbs and spices. The doctor looked at Emma through the misty glass lenses in the hood. He could tell from his recent experiences that she was near death, but knew that he had to carry out some pointless procedures to justify his fee from this wealthy merchant. Opening his surgical bag he extracted a bowl and scalpel and proceeded to lance the buboes on Emma's neck and drain the evil smelling contents into the receptacle. Adam tried his best to both reassure his frantic wife whilst at the same time restrain her, to enable the doctor to carry out this painful procedure.

He momentarily forgot his own pain and discomfort as he watched the doctor dress the now exhausted Emma's wounds and fill a saucer with milk. Adam strained to make out the doctors muffled words as they came from within the hideous crow mask:

'The milk will absorb the poisonous air, Mr Thackery. Sadly there is no more that I can do for your wife; I fear she is near death and would not be helped by further bleeding. I shall however apply the leeches to yourself as you are not yet ready for the lance.'

The doctor took from his bag a jar containing the wriggling creatures and without removing his gauntlets clumsily applied them to Adam's body. As the leeches did their work the doctor retrieved his walking cane from where he had rested it next to the door and clasped his hands over its top, as if in prayer. Adam lay still, feeling the bite and draw from the hideous parasites that squirmed over his once well nourished body, now a sickly pale torso glistening with sweat, down which ran tiny rivulets of blood produced by the gorging worms.

Having returned the leeches to their jar, the doctor hurriedly cleaned his bowl and scalpel in the Thackery's washbasin, using water from its matching jug. He then repacked and closed his bulky leather bag.

'I have done all now within my power, Mr Thackery, and must take my leave of you. As much as it pains me to ask good sir, my payment?'

Adam waved a tired hand towards a pile of coins

on a side table. The doctor re-opened his bag and took out a jar, half full of *four thieves vinegar*, into which he expertly scooped the coins before stowing the bounty safely away.

'Good day to you, Mr Thackery, and pray God be merciful.'

The doctor opened the door and briskly swept out of the room. Adam fell back exhausted onto his pillow, and gazed at the yellowing ceiling as he spoke.

'Many will benefit and become rich due to this pestilence, Emma, they will profit from the misery of others, as I suppose in some way have we. The difference being that some will survive to enjoy their riches. So many plans my dear one, so many dreams. You have been my life my angel, and although God has not blessed us with children, I have found joy and contentment in your company alone.'

Adam rolled over onto his left side and looked at Emma. The pain had vanished from her face; maybe the doctor's procedure had delivered some benefit. She lay peacefully on her back, her eyes open, staring heavenward; she seemed somehow serene. He reached gently for her hand to express his affection and his touch was met with an icy stillness. Emma was dead.

The cart lurched heavily as the iron rim of the wheel bounced in then out of a large pothole as they entered Leadenhall Street. William grasped the hard wooden seat with both hands to steady himself, yet still fell heavily sideways against Thaddeus's shoulder. This was their second journey into the city that night, and the unusually warm air had, despite the plague, brought many people out onto the streets. The alehouses and theatres had been ordered closed in May and those of the population untouched by the plague were getting restless. Small groups were forming around doorways; despite the already sultry heat they stood or sat on stools in twos or threes around smoking braziers in the belief that sweating was efficacious. Their conversations were conducted in raised voices as they distanced themselves by a matter of feet from all but family, as if to create a firebreak from the possibility of infection. Most were smoking pipes as this had also been encouraged in the belief that the tobacco fumes kept the pestilence at bay.

On seeing the cart many started to back away into their open doorways, and most covered their noses with their hands or pulled their loose collars up across their faces. Thaddeus reined in the cart outside a substantial four-storied house; by the fine carving around the ornate door it was apparent that it belonged to someone of wealth. The first, second and third storeys projected outwards like an upturned wedding cake, as was a common sight in the city, and the white daub panels set within the black oak beams were well maintained and recently painted. There was a searcher standing by the door; at first Thaddeus thought it was Mary, but on second glance this woman was slightly younger. She raised her white stick in acknowledgement of their arrival and pulled heavily on her clay pipe before blowing out a stream of aromatic tobacco smoke.

'You must be, Mr Cleaver. Mary has mentioned you kindly. I'm Alice, only been on the job a couple of days; the parish took another two of us on this week. We've got one inside dead and one at death's door.

He's desperately holding on until he sees you; asked for you by name he has. I'd get up there quick he could go at any minute.' Thaddeus looked up at the open windows.

'Which room, Alice?'

'I'll take you up, Mr Cleaver, It's a lovely house, simple but speaks of money if you know what I mean.'

He gestured to William to look after the empty cart and proceeded to follow the woman into the house and up the narrow wooden stairs. Adam Thackery lay beside the body of his wife. In the few short hours since her death his own condition had worsened and his face was now a mask of pain and despair. His eyes looked down from the ceiling and fixed upon Thaddeus as he entered the room behind the searcher.

'Come, come,' he whispered beckoning with his fingers, too weak to raise his hand from the bed. 'I must speak with you alone.'

Thaddeus looked back at the searcher, and nodded a gesture towards the door for her to leave the room. Tightening his scarf around his face he approached the bed, and turning his face away from Adam he lowered his head so that he could hear the dying man's words.

'They call you, Cleaver? I understand that you are a good man.' Adam was struggling for breath now and his chest rose and fell rapidly.

'Are you a good Christian, Mr Cleaver?' Thaddeus nodded.

'I do consider myself to be, sir, although these days I see the outside of churches more than the inside.' Thaddeus was conscious of the scarf muffling his speech and tried to speak as clearly as he could.

'I believe in God, Mr Cleaver, and for me the Bible

is the truth. My poor wife and I have lived pious lives despite our good financial fortune, and as such we believe that we have a place in Heaven. Can you understand that, Mr Cleaver?'

'Yes, sir, there is comfort in knowing that we will meet our maker.'

'But will we, Mr Cleaver? Will we without a true Christian burial?' Adam was getting very distressed now, which was making it harder for him to speak. Thaddeus looked around and saw a glass half filled with water on the nightstand; he picked it up, and putting his rag-covered hand behind Adam's head encouraged him to sip the cooling liquid.

'I have very little time, Mr Cleaver, I do not want for my wife and I to be thrown anonymously into a communal pit. We have done nothing to deserve being cast into hell that way, do you understand?' Thaddeus nodded.

'The clergy have deserted me, Mr Cleaver. They would not dare call. My servants, save one, have fled and therefore cannot communicate my wishes, nor would they have any influence in getting them carried out. In this unholy and confused time, roles are being reversed. People once with power and authority have deserted the city, and their distance negates their worth. Forgive me, but now lowly souls such as you carry more weight in certain circles than absented kings.'

Thaddeus could see that Adam was struggling now to stay conscious, his voice was getting weaker by the second and his eyes were starting to mist over.

'What is it that you want of me, sir?'

'Mr Cleaver, I want you to ensure that my wife and I

have a true Christian burial within holy ground, and that we have a marked grave. I know that you walk with those that can arrange that, and I can now only put my wishes into place with your help. As you can see I am not a poor man, but I have no access to coin to pay you. Having no children or surviving family the house will revert to moneylenders, and what trinkets we had have disappeared with the servants. But, Mr Cleaver, what I do have is more precious than gold, and I will give it to you if you promise to God that you will arrange to have my final wishes carried out. Will you make that promise to me, Mr Cleaver?' Thaddeus looked at the dying man and felt his pain and desperation.

'I promise, sir that I will do all within my means to fulfil your wishes.'

Adam Grabbed Thaddeus's wrist with the last of his strength and with his left hand pointed to a large cabinet in the corner of the room.

'In the top drawer of that cabinet is a key. It will unlock the door of my rented warehouse by London Bridge; the address is in there too. Take what you find in the warehouse, Mr Cleaver, and may it bring you happiness in this life as long as you ensure that Emma and I find happiness in the next.' Adam's grip on Thaddeus's wrist suddenly relaxed as having fulfiled this final act of devotion to Emma he slowly exhaled his last breath.

Despite its external rusted appearance, the mechanism of the heavy iron lock moved easily as Thaddeus turned the key. He and William had delivered the corpses of the Thackerys to St Bride's,

17

and with the promise of a substantial reward, the clergy ensured Thaddeus that they would receive a good Christian burial. He was in two minds as to whether or not to involve William in the exploration of the warehouse, but decided to do so as he was unsure as to what he would find and felt that he may need some assistance in either gaining access or moving the potential treasure trove, whatever it may be. He decided to tell William very little about what had transpired between himself and Adam Thackery, and just indicated that he would make it worth his while if he gave him a hand with 'a little bit of business.'

Thaddeus opened the right hand door of the heavy double pair on the warehouse, just enough for them both to slip inside, and they stood still for a moment trying to accustom their eyes to the faint illumination produced by the early morning shaft of sunlight which spread out like a carpet onto the warehouse floor, above which floated a fine haze of dust particles. He lit a lantern as William closed the door behind them. The first thing that they noticed was the smell, a combination of the many spices that had, over time, been stored and traded within this old wooden and brick construction. The ground floor was some sixty feet wide by one hundred feet deep, and half way along the right hand wall there rose up a wooden staircase to a wooden loft which was half the warehouse depth. Reaching from the back of the warehouse to the rise of the stairs, piled up from the ground to the height of the loft floor, were bulging rough Hessian sacks, in front of which were about half a dozen large sealed barrels.

Thaddeus drew his knife from his belt and made a cut into one of the sacks taking from it a small object, which he immediately scraped with the blade and then held to his nose and smelled.

'Take a sniff, William.' He held the object towards the boy as William dutifully lowered his nose onto it.

'That's nice, Thaddeus, spicy like, but what is it?'

'My new found fortune, William, it's nutmeg.'

'Nutmeg, I've heard of it of course but never seen it before; is it valuable then?'

'Since the plague has spread, one pound of this stuff is worth as much as a trooper's daily pay. It's more valuable than gold, William, for one reason the rich believe it keeps the plague at bay. And here I am, surrounded by tons of the bloody stuff.' Thaddeus started to smile. 'Did you know that the Dutch have the monopoly on nutmeg? They keep the prices high; I learnt that when I was in Holland.'

'When were you in Holland?'

'That's another story, lad. They grow this stuff on an island called Banda in Indonesia, and just before I was born, the Dutch enslaved the islanders and massacred all men there over the age of fifteen just to keep control of the trade and to prevent the seeds being smuggled off and grown anywhere else. This little seed stone has a bloody history, but it's worth a fortune.' Thaddeus slipped the nutmeg into his belt purse and started to carry out a rough count of the sacks. By his estimation he would never have to work again; yet he wondered why with such a rich consignment Adam Thackery's house would be taken by moneylenders. Maybe he had pledged the house against a loan to purchase the shipment, a risk, but for a gambling man, at current values, maybe a once in a lifetime opportunity.

William was now halfway up the stairs as he had decided to investigate the loft, and had just stepped off the top step onto the boarded floor when a bulky figure threw itself snarling against his legs, pushing him backwards. He managed to grab the rough wooden banister rail and prevent himself from falling, but he was visibly shaken.

'Mr Cleaver!' He clung to the rail, his eyes fixed straight ahead, breathing heavily. Thaddeus raised the lantern and ran noisily up the wooden stairs to stand beside William. On the floor ahead of them, now lying on its side panting heavily, was a large dog. Around its neck was a thick leather collar, attached to which was a substantial chain, which had prevented it from furthering its attack on William. The dog was a mastiff and looked half starved; its large eyes looked demonic with the reflected glow from the lantern, but its energy was spent. Thaddeus walked towards the dog and knelt down beside it, it was too weak to resist as he gently stroked its large head.

'Thackery, must have hidden the poor creature here to avoid the culling and then got too sick to feed it. I don't think I've seen a live dog for weeks now, or even a cat for that matter; they're killing them in their thousands any way they can since the order went out, clubbing, poison, you name it. I can't see them being responsible for spreading the disease; in fact the more they kill the more human corpses we seem to be carting.'

'What are you going to do with it, Mr Cleaver, kill it?'

'No, lad, what's the point; anyway if we feed it up it can stand guard over this lot. You were lucky, William, I think it summoned its last ounce of strength to throw itself at you. I don't think you would be smiling now if it had been well fed. Go out to the cart and get those scraps of mutton from under the seat that I was saving for the pot; oh, and while you're there, grab the ale flask.' William dutifully descended the stairs and the bright shaft of sunlight reappeared as he opened the door and walked out onto the filthy street.

Thaddeus walked around the loft and it was obvious from the piles of faeces that the dog had been here for some time. The smell had not been noticeable at the lower level, and was masked by the aroma of spices, but up here it was rank. There was a small office in one corner and Thaddeus set the lantern down on a tall wooden desk and started to peruse the papers and documents that were strewn carelessly over it.

It was apparent that Adam Thackery, if not tidy, was a very good businessman. He had contracted for the sale of the bulk of the nutmeg with a wholesaler in America, and the merchant ship was due to dock on the Thames the following week where the consignment of nutmeg was due to be loaded and paid for once on board. Adam, it appears, was untrusting of banks and promissory notes, preferring to take the risk of trading with cash. This may have meant that he was planning to leave the country, but not in the wake of the plague, as the transaction would have been agreed long before the outbreak. Possibly he may have secured passage on this or another merchant ship, but there was no documentation to this effect. Thaddeus cast his eyes quickly over the documents, aided by the dim orange light from the lantern. He could not believe his luck as he turned over a paper to realise that it was a note giving the bearer title to the consignment, which had obviously been prepared in advance to enable Adam to exchange the nutmeg for money on board the ship. He also found a book in which was listed the names and addresses of apothecaries and other individuals to whom the merchant had agreed to supply smaller quantities from the main consignment. Everything Thaddeus needed for a comfortable life was here in this warehouse.

He realised that he needed to secure the documents. It would be dangerous taking them back to St Bride's as their shack was totally insecure. He could just stay here with the goods until the ship arrived, but what if for some reason the trade fell through, he would have nothing, and as horrendous as his current employment was, it kept him fed. He looked around the small office for somewhere to secrete the documents; under the floorboards was not an option as there was only one plank thickness separating the office from the storage area below. He held the lantern up at head height and it was then that he noticed a dark shelf above the office door, not an impenetrable hiding place but at least not an obvious location. He piled the papers together and laid them flat on the shelf, then weighted them down with the book. In the dim light he felt sure that no one would easily fall upon them.

William had returned with the food for the dog. Thaddeus found the animal's drinking bowl and poured some ale into it which the dog gulped down. It had managed to stand, albeit shakily, but was too weak to challenge them. The ale seemed to revive the creature enough for it to be able to eat the mutton scraps, and it even managed a wag of its tail.

'We need to get back to St Bride's, William, and get something for *us* to eat, and then some sleep; we have another busy night ahead of us carting corpses.'

'But I thought you were rich now, Mr Cleaver, why would you go back to doing that?'

'I have my reasons William, and don't worry, I won't see you go wanting. Now listen, lad, whatever you do tell no one about what you have seen here, do you understand?'

'I understand, Mr Cleaver, what are we going to do about the dog?'

Thaddeus looked across at the animal that was now lying on its stomach on the floor with its head on its crossed paws.

'We can drop by this way tonight and give it some more food, and if we can find some, clean water. Ugly looking bastard isn't it with all those warts on its face. It reminds me of Cromwell.'

'That's it, Mr Cleaver. We can call it Oliver.'

3 THE CHOCOLATE GIRL

London - March 1665

Lizzie Jephson stood nervously outside the rear door of the chocolate house; today was her first day as a chocolate girl. At seventeen she had already worked in a number of establishments as both kitchen and tavern maid but she was ambitious. On seeing the advertisement in the newly published *London Gazette,* for young ladies to wait on rich customers at the tables of one of these new fashionable establishments, she applied immediately, and possibly more because of her good looks than relative experience, she managed to get the job. She lived close by to the Bishopsgate address and had arrived early to try to make a good first impression on the French owner Monsieur Coultier.

She knocked on the door and was ushered inside by a young lady of similar age.

'You must be, Lizzie, glad to see you're early, hates tardiness does, Monsieur Coultier, makes him really annoyed it does. I'm Sally. Go through there and get your cap and apron on and then I'll show you what's expected of you.'

Lizzie walked as directed into a small room that appeared to be used for changing, as there were capes and scarves hanging from a row of pegs on the white plastered wall. On a chair in the middle of the room was a long crisp white apron, on top of which, lay a white coif cap. After pinning up her long black hair she put them on, smoothed down the apron which she had tied below her tight bodice, and walked back into the empty hallway. A door opened and Sally, with a broad smile on her friendly face, reappeared, beckoning Lizzie to follow her into the main salon. Lizzie breathed in the aroma of coffee and cinnamon and the heady smell of stale pipe tobacco. The walls of the room were panelled in oak and long tables were arranged in rows, alongside which were upholstered benches. There were framed landscape paintings on the panelling, and although it was eight o'clock in the morning, wall lamps had been lit and flickered in their holders. Sally stood with her hands on her hips, her eyes panning the room as she spoke:

'The merchants start to come in from about half past eight, some wanting nothing more than coffee and some light refreshment for breakfast, then later in the morning we get the gentry, they come in to take chocolate and will stay talking for hours. It can get a bit noisy, and you have to watch your arse with some of them; gentry they may be but gentlemen they are not.' Sally laughed as she saw the worried expression on Lizzie's face. 'I'm sure you have seen worse if you have worked in the taverns, Monsieur Coultier, won't stand for any nonsense, well from most of them anyway, well not down here.'

Lizzie looked at her inquisitively 'Down here; are there more rooms upstairs then?'

'Two more smaller salons, that's where the special customers go, private dining and private philandering, but don't tell, Monsieur Coultier, I said that. There are also a few small private rooms but we are not allowed to go in there. You'll get the hang of it soon enough; just watch out for groping hands and skirt lifting canes and you'll be fine. Now come through here into the kitchen and I'll show you where they prepare the food, coffee and chocolate.'

By nine thirty the main salon was full, and as Sally had intimated, it was vibrant and raucous. The little Frenchman stood by the ornate serving bar watching the chocolate girls come and go, as they picked up food and beverages sent through from the kitchen, and he directed their attentions to clients needs with a quick wave of his hand, a wag of a finger or a firm nod of his periwigged head. Lizzie was not as yet taking orders from the customers, but delivering the hot beverages to tables as directed by the more experienced girls. The predominantly male clientele were in the main benign and most ignored her, engrossed as they were in deep conversation. A man of about thirty, finely dressed and wigged caught hold of Lizzie's slim wrist as she placed his order on the table in front of him.

'Fruit with our chocolate now I see, the firmest of peaches if my eyes do not deceive me.'

The man kept a tight grip as he held the girl at arms length, looking her petite frame up and down whilst smirking at his companions.

'Are you juicy, my girl? Are you sweet on the tongue?' She tried to wrest herself free.

'Please, sir, you're hurting me; I have other customers to attend to.' Quick as a flash Monsieur Coultier appeared as if from nowhere.

'Unfortunately my dear, Mr Harper, some fruits are not yet in season, but as you well know the house does offer exotic spices to those with a full purse. Now, Lizzie, is new to our establishment and needs to attend to others, off you go my dear; vite, vite.'

The morning passed without further incident, yet Lizzie had been visibly shaken by the rake's unwanted attention and was wary of lingering beyond necessity within close proximity of the customers. She worked solidly until early afternoon when she was allowed a short break. As she sat on a hard wooden stool in the busy warm kitchen eating a light meal of bread and cold meats, Monsieur Coultier entered to speak with an older lady who was preparing drinks for the customers. He saw Lizzie, and picking up a jug, poured a small amount of a dark, hot liquid into a small glass before walking towards her.

'I hope that, Mr Harper, has not spoilt your day; he is not a bad man, but one who likes to foster a reputation as one who is successful in the art of attracting ladies; personally I think his actions have the opposite effect.' Lizzie just nodded coyly as she had just taken a large bite from a chunk of bread. 'As you will be serving the finest chocolate in London I thought it would be a good idea if you sampled it, it will assist you in the future in promoting its delights to our customers.' He raised the glass to the light and looked intently at the dark brown liquid. 'Did you know my dear that ancient civilisations such as the Mayans and Aztecs of the South Americas used the humble cocoa bean as currency. May I offer this exciting beverage to you, as did, the Emperor Montezuma, to, Hernando Cortez, so that you will not think ill of our establishment and its elite society.' Lizzie accepted the proffered glass and took a sip; her face grimaced at the initial bitterness on her tongue, but she sipped again and this time smiled as the fusion of cinnamon and powdered cloves started to present itself.

'I've never tasted anything like it, Monsieur Coultier, thank you, it's wonderful.'

'Wonderful it most certainly is my dear, and as you will learn, we mix the chocolate to many recipes, some well known and others a secret to ourselves. Having now tasted its delight you have some experience of what it is to be rich, do you not?' He smiled kindly at her and took the now empty glass. 'It is my desire to make *Le Puits de Chocolat* the finest chocolate house in London, and for you, it is the opportunity to serve London's elite, so if occasionally they are, how shall I say, a little forward, just smile and enjoy the privilege of attending to such fine people. Now enough of our idleness, we must both return to the salon and serve, serve, serve; off you go.'

By five o'clock Lizzie was feeling exhausted; the atmosphere in the main salon had become heady with tobacco smoke which swirled each time the main wooden door opened as customers came and went. She had little time to chat with the six other serving girls, but occasionally had the feeling that they were casting glances at her and whispering to each other.

'Lizzie, isn't it?' A plump redheaded girl had sidled up to her, and unsmiling stood looking her up and down. 'Monsieur Coultier, wants you to clear some tables upstairs, urgent like.'

'Oh, I haven't been up there yet; I've spent all day getting to know my way around down here.' Lizzie gave the girl a friendly smile, which was not returned.

'You need to go up them stairs, turn right along the corridor and it's the little room right at the end; no need to knock, just go in.' Lizzie noticed the girl look past her, over her shoulder towards a group of the other girls as she spoke, and she detected a sly grin.

'Off you go, don't hang about, Monsieur Coultier, don't like to be kept waiting.'

Lizzie slowly climbed the stairs, feeling the nervousness of a new recruit experiencing the unfamiliar. Immediately at the top of the stairs to her left was an open door into the first small salon, then to her right was a long corridor, which in keeping with the downstairs salon was oak panelled. As there were no windows, two wall-mounted lanterns illuminated it, and along its length there were four closed doors, two on either side. At the very end of the corridor was the final door, above which, on the oak surround, was a carved lion's head. Lizzie smoothed down her apron and straightened her cap before reaching for the large brass doorknob. As her fingers closed around it, the door behind her, to her right, swished open and there stood Monsieur Coultier. His expression on seeing her there was initially surprise but immediately turned to anger as he walked forward, grabbed her wrist and pulled her roughly away from the door.

'What on earth do you think you are doing girl, why are you here?' Lizzie tried to explain but he had grabbed her shoulders and was now shaking her furiously.

'You must never, never, ever come up here without my personal permission, and under no circumstances will you ever go into this room; do you understand me, you foolish girl?' He raised his open right hand as if to strike her, but snapped it shut, and then, slowly, lowered it to his side.

4 A CONTESTER

London – August 1665

Bartholomew Mobbs was not a practical man. He was a man of letters and the law. He stood in the street opposite Thackery's warehouse and pondered as to how he could gain entry to the building without a key to the large iron padlock. The thought of forcing the lock did not enter his head. Yet, he was a man of determination, and his curiosity as to what was inside had fired his desire to visit the premises in person to investigate. Some time later he walked beside Father Turnbull as they made their way briskly through St Brides's churchyard to the modest stable where Thaddeus was feeding the carthorse.

'Thaddeus, this is Mr Mobbs. He is a solicitor working on behalf of a nephew of Adam Thackery who we buried here with his wife only this morning. I don't think we have even filled in their grave yet. But it appears that the law works very quickly when the stakes are high.' Mobbs tried to exert his status by acting as officiously as possible, but in doing so only managed through his pomposity to appear comical.

'You have a key I believe, Mr Cleaver. A key that you unlawfully took from the home of the Thackerys.' Thaddeus continued to feed the horse, not looking directly at the man.

'I have a key that was given to me in good faith by Adam Thackery upon his death bed. I know nothing of the law but I do know about honour and it was his last wish that I should have it and all that it unlocks.'

'But it is not rightfully yours, Mr Cleaver. The Searcher, Alice, witnessed you rifling through drawers after Thackery had died and saw you steal the key.' Thaddeus put down the feed bucket and squared up to the solicitor.

'Mobb, is it?. Firstly, I am many things but a thief is not one of them. Secondly, Alice the searcher knows full well that it was Thackery's last request that I took it as she was standing at the door listening for the whole time that I was with him. He told me he had no family, so where has this nephew come from so quickly?' Mobbs's face adopted an air of smugness.

'Isaac Cornell is the son of Adam Thackery's sister. She is long dead, but he lives and is known to the searcher, hence the promptness of my visit. I have learnt to act with speed, as these are unusual times, Mr Cleaver and lines of succession are being terminated daily.' Thaddeus's heart sank. He was so close to good fortune only to be thwarted at the last minute. Father Turnbull touched Thaddeus's arm.

'Thaddeus, you can't argue with the law. But tell me, Mr Mobbs, is there a will naming this man Cornell as beneficiary?' The lawyer look flustered for a moment and then declared:

'Yes a will has been found. The searcher found it in the house this morning and it leaves all to Isaac Cornell.' The priest glanced at Thaddeus and then back at Mobbs.

'Well can we see it?

'Well I don't have it with me. I have it in my office for safekeeping.' Thaddeus was now getting annoyed with the man. He had felt his spirits lifted by the bequest and now he was feeling extremely anxious that it would be whisked away from him. He challenged Mobbs again.

'So, Mr Mobbs. If we can't see it, then tell us, what exactly does the will leave to his supposed nephew? You see I know what's in the warehouse because as you rightly say, I have the key.'

'All of Thackery's worldly goods, Mr Cleaver. He hasn't been specific. The will was made a long time ago.' Thaddeus picked up the empty feed bucket and stroked the horse's nose before turning back again to Mobbs.

'The key is mine, Mr Mobbs, along with all that the warehouse holds. So if you must, sue me.

Some time later Father Turnbull sat behind the oak table in the vestry. Open in front of him was a large volume of the parish records. His index finger slowly travelled from top to bottom of the page and then, wetting it upon his tongue, he used it to turn the yellowed paper to repeat the exercise upon the other side.

'The Thackerys should be in this volume somewhere unless they were incomers.' His finger stopped it's descent and then began to travel from left to right. 'Ah, here they are. Adam Thackery, born to Joseph and Eliza. It is written here that he was an only son. He hasn't, or never has had, a sister, Thaddeus. As you suspected, Mobbs is a liar.' Thaddeus moved behind the priest to peer over his shoulder at the page and like a slowly opening flower bud a smile appeared upon his face as he read the written entry.

'Bloody chancer. Can we connect him to the searcher?' The priest snapped shut the record book and walked towards the large wooden coffer where it and similar others were stored. He placed the book on the floor beside it and began to lift other volumes from the box inspecting the legend on the spines as he did so.

'Alice's name is Cartwright, but I believe that is by marriage. Bare with me, Thaddeus, for a moment.' Eventually he found the volume that he sought and placed it on the table. After a few moments he began to tap his finger on an entry. We have them, Thaddeus. We have them. Her maiden name is Mobbs. It wouldn't surprise me if they are brother and sister.'

'I wonder how many times they have tried this deception?' Thaddeus was feeling energised now by the positive news. The lawyer's attempt at fraud and the physical fatigue of his own gruesome occupation had left him in low spirits, but now he was experiencing an adrenalin rush brought on by both anger and the renewed anticipation of a new found wealth. Father Turnbull closed the book and looked up at Thaddeus with a concerned look on his face.

'You still haven't told me what is inside the warehouse. You are a good man, Thaddeus. I hope the contents are not such that they will take you along a dangerous or corrupt path.'

'Nutmeg, Father. A very precious commodity. It will make me a rich man.' The priest began to shake his head and look disparagingly at him.

'Riches. You would make profit from the very thing that is believed to keep away the plague? Surely you should make this available freely to the people.' Thaddeus had not even considered the dying masses of London. He had been swept away by the euphoria of his own good fortune.

'Do you believe nutmeg to be efficacious, Father?' The priest replied without a moments hesitation.

'Hope, Thaddeus. It gives the people hope. Whether it keeps the plague at bay or not, if the people believe in it then it will give them an alternative to despair.' Thaddeus was now desperately trying to justify his reason for selling the nutmeg, not only to Father Turnbull but also to himself.

'But there are so many old wives tales telling of cures and remedies, none of which have been proven. I have spent my entire life fighting for and defending others. And what do I have to show for it? Nothing but scars, Father. Some that are visible and some that the eye will never see. Suddenly a man gives me a future in return for a simple kindness. An opportunity for me to live a good comfortable life after so many years of experiencing carnage and destruction in the service of my country. Wouldn't you take it, Father? Wouldn't you?' The priest looked down at his now clasped hands and was silent for a moment before looking up.
'God sets us many trials, Thaddeus. I know that as a soldier your body has been put to the test many times. Maybe this is God's way of testing your soul.'

Thaddeus had not spoken much that night as he and William had loaded body after putrid body up onto the cart. As they passed through the gates of St Bride's, William grabbed Thaddeus's arm and pointed towards the direction of their tarred hovel. Normally invisible in the pitch-blackness of the churchyard, it was now swathed in light. Thaddeus pulled on the reins and brought the cart to a standstill, then both he and William jumped down from the drivers seat and began to run towards the hovel.

As they got nearer they could make out the thin figure of a man standing at the entrance holding a lantern, whilst another figure could be seen rummaging through the pairs meagre belongings in the shack.

'Isn't that Mobbs, Thaddeus?' The boy was checked in his stride as Thaddeus's strong arm grabbed his.

'Nice and easy, William. Let's just make sure we know what we are up against. There may be others.' The two watched from the shadows as Mobbs disappeared into the hovel only to exit moments later with Alice the searcher.

'Well it's definitely not there. He must have it on him.' Alice looked angry as she scolded her companion.

'If you were more of a man you would break the lock open or smash the doors down, then we wouldn't need the bloody key'. The lawyer turned on her and grabbed her face in his hand.

'Your rashness will find us undone, Alice. We don't know exactly what's in there. Until we find out we don't have a clue as to how we are going to get it out. We can't come away to arrange suitable transport if the place has been busted wide open. If you were capable of thinking things through you wouldn't be prodding corpses for a living.' The woman pushed his hand away from her face only to see out of the corner of her eye Thaddeus and William walking towards them.

'Mr Cleaver, Sir. This gentleman was looking for you so I brought him over here on the chance that you might have finished early like.' Alice looked nervous as she tried to bluff an explanation for her being there. Thaddeus stood in front of the pair, his arms folded and his feet apart.

'A family reunion, Alice? What is Mobbs here, your brother? Or a cousin maybe?' Alice, realising she was exposed responded aggressively.

'We want the key, Cleaver. Mr Mobbs here is authorised to collect it for his client under the terms of Thackery's will.'

'Ah, the non-existent nephew, Isaac Cornell. We've checked the Parish records, Mobbs. Thackery has no nephew.' Mobbs shot a glance in panic at Alice and then bolted, only to be tripped over by William to end up laying face down on the gravelled path. The woman had by now become hysterical as she threw herself bodily at Thaddeus and began to strike him. Thaddeus, not wishing to strike a woman, fended off her initial blows, but she then produced a knife and lunged at him. Being skilled in street fighting, Thaddeus side stepped and the woman, sailing past him, over balanced and fell face down onto the path. Mobbs by this time had recovered from his fall and rushed to her aid. The woman lay motionless, her head was turned to one side and her face hard pressed into the gravel. As Mobbs attempted to roll her over and lift her, he felt a warm stickiness on his hands before seeing the knife embedded in her breast. Consumed with grief the man jumped to his feet and threw himself at Thaddeus, wildly throwing untrained punches which the ex soldier fended off as if the lawyer were nothing but a child. Placing himself behind Mobbs, Thaddeus thrust his arm under the man's armpit, placing his forearm across the back of his neck to restrain him. It was then that he noticed the tell tale black buboe on the man's neck. Instinctively Thaddeus released his grip, which gave the lawyer the opportunity to slip free and stumble away into the darkness. William was about to give chase but Thaddeus grabbed his arm.

'Aren't you going to get him?'

'No point, William. He's a dead man.'

5 LOOSE TALK

London- August 1665

Thaddeus lay dozing in the shade given from a monumental gravestone outside their shack in St Bride's churchyard. There was no breeze, and the blistering heat was melting the pitch from its canvas roof, the smell of which, held static in the warm air, he found not to be unpleasant to his nostrils. William, unable to sleep in the daylight hours, had wandered off to try to purchase a jug of ale, and this time alone gave Thaddeus an opportunity to ponder on the events of the previous twenty-four hours.

They had revisited the warehouse the previous night whilst body collecting, and fed the dog from scraps left over from their own meagre meal. This had consisted of cold meat pies, which they had managed to acquire from a local butcher who, known to William, was still brave or foolhardy enough to be still serving the public. Thaddeus had coerced William to clean up the dog mess whilst he had a closer look at the rest of the goods stored in the warehouse.

Taking his knife, he set to work prising the lid from one of the large barrels that had been grouped in front of the nutmeg sacks. It took some effort as it had been well sealed, but with no heavier tools to hand he could do no more than persevere. Eventually the round wooden lid yielded to his labour and once removed, exposed tightly packed valuables, presumably from the Thackery's home. So, Adam had been planning to leave the country, or at least London. Maybe he was just escaping the plague, and was intent on following the example of the king. Charles had fled for Salisbury in July, but when an outbreak of the plague occurred there, he had decided to re-locate again, this time to Oxford, from where, in relative safety, he now received regular reports as to the declining numbers of his beleaguered subjects. The barrel was full of the trappings of wealth; silver plate had been hurriedly wrapped in fine clothes, and a gilt framed portrait of Emma Thackery had been wedged securely in place by bundles of linen. There were five more barrels to be investigated, but this wasn't the time. Thaddeus felt the warm glow experienced by those who had overnight, had a change in their fortune. The content of the barrels had now given him some quickly disposable assets.

He replaced the lid as tightly as its now damaged condition would allow, and called to William to hurry down as their night's grisly work still had to be undertaken.

'Look, Thaddeus, Oliver likes me.' William was kneeling at the top of the stairs with one arm around the mastiff's shoulder, stroking its head with his free hand. The dog had rallied tremendously since being fed and watered, and had obviously taken to its saviours.

'Come on, lad, don't get too attached as you never know, with the food shortages we may end up eating the bugger.' He laughed as William clattered down the stairs; the dog, straining at its chain in an attempt to follow him.

The night, as usual, had presented images that Thaddeus would rather forget, and now, in the churchyard, resting in the shade, he tried to shut out the vision of a child's gangrene blackened fingers clutching in death a rag doll as they had gently taken her from her distraught parents and carried her to the cart. He was abruptly brought back to the present by the sound of a heavy thud and a curse from behind him. He turned as he sat up to see William, face down on the stony path, obviously the very worse for drink. William lifted his gravel-pitted face and gave an inane grin as once again his head thudded back down onto the ground. Thaddeus got up and pulled the boy into the shack, dropping his slim yet muscular frame onto his straw filled mattress to let him sleep off the effects of his indulgence.

Hours later William slowly emerged from the hovel into the sunlight, squinting his eyes, with a pained expression on his face as he picked at the small stones embedded in his grazed cheek.

'You had fun I see.' Thaddeus gave him a patronising glance as he bit off a piece of hard bread.

'My head's been hit with a spike I'm sure of it.' William looked pale as he sat down on the grass beside Thaddeus.

'Drink has that effect you know; where the bloody hell did you get to? And I see you didn't bring a jug back for me, I'm not drinking rancid water.' William was now looking shame faced and his chest convulsed slightly as he began to vomit.

Earlier that morning William had left the churchyard intent on getting their ale jug filled. He had become the provisioner as he had knowledge of the local traders in the area from his days as apprentice in the butchers shop. Many had now vanished, either dead from the plague or having fled away from the city to less populated safe havens. Those that were still in business carried out their trade with caution, and as he approached the Angel Tavern he could see the taverner handing over a jug of ale to someone through a half opened door. With his face half covered by a scarf, the man urged the customer to drop the payment into a wooden bucket just inside the door by his feet. The coins plopped into the vinegar which quarter filled the receptacle; in exchange, the customer's replenished jug was handed over as the taverner then gestured to the next in line to hand him theirs, before closing the door to get it filled.

A brazier burned outside the tavern door filling the air with smoke, which gave the small ragged group standing around waiting to be served some false sense of protection. William adjusted his scarf as he walked over to the waiting men clutching his empty earthen pottery ale jug. He nodded a greeting and folding his arms leaned his back against the tavern wall, against which he placed the sole of his right boot. The men amiably chatted and joked amongst themselves, each waiting their turn to get their jugs filled. From their conversations he made out that most were local tradesmen, now short of work and with time on their hands. William waited patiently, tasting the smoke from the brazier as it eventually permeated the fabric of his scarf. The morning chill was now giving way to the sun, which was beginning to shine onto the street from between the overhanging stories of the black and white wooden buildings. A sudden movement caught his eye as a group of four large men stepped out from an alleyway and started to walk towards the tavern.

They were loud and coarse and their attitude made William feel slightly threatened. William was obviously not alone in his perception of the newcomers as the original group of customers backed away from the door as the new arrivals started to pound on it.

One of the men at the back of the group glanced over at William as if he recognised him.

'Don't I know you, lad? Your girlie locks seem familiar.' William felt uncomfortable and was sure that there was going to be trouble, yet he mumbled out a reply through his scarf:

'I don't think so, mister, I mainly come out at night, I wouldn't come too close if I was you, I'm a body bearer.'

'That's where I know you from, the pit at St Bride's, we're diggers. Hey, lads this one's one of us.' The door of the tavern slowly opened and the leader of the group pushed his way roughly past the startled owner.

'Gentleman, please we are closed except for sales off premises. It's not my fault, as you know it's now the law.' The rest of the group had now piled through the tavern door and their leader looked around totally ignoring the innkeeper's pleas.

'Laws don't apply to us do they, lads? Go fill us some jugs, and bring us something solid to fill our bellies; I think this room will do us nicely.' As William stood outside the tavern looking in at the poor man's plight, the digger he had been speaking to stepped back outside, put his arm around William's shoulder and pulled him inside through the door.

'Come on, lad, you're with us now; we all stick together. We're like the living dead ain't we; none of us might be here tomorrow. We could all be passengers on your cart, so today we get pissed, right?' The man gave William a friendly smile, which put him at his ease as he sat down with the group at a rough table. The innkeeper returned with two large jugs of ale and some mugs, and then started to leave with a promise to return with cold cuts and bread. One of the group called after him: 'Keep the ale coming it will take all you've got to get rid of the taste of St Bride's.'

'And Newgate.' Chipped in Williams's new friend. They all started to laugh as they quickly downed their first drink and proffered their empty mugs to their leader for a refill.

'So how long have you all been gravediggers?' William was now feeling more relaxed in their company and the first effects of the ale were slowly starting to kick in.

'We've been digging our own graves all our lives, haven't we, lads?'

'One way or another,' one of them replied. They all laughed at him and then carried on their separate conversations, their loud voices sporadically giving way to more bursts of laughter and mimicry as they entertained each other with bawdy tales.

'I'm Samuel, by the way, that's all you need to know; men with pasts we are, and maybe no futures. Have you lost family to this bloody pox?'

William looked at the big man whose broad open face and hairless head gave him the appearance of a giant baby.

'Not family, but a few acquaintances.' He then went on to tell him about his time with the butcher and his experiences living on the streets.

The Innkeeper had returned and Sam started to

devour hungrily the thick slices of cold meat washed down with the never-ending supply of ale.

'We were all in prison together; all innocent of course.' He shot William a knowing grin.

'They gave us a choice, stay locked up until we died from prison fever or dig pits in the open air until we die from the plague. At least this way we get to see the sunshine and get pissed. So, no contest really.'

'Aren't they afraid you'll run away?'

'They take a chance of course, but like yours I'm sure, the pay is good, so they hope we'll make the most of the situation and live a merry life, albeit possibly a short one.'

William by now was starting to slur his words slightly and he felt very relaxed as he ate his share of the simple meal, listening to Sam, and taking in the snippets of conversation coming from the others.

'I'm going to be a butcher' he suddenly blurted out, staring straight ahead, trying to focus his eyes on the empty jugs littering the table.

'If I survive, I'm going to have my own shop. I've got the money you know; well almost, but when Thaddeus trades the nutmeg he's gonna see me alright, he said so; he's my mate you know.' The conversation of the others suddenly started to diminish as they all looked at the drunken boy slowly sliding lower and lower down into the wooden settle on which he was sitting.

'Tell me about the this nutmeg then?' Sam looked at the others as he spoke, raising his eyebrows and cocking his head to draw their attention to William.

'It's a secret.' William was slowly closing his eyes with a big satisfied smile on his face.

'But we're your mates, you can tell us; is it a lot of nutmeg or just a few seeds?'

'As Thaddeus says, "there's tons of the bloody stuff." Going to set us up for life. But sssshh don't tell anybody though.' William now started to giggle to himself as he placed a finger to his lips. 'It's a secret.'

Sam put his arm around the boy's shoulders and ruffled his hair, as smiling, he looked across the table to the group's leader.

'Did you hear that, Ned? It's a secret.'

6 TO THE BEARER

London – August 1665

Under normal circumstances, Captain Abraham would have sought lodgings ashore, but hearing from the quay owner that the plague was present, and its death toll increasing daily, he decided to confine himself and his crew to the ship. He had navigated the vessel through the Pool of London, which was less busy than he had seen on his previous visits, before securing her in one of the twenty legal quays near the Tower of London. He was not yet sure how he was going to unload his cargo of tobacco without endangering his crew. Since the outbreak of plague, the value of the cargo had probably doubled whilst they were at sea as even children were now being encouraged to smoke to ward off the disease.

He felt for the crew who had been cooped up on this creaking vessel for many months. Many of them had families in London, and now, on hearing of the outbreak of the plague, were desperate to find out if they were alive or dead. They had assembled on deck and stood around noisily as they waited for their captain to address them. As he came out onto the stern castle of the old caravel the men fell silent.

'Gentlemen, you have doubtless heard by now of the plight affecting the citizens of London. I am informed that the death toll from this plague, which is of the type known as bubonic, is in the many thousands and rising daily.' The men started to speak noisily amongst themselves.

'What about our families?'

'Are we safe going ashore?'

The men started to fire random questions at him voicing loudly their obvious concerns.

'Gentlemen, please. I appreciate your concerns as they mirror my own. All I can say is that whilst we are on board this ship and not in contact with the land based population we are safe. I realise that many of you have family within London, wives, children, and that your concern is for their well-being. Should you decide to leave this ship to be with them I completely understand. But what *you* must understand, is that I cannot, for the safety of the rest, let you return on board this ship.' The men once again turned to each other and started to discuss noisily what the captain had said. He stood for a moment watching the anxious men below, and then raising his voice above the cacophony continued:

'Gentlemen, although I have a responsibility towards you, I also have an obligation to carry out the duties for which I was hired by the owners. We have a cargo to offload, and should it all arrive in the next few days, a cargo to take onboard after which, with a certificate of good health, we shall set sail once again for the Americas and can sleep easy knowing that we will have left the pestilence behind us. If you leave this ship in vast numbers we will be unable to recrew from the dockside as I am not prepared to take the risk of letting the disease on board. This will mean that we will be unable to set sail, and will have to remain on board at this quayside until such times as the plague is considered passed. This action, gentleman, will ruin us all financially, as the owner I'm sure, will not pay wages for a job incomplete, so think hard. I am trying to be unusually democratic in my actions, but in these extreme circumstances, as a Christian, I feel that I have to give you a choice. I will be in my cabin for the next hour; those wishing to leave, assemble here on deck during that time and I will get you signed off the ship's register and wish you well. The rest of you may take recreation on board whilst I consider my options for getting us paid. Good morning, gentlemen.' He turned briskly and made his way back to his cabin where he poured himself a large brandy and sat deep in thought at his small desk.

This was not the way to conduct business, but with the threat of the plague, Captain Abraham could not allow anyone to board his ship. He walked halfway down the gangway, and placed carefully in the centre of the wooden boards a small wooden box containing a banker's draught from a spice dealer in America. He then retreated to the top of the planked walkway, where he turned to watch two well dressed men alight from inside a horse drawn coach from which, they pulled a small but heavy looking chest. The men carried the chest between them up the gangway, and set it down in front of the small box deposited there by Captain Abraham.

'I apologise for my lack of hospitality and the unconventional manner in which we are conducting business, but as I am sure you appreciate, I can allow no one on board my ship, for in doing so, we would not be allowed to set sail for our return voyage to the Americas.'

One of the men unbound the scarf from across his nose and mouth, and looked up towards the captain.

'These are unconventional times, my dear sir, yet business must carry on lest we all die as beggars.' He gestured toward the small wooden box. 'The banker's draught I assume, may I?' The captain nodded his approval and the man knelt down and extracted the document from the box, and then proceeded to read it intently. 'All seems to be in order, now if you wish to count the gold?'

'Please, gentlemen, if you would kindly retire from the gangway I will have the chest brought aboard unopened. Your bank has a solid reputation built on trust, so I will not dishonour you by making you wait as we count its contents; I will leave that task to the merchant when he delivers the shipment for which this is payment.' The banker looked across to his colleague and whispered.

'If not for the pox he would bite every coin.' He turned his eyes again to Captain Abraham. 'Thank you for that compliment, we shall take our leave of you now and pray that you have a safe return voyage.' At that, the two men returned to the carriage. The driver sharply cracked his whip, and the two well-groomed horses broke into a trot pulling the vehicle noisily over the cobbles back towards the city.

It had taken two days for the ship's crew to unload the consignment of tobacco, which now sat under canvas on the dock. The redundant quayside loaders stood by idly at an enforced distance, watching the sailor's exertions, occasionally jeering at any little slip, and feeling bitter that their livelihood had been impacted by this overcautious seafarer. The transfer of banker's draught and title had been conducted in similar fashion to that of the gold, and the captain felt comfortable that this unorthodox system of exchange would be an adequate protection for himself and the remainder of his crew.

Nearly half of the ship's crew had signed off, deciding to take their chances in the city with their families. This would make any voyage out into open waters impossible, as the large square-rigged sail needed many hands in its management. Captain Abraham had given much thought to his dilemma, and had decided that once he had taken his new cargo onboard he would leave the Pool of London and try to dock again near the estuary of the Thames, well away from the city, where he could take on un-contaminated supplies and healthy replacements for his departed crew members.

Thaddeus knew that he didn't have long to shift the nutmeg. By his reckoning it would take three sturdy wagons to transport the sacks down to the quayside. Their hire would not come cheap, especially with drivers, but he had little choice as although he had the use of the plague cart, it was not adequate for this task, and he could not afford the time to make multiple trips. William was now feeling better after his over indulgence, and they sat in the late afternoon sunshine amidst the gravestones.

'Get all the rest you can, lad, we have a busy time ahead of us, but if all goes well, tonight will be the last time we drive the plague cart.'

'Will I have enough money for my butchers shop, Thaddeus?'

'That, and more, lad. If you buy now while the city shakes in its boots, you will buy cheap. Then, when we see the end of this pox and things get back to normal you will own a valuable business, and I know it will end, William, just like I saw in Amsterdam. The ship should have docked by now, the *Crimson Star* down at Addison's quay, it will be there for many days, unloading and loading. First thing tomorrow, we get down to the carter's and hire some wagons with drivers, then get the bulk of the nutmeg down to the ship. Tomorrow night the only sore head you will have will be from counting money.'

The relative silence at the water's edge was shattered as three large wagons rumbled from between a row of small warehouses onto the cobbled quayside. Captain Abraham watched as despite the heat, two men clothed in rough hooded capes and with half covered faces, jumped down from the driver's seat of the lead wagon and walked towards the ship.

'Stop there. Are you the merchant, Thackery?' The captain stood with authority at the head of the gangway, looking down at the men.

'Thackery is dead, but we have his note giving us title to these goods. We understand that you have payment for us ready in gold, is that correct?'

'Aye, sir, if as you say you have title. I cannot unfortunately allow you on board, but bring the note halfway up the gangway, weight it down, and I will inspect its authenticity.'

The captain watched as the man, holding tightly onto the roped support, slowly walked up the wooden boards, bent down, and placed the note against a cross braced tread before placing on top a large stone that he had picked up from the quayside, before turning and walking back to his companion. Captain Abraham walked down to the note, lifted it from beneath the stone, and read its contents.

'It all seems in order. Please get your men to unload the consignment onto the quayside from where my crew will carry it on board later. Meanwhile, gentlemen, I shall bring to you your payment.' The captain nodded to two burly sailors who were standing at his side, and they proceeded to carry the heavy wooden box left by the bankers down to the halfway position on the gangway. The two hooded men ran up to retrieve it, and after slowly manoeuvring the box down the narrow walkway they set it carefully down on the ground, where one of them raised the lid. The man stood up, and both he and his companion lowered their hoods and unwound the scarves from around their faces.

'I will count it later, but tell me, captain, we carry certificates of health, how much would you charge us for passage to the Americas?'

Captain Abraham considered the prospect carefully. His eyes fell on the open chest as the sun glinted on its contents, then he looked into the faces of the two men standing over it. Both were in their late thirties. The leader was a thin swarthy looking individual with a disfigurement around his right eye and temple. His colleague was more heavily built and his broad open face and hairless head gave him the appearance of a giant baby.

Thaddeus pushed the half open warehouse door. The old iron lock had been hammered, and pieces of it lay strewn on the cobblestones. Inside, in the half-light, he saw that the contents of the warehouse had been taken; even the barrels were gone. He lit the lantern and made for the stairs, almost falling over the body of a man lying twisted on the floor at the foot of the narrow wooden staircase. Stepping over him, Thaddeus ran up the stairs to be greeted by the sight of Oliver lying motionless on his side. The big mastiff had been stabbed to death; his large head lay in a pool of blood and dark sticky footprints lead off to the small office. He ran into the room and immediately felt above the door for the documents, but as he suspected, they had gone.

William was kneeling on the floor by the injured man as Thaddeus ran back down the stairs.

'The bastards have taken the lot, documents and all. Is that one still alive?'

'Just about; looks like Oliver went for him.' William lifted the man's head by his hair and gulped as he recognised him as one of the diggers from the tavern. From his contorted position on the floor it looked as if his back was broken, and now slowly coming out of unconsciousness he started to groan in agony.

'The dog's dead, William.'

'Bastard'. William slammed the man's head hard onto the floor as Thaddeus put his foot on the man's back and pressed down hard causing him to scream out in pain.

'Where have they taken the stuff?'

'To the quayside, help me, help me please.' The man was in no shape to lie or deceive, so Thaddeus carried on pressing with his foot.

'Who should I be looking for? Who's the bastard in charge?' The man screamed as his face contorted into a hideous mask of pain.

'Ned. Ned Bennet.'

Thaddeus stepped back from the man and grabbed the stair rail behind him to steady himself; the colour had drained from his face.

'You alright, Thaddeus? Do you know this Ned Bennet then?'

'Know him, William? I thought that I had killed him.'

7 LE PUITS DE CHOCOLAT

London- April 1665

It had been some four weeks now since Lizzie had first come to work at the chocolate house, and despite her cruel inauguration by the other chocolate girls she had settled in well, and was thoroughly enjoying the work. Monsieur Coultier had soon realised that Lizzie had been sent up to the forbidden room by her co-workers, and had made sure that their lives were made difficult for a few days; for although he had no interest in any horseplay that the girls undertook amongst themselves, he was adamant that no one should enter the small rooms on the first floor.

It was around 10:00am when Monsieur Coultier approached Lizzie in the main salon, and took her to one side.

'Lizzie, my dear, a moment if you please. This afternoon I will need you to wait tables in one of the first floor salons; I think that you are now ready. Young Sally has failed to arrive this morning; very unlike her. I will expect you to be at your best, and also to be discreet as we reserve these salons for the elite. You will possibly see some very important people, and maybe even those that are fashionable or famous. Under no circumstances look surprised at them or what they do; I want you to act as if you mix with people of their status every day, which of course now you do. Now run along and report to me in the kitchen at one o'clock.' He clapped his well-manicured hands and ushered Lizzie to get back to work.

At the appointed time the little Frenchman

outlined Lizzie's duties to her, which consisted mainly of waiting table as she had done previously, but with the addition of taking orders back to the kitchen. She was given a new apron and cap which were both delicately edged with lace denoting her, and the service that she now delivered, as being a step up from that found in the lower floor salon. She realised that she had not at any time seen these so called elite enter the chocolate house via the main door as none of the faces were known to her, and she would over the previous weeks have seen them come in and go upstairs if they were regulars. It was then that she realised that one of the doors along the panelled hallway led to another staircase, at the bottom of which was a door leading to the street at the back of the building.

The clientele was very different in these two rooms. The men were finely dressed and wigged, but to a much richer standard than those in the salon below. There were also many more women, elegantly dressed, most of whom sat around in small groups laughing amongst themselves, whilst casting non-discreet glances at the many groups of gentlemen who did likewise. In the blue salon at the top of the stairs, where Lizzie was assigned, one particular lady stood out from the others, as she was the only woman sat amongst a group of standing men. She was in her early thirties, classically attractive and wearing a beautiful gown cut low at the shoulders, which emphasised a necklace of precious stones, the like of which Lizzie had only dreamed of. She was very much holding court with the gentlemen who were posturing and competing for her attention. As the afternoon progressed, Lizzie made countless trips back and forth, taking orders from the salon to the kitchen and returning with glasses of spiced chocolate, coffee or glasses of wine. She was also instructed by Monsieur Coultier to move amongst the guests with a large silver tray, upon which sat delicate sweetmeats and fancies which the assembled ladies and gentlemen took when proffered and popped into their mouths, mostly without a second glance at Lizzie.

She approached the group of standing gentlemen amongst whom the fine lady sat, and as taught, tried to discreetly catch the eye of the individuals while smiling and offering the food from the tray. As she did so, one of the men took a step backwards, wildly waving his arms as he animated a story to his fellows, and as a consequence, struck the tray from underneath, sending it hurtling up into the air. Lizzie stood open mouthed as the food flew from the tray in a prescribed arc as if in slow motion, to land in the lap of the seated woman, who immediately jumped to her feet and screamed. Without exception everyone in the salon turned towards the noise emanating from the startled woman, who proceeded to launch herself in a frenzied attack on Lizzie, punching and kicking the poor girl to the ground. Lizzie instinctively covered her head with her hands as the woman rained blows and kicks upon her, whilst screaming abuse at the top of her voice. Two of the attending men set about pulling her as delicately as possible away from Lizzie, and then distracted the woman's attention by attempting to brush down her gown as a third member of the assembled group swept Lizzie up and rushed her out into the corridor.

'Are you alright, girl?' Lizzie did not look up but

stood cradling her face in her hands, still in shock.

'Mrs Fitz-Herbert is known by most to have a very fiery temper as unfortunately you have now experienced.' The man's voice was soft and comforting, and Lizzie found his tone quite hypnotic. She slowly raised her head, at the same time lowering her hands and looked up into the stranger's eyes. Framed by the curls of his periwig his smiling face was very pleasing to the eye and his steely blue eyes seemed somehow to draw her in. He raised his hand and gently with a lace handkerchief, wiped away a small trickle of blood from a small cut on her lip.

'Thank you, sir, you are very kind.'

'You did nothing wrong, girl, that oaf Carlisle should have watched where he was going. I'm Richard Valletort and I will be quite prepared to speak in your defence to Coultier as I'm sure he will come down on the side of Mrs Fitz-Herbert. He will do as I say so have no fear for your position here.'

Lizzie composed herself and thanked the man before making her way downstairs and into the kitchen where she sat nervously on a stool unsure of what to do next in anticipation of a reprimand or worse from Monsieur Coultier. Very soon the kitchen door opened and a very excited Emily, one of Lizzie's co-workers, entered the room and made straight for her.

'Oh there's been ructions upstairs, Lizzie, from your Mrs Fitz-Herbert; she right tore into Monsieur Coultier she did. I think she wanted you hanged at least, and I think he would have obliged her to save face if it hadn't been for Mr Valletort. He explained in no uncertain terms how it wasn't your fault, and said that he and his circle would stop coming if Monsieur

Coultier took any action against you. He even went so far as to say that you should be paid extra for today's work in compensation for the distress that Mrs Fitz-Herbert caused you. She just looked at him and stormed out of the salon like a ship in full sail with three or four rakes fawning after her.'

'Emily, I feel terrible, it wasn't my fault; I thought that dreadful woman was going to kill me. If it wasn't for Mr Valletort I think she very well may have. Who is he?' Emily gave Lizzie a knowing wink.

'Lovely ain't he. He is always the perfect gentleman, even when the other men are being lewd with the ladies or start acting like buffoons he always stands apart, distances himself like. He just stands there like a handsome god, impeccably dressed; just sort of, well lovely. He could have me across one of those tables any time.' Lizzie feigned a shocked gasp.

'Emily Harris, you'll lose your place in heaven speaking like that, but what does he do?'

'Well nothing really, some say that he is a close friend of the King, but he has no title. Rumour is he lived abroad for a while after the war and came back at the same time as Charlie, but all in all he is a bit of a mystery. You've taken a shine to him haven't you?'

Lizzie felt her face start to flush.

'His voice is like, it's like, oh I can't explain, but when I looked into his eyes….'

Emily started to laugh. 'You're smitten my girl, but be careful, don't spend your life wanting what you can't have; it'll only end up in tears. Anyway Monsieur Coultier wants you back upstairs to clear tables in both rooms; best not keep him waiting.'

'Best not I suppose. But, Emily, Mrs Fitz-Herbert, I

need to be careful around her from now on; how important is she?'

'In the scheme of things not very, but she does have some important admirers. Her husband is a Colonel, away at the moment preparing to make a stand against the Dutch, while she plays the Queen around London, stroking the stand of any man wealthy enough to afford her, if you take my meaning. Best be careful of her, but go on now or you won't have a job where she can bother you.'

Lizzie was apprehensive as she opened the door of the upstairs blue salon in which she had earlier encountered the extreme displeasure of Mrs Fitz-Herbert. She was concerned that she would be stared at when she entered the room, but she need not have worried, as these people were in the main self-obsessed. She found herself looking around the room hoping desperately to catch sight of her saviour, but Richard Valletort was nowhere to be seen.

As late afternoon approached, and both salons started to slowly empty, the elite clientele began to noisily make their way along the corridor and leave the building via the back staircase. Lizzie knew that she still had an hour or two ahead of her in which to tidy the rooms in preparation for the evening trade. She cleared empty glasses onto a tray from the blue salon, and then walked out into the hallway to see the last of the customers disappearing through the far door. As she passed the green salon to her left, its door suddenly opened inwards, and framed in the doorway was the man she had encountered on her first day at *Le Puits de Chocolat*, the man, that Monsieur Coultier had referred to as Harper.

'Ah, the girl with the beautiful peaches.' Harper grabbed her arm with his right hand whilst supporting the tray that she was carrying with his left as he pulled her back into the salon. But for them, the room was now empty.

'Now, my girl, you and I have unfinished business.'

8 AN OLD ADVERSARY

London - September 1659

Captain Benjamin Henderson slowly dropped the coins held in the palm of his hand into his purse. Eight shillings; this was not a lot to show for his loyalty to Cromwell. Since January he had only received one month's pay, and the army was close to waging war upon itself as disputes between the generals were dividing loyalties. That day an opportunity had arisen for him to make a little money on the side, and he had sent for one of his most trusted men to undertake a simple mission of private enterprise.

There was a sharp knock on the door of his small office, and he called to the waiting soldier to enter the room.

'Sergeant Cleaver, I have a job for you, sit down and listen well.'

The stocky young sergeant pulled out the simple wooden chair, brushed back his Venetian red coat and sat down. He wasn't sure why he had been summoned, and was suffering from an apathy spreading through the ranks brought on by the uncertainty of not knowing whether Cromwell's New Model Army would survive the turmoil it was currently going through. Cromwell's son Richard had taken on the title of Commander in Chief the previous year after his father's death, but was not held in high regard by the men, and since April, when Richard was deposed by a military junta headed by Lieutenant General Fleetwood, it was becoming obvious that there were politicians who were seeking its dissolution.

Sergeant Thaddeus Cleaver, like his compatriots, had grave concerns for his financial future. Soldiering since the age of thirteen had not made him financially secure, and much time was currently spent in barracks and taverns dreaming up schemes that would put food in his belly in the short term, and provide for him a home and comfortable life in the future. Sitting back in his chair, Captain Henderson spread out his long legs. On the table in front of him lay the remains of a cold sparse meal and he toyed with a knife that he had taken from the battered pewter trencher.

'Sergeant Cleaver, I know you as a man that can be trusted.'

'Thank you, sir, I...'

'Don't speak, man, just listen.' He held the knife suspended between the thumbs and forefingers of both hands, slowly twirling it around.

'An opportunity has come my way to, how shall I say, take on some private security work for a very rich client. If this proves to go well and without incident, it could lead to further work of this nature for the right men. Do I have your attention so far?'

'Yes, sir, very much so.' Thaddeus leaned forward in his chair parting his legs and placing one hand on his knee while his forearm loosely rested on the other; he listened intently.

'Good, I thought that I might. As you know under the Navigation Acts, goods from the Americas may only be imported into this commonwealth on English ships. Unlike my silver spooned Royalist counterparts who could buy their rank, I was elevated to captain from a background which saw me working for a merchant; thank God for the meritocracy of

Cromwell's army eh! An acquaintance of mine from my previous life is a Dutch ship owner who wishes to transport goods to and from the Americas under an English flag, and as you can imagine, to arrange such a thing will mean that he will have to grease quite a few palms in the custom houses. This will require him to move a large amount of gold around the city. Fortunately bullion is excluded from the Navigation Acts, so one of his ships can legitimately dock with such a consignment.' Thaddeus raised his eyebrows.

'I see that now I really have your attention, Sergeant Cleaver. The gentleman is quite rightly nervous of transporting the gold from the relative safety of his own ship to the rendezvous with the bent officials, so he has approached me to provide an armed escort for the short journeys, for which, in return he is prepared to pay a reasonable sum, a proportion of which I will pay to the armed escort. I would like you, Sergeant Cleaver, to recruit and lead that escort, which I want you to select personally, but only from trusted men who have proved their worth. I would think about six in total including yourself.' Thaddeus let out a low whistle.

'That is an opportunity, but not without its risks of course; when will this take place, sir?'

'His ship is due to dock from Amsterdam in three days time, so you do not have long to recruit some good men. Needless to say this conversation has not taken place. I will arrange for you to receive payment from which, as I said, you will pay your men; I want no contact with them at all, is that understood?'

'Yes, sir, totally understood.'

'Good, I know I can rely on you, Sergeant Cleaver,

now go and select your men; I will give you details of the ship and timing the day before it docks.'

Thaddeus stood up, saluted and left the room. This was an opportunity he had not foreseen, and one that could deliver a positive outcome to his current financial concerns.

Simon Wainwright, John Jephson, David Hawkins, Robert Potter and Thomas Wright had all proved their worth as troopers in the New Model Army, and although they were somewhat rough and ready individuals, Thaddeus had no doubt that they were honest, and like him hungry, hungry enough to take a risk carrying out a private mission that could put their lives in danger. Thaddeus sat at an oak planked table in a tavern close to Tower Hill, waiting for his men to arrive. He was not in uniform, but had selected clothes from his meagre wardrobe that gave him an air of authority, dark brown breeches, and a simple white shirt over which he wore a long leather waistcoat with his sword belt across his shoulder. He had also tucked into his breeches a loaded pistol.

One by one the men began to arrive and joined him at the table. First were Robert Potter and John Jephson. John was a good family man who couldn't wait to get back to his old job as a boot maker; his skills had often been put to use keeping the troopers in marching order, and he and Thaddeus had shared both good and bad times together over the last few years. David Hawkins and Thomas Wright were next to enter the tavern and help themselves at Thaddeus's invitation to a mug of ale from the jugs in front of him. These two were inseparable friends, not great thinkers, but took orders well without question. After five minutes or so of general conversation Thaddeus quizzed the others as to the whereabouts of Simon Wainwright. It was unlike him to be late; although he had a reputation as a reveller he had never been known to let Thaddeus down.

As they chatted amongst themselves the tavern door opened and a thin swarthy looking man entered, looked around, and finally approached them.

'Is anyone of you, Thaddeus Cleaver?' The man had a surly attitude as uninvited he picked up a mug and started to fill it.

'And who might you be?' Thaddeus replied. He didn't like the look of this man who gulped back the ale from the mug in one motion.

'I was sent here by Simon Wainwright, he's somewhat indisposed at the moment; he got drunk last night, got into a fight and got his leg broken. He was concerned about letting you down so he asked me to take his place. He mentioned escort duty or something; he said Cleaver would pay me, is that right?' Thaddeus looked the man up and down. His clothes were none too clean and slightly tattered.

'Are you army?' Thaddeus looked straight into the man's narrowed eyes and awaited a reply. The man sniffed and reached out again for the ale jug, but Thaddeus grabbed his hand and held it pressed against the jug's handle.

'Used to be, we fell out, you know how it is, but I can handle myself if needs be; I've been around a bit if you know what I mean.' The man gave a half smile, which made him look all the more sinister. Thaddeus had taken an instant dislike to the man but had little choice.

'It's bad news about Wainwright but I promised an escort of six and I really don't want to let the client down. If you can behave yourself, act like a soldier and take orders from me you're in.' The man nodded,

'That won't be a problem as long as I get my money when it's over.'

'You will if you do your job and do as I say, What's your name?' Thaddeus released the man's hand, which he quickly withdrew and rested on top of the handle of his sheathed sword.

'It's Bennet, Ned Bennet.'

Frederik Evertsen sat on the hard ship's bunk as he tied his stacked heel shoes. He was a short red-faced man, overweight and unfit, but at the age of fifty-four he had a strong drive and determination to add to his already considerable wealth. He looked across the small cabin at his daughter Catharina, who although small in stature like her father, looked nothing like him. She was slim, elegant and incredibly beautiful. He had built his shipping business up from nothing, letting no one or anything stand in his way; consequently he had no qualms at all about bribing English custom officials to enable his ships to operate as English vessels at a time when England was doing all it could to diminish Dutch trading around the world.

Frederik had decided to let Catharina accompany him on this trip to give her some experience of the business, that one day, he hoped she would take over and control. He also thought that her good looks would soften the hearts of the custom officials, and distract them as he negotiated their *under the table* fees. They had arrived from Amsterdam the previous afternoon. Catharina had been given the small passenger cabin which she had found somewhat spartan, and Frederik commandeered the captain's, leaving the poor deposed seaman feeling extremely put out as he had now been forced to bunk in with the first mate.

Frederik went up on deck and stood looking out over the quayside with his arms outstretched, his hands holding on to the ship's rails impatiently drumming with his fingers. Two men on horseback came into view followed by a large carriage with a further two men on the driver's bench seat and yet another two standing on a platform at the rear. Precisely on time he thought, a good start to the morning's business. Thomas Wright reigned in the carriage horses, and Thaddeus jumped down from where he had been seated next to him to make his way towards the ships gangway. Thaddeus walked up the wooden structure and extended his hand in a greeting to Frederik who now stood at its top.

'Mr Evertsen. My name is Thaddeus Cleaver; you are expecting my men and I.' Frederik responded in thickly accented English:

'Mr Cleaver, you come highly recommended by my good friend Benjamin Henderson, or should I say Captain Henderson. War changes many things, especially the title by which a man is known, but hopefully not the essence of the man himself; Benjamin and I shared much in happier times, Mr Cleaver. Come, please follow me to my humble cabin and I will instruct you in the detail of the day.'

Thaddeus followed a few paces behind up onto the stern castle, and ducking his head entered the low, dim cabin. His eyes quickly adjusted to the poor light, and his gaze immediately fell and lingered for much too long on Catharina.

'Mr Cleaver, my daughter, Catharina, she will be joining us today as I am instructing her in the ways of my business for I get no younger, and one day I would like to think that she will take over from me and treat me kindly in my old age.' He laughed as he gestured for Thaddeus to be seated. He and Frederik sat around the captain's small table whilst Catharina made herself comfortable sitting on the bunk.

'Some wine, Mr Cleaver?'

'Thank you, sir, but no, I need to keep a clear head.' Frederik nodded approvingly

'Very commendable, I see you take your duties seriously.'

'I consider myself to be a professional, sir, and conduct myself accordingly.' Catharina shot a glance at her father, nodded slowly, and smiled.

'Well, as you know, Mr Cleaver, I have payments to make to certain people today to further my business; this will involve the transportation of a large sum of gold coin to three specific destinations within the city. I have no reason to suspect any form of incident, but with the sums involved it always pays to err on the side of caution, I'm sure you will agree.'

'Most definitely, sir, rest assured that your coin and your persons are in safe hands.'

Catharina looked across at Thaddeus and met his gaze as she spoke:

'I'm convinced that your hands are safe and strong,

Mr Cleaver, but what of your men?'

'I can vouch for them all madam; I can and have trusted them all many times with my own life.' Thaddeus immediately turned his thoughts to Bennet, for as soon he had spoken the words he realised that this man was an unknown quantity.

'Then there is no more to be discussed, Mr Cleaver. Here are the addresses that I wish to visit, and you shall receive your payment upon completion of our little mission.'

Having overseen the loading of the box containing the gold safely and discreetly inside the carriage, Thaddeus approached the two horsemen. He had paired Bennet with John Jephson, not wanting the former to be in close proximity to either the gold or the Dutchman. He knew that Jephson would keep an eye on him, and ordered them both to ride on ahead to the first address to reconnoitre the route for any potential problems or hi-jackers. Frederik and Catharina settled themselves inside the black leather seated vehicle, and Frederik could not help smiling benignly as one of the two riders leaned forward across the neck of his mount and thrust a coin into the hand of an imploring beggar before wishing the ragged man well and then, with his fellow horseman, riding off. Kindness Frederik thought, is not restricted to any particular race of people, the English like the Dutch carry compassion in their hearts.

The streets of London were busy with carriages and carts of all descriptions as well as occasional small herds of livestock heading for the markets. People loitered on corners and pedlar's cried out selling their wares, all of which meant that Thomas Wright had at times to carefully manoeuvre the carriage between people and around obstacles, making their progress very slow as they travelled along the relatively short distance from the Pool of London, to London Bridge. Their first destination was to be the home of a customs official that lived on the bridge, a short way along from the gatehouse. They had drawn the carriage to a halt just before the gatehouse as to drive it onto the bridge for such a short distance would have cost them much in the way of time. On a bad day it could take an age to cross, due to the chaotic mêlée of carts, pedestrians and animals ponderously shunting over this ancient wooden structure, which at most was only a few metres wide. The bridge had, built upon its span, a vast number of multi storied shops and houses, many of which required traffic to pass underneath them through arches, and although there were now gaps between some buildings, due to a fire some twenty-six years earlier, none of them were sufficient in width to allow for the easy turning of a carriage and horses.

Thaddeus, as the most trusted, was instructed by Frederik to stand guard over the carriage and consequently he delegated David Hawkins and Robert Potter to escort the Evertsens to the home of the official, where they would, in private, negotiate the bribe, after which, they would return to the carriage and count out the payment before Frederik would go back with Hawkins and Potter to deliver it. Frederik considered this methodology clumsy, but logistically they had little choice, as at this stage the amount of the bribe was negotiable and had to be paid on the day in gold coin.

Frederik and Catharina had been gone some thirty minutes, and Thaddeus having pulled down the blinds to stop prying eyes, stood by the carriage door contemplating the transfer of the gold from the box within. Thomas Wright stood holding the bridles of the carriage horses, patting their noses gently and trying to keep them calm, whilst John Jephson and Ned Bennet sat upon their mounts, one at either end of the carriage, looking slowly up and down the noisy street, apparently trying to determine which of the ragtaggle of passing citizens looked any more suspicious than the rest. Thaddeus caught sight of the Evertsens returning, closely followed by Hawkins and Potter. As Frederik and Catharina stepped into the archway of the gatehouse, two heavily built men emerged from the shadows, separating them from their escort; two more figures appeared as if from nowhere and grabbed Frederik and Catharina from behind, placing knives against their throats as Hawkins and Potter both dropped to their knees, both fatally stabbed in the chest. Catharina struggled as her ragged captor clasped his hand across her mouth. Thaddeus instantly recognised him as the beggar on the quayside, the beggar that Bennet had spoken to as he had handed him a coin.

Thaddeus turned his head at the sound of horse's hooves to see Ned Bennet, riding sword in hand towards John Jephson, who reared his horse as his assailant, crouching low in the saddle, thrust his blade into the soldier's side causing him to slump over the animal's neck, writhing in agony. Thaddeus drew his sword and pistol and crouched low in a defensive stance, unsure as where best to concentrate his counter attack as Tom Wright stood exposed, vulnerably struggling to hold the bridles of the startled carriage horses as their wild eyes darted from side to side. A cry filled the air as Catharina bit deeply into the hand of her captor, which caused him to momentarily lower the knife from her throat. At this opportunity Thaddeus darted toward the beggar and thrust the tip of his sword up under the man's rib cage, at the same time pulling him away from the girl and letting him drop lifelessly to the floor. Catharina fell back into the shadows against the internal wall of the gatehouse arch as her father was thrown heavily onto the floor by the thug that had been holding him. Thaddeus was spun around as the thugs, now intent on stealing the gold, barged into him as they ran towards the carriage, two of them quickly clambering inside as the third pulled himself up onto the driver's seat. A shot rang out and Tom Wright fell to the ground, clutching his chest as Bennet, smoking pistol in hand, leaned down to grab the hanging reins of the carriage horses and pass them up to the new driver. He then grabbed the bridle of one of the pair and riding close by its head, pulled the horse to start the vehicle into motion.

Cursing Simon Wainwright for delegating to this man, and cursing himself for allowing the insubordinate scum to trick him, Thaddeus made for the carriage sheathing his sword as he ran, and seeing the iron step, sprung himself up onto the drivers seat where, still clutching his pistol, he pulled hard on the reins, wresting them from the hands of the thug sitting beside him. The horses veered towards the wall of the embankment, hemming in Ned Bennet's mount. The driver was now raining blows on Thaddeus who, whilst defending himself the best he could, took rough aim with the pistol and fired at the lone horseman. Through the powder smoke he saw Bennet clutch his face as he lurched from the horse and tumbled over the wall of the embankment into the swirling water below. Still struggling with the driver Thaddeus caught a quick glimpse of Bennet being pulled by the current into the paddles of the waterwheel that operated under the first arch of the bridge. Then a blow to the jaw from the driver's massive fist propelled Thaddeus from the carriage onto the low stonewall where he lay motionless as nausea and a white mist preceded oblivion.

Thaddeus was aware of a gentle rise and falling motion as he painfully opened his eyes. He was lying on a bunk and his chest felt as if a brick wall had collapsed on it, touching it with his hand he realised that it was tightly bandaged. His head ached, his mouth was dry and he could hear the faint sound of seabirds. He heard the latch lift on the door and in the dim light he could see a figure approach him.

'You're awake then, I thought that we had lost you.' It was Catharina, her beautiful face broke into a smile as she softly stroked his forehead.

'What about the others?'

'The two men you sent to escort us were both killed, as was your driver. One of your horsemen rode off, I think his horse bolted, and of course the other you shot, he ended up in the river.'

'Your father, is he alright?'

'Bruised and sadly, much poorer, but alive, thanks to you. We carried you back to the ship, as we obviously did not want to get involved answering lots of questions; the bribery of officials would be a difficult thing to explain to your magistrates, as would the reason you had killed two men, albeit in self defence.'

'So I'm on your ship; it feels as if we are at sea.'

'We are, Mr Cleaver. We could not risk staying in London; your authorities could trace the incident back to us from the carriage hire and we thought it best if you came with us, we owe you that. We are on our way back to Amsterdam.

'Please, Miss Evertsen, after our recent experience together and with our present circumstances confining us together, would you please do me the honour of calling me Thaddeus.'

'And you must call me Catharina, Thaddeus.' She smiled at him, and to his amazement lowered her face to his and kissed him tenderly, full on the lips.

Frederik adopted his customary pose on the stern castle, arms outstretched, gripping the rail, and looking across the lower deck at the sailors carrying out their duties. He was inwardly hoping that his daughter would not get too attached to this young soldier, as was her habit with gallant young men. Arguably Sergeant Cleaver had saved their lives from the robbers, but had it not been for the man's poor judgement of character, they would not have been at risk in the first place. Frederik was having serious doubts as to Catharina's suitability to take over the management of the business from him; her heart ruled her, and in the absence of a son he needed someone that was naturally hard-nosed and bullish if the business was to survive and furnish him with a good income in his old age. Someone possibly like his nephew Johan.

9 A NEW LIFE

Amsterdam - October 1663

Four years had passed since Thaddeus arrived in Amsterdam. His relationship with Catharina developed quickly, much to her father's displeasure, but Frederik found employment for him within the family business. Frederik used him constantly for any errand or project that needed a soldier's strong right arm, and this meant that Thaddeus was constantly facing danger, a fact that hadn't gone unnoticed by Catharina who pleaded with her father to find him work of a less perilous nature, for she was convinced that her father was intentionally trying to get him killed. Thaddeus also spent long periods away from her, as often he would be given assignments that took him abroad. Frederik had been fortunate enough to secure a contract with the government to supply vital supplies to Copenhagen, which was trying to rebuild its fortunes after the Swedish siege in 1659. Holland, as an ally of the Danes had secured trade routes, but Frederik insisted that his ships carried a small armed contingent in case Sweden broke the treaty of 1660 and took to attacking trade ships supplying Denmark.

Upon her marriage to Thaddeus, some twelve months after their first meeting, Catharina's cousin Johan had usurped her from any executive role within the business. She hoped that her new husband would be treated well by her father now that he was officially part of the family, but this had sadly not been the case. Frederik would not dream of openly denying his daughter's hand to the soldier as he knew that he would lose this strong headed woman forever if he did so. Instead he lavished a lifestyle on her that he knew Thaddeus could not match, or indeed be comfortable following, in the hope that his daughter would tire of the Englishman and find a more appropriate match from amongst the wealthier eligible men within the cream of Dutch society.

Johan Evertsen was a disagreeable man, a bully by nature with a taste for gambling and young girls, both of which had got him into more than his share of trouble in the past, but Frederik liked him. He believed his nephew had the drive and ambition to grow the business, and that he was obviously a man that was not afraid of taking risks, unlike Catharina. Thaddeus was very wary of him, and over the last few years, since he had been in the Evertsen's employ, he had had occasion to witness both his brutish treatment of employees and his rough use of women. The big Dutchman had invited his cousin and her husband to a dinner at his affluent home where he was to entertain a number of the city's wealthiest merchants in an attempt to win business for the company. Catharina looked, as always, beautiful, but in a formal surrounding, dressed in a gown of the finest Italian silk, she stood head and shoulders above the overfed wives of the corpulent traders.

Feeling somewhat ill at ease in the rich surroundings, Thaddeus stood by her side, listening disinterestedly to the bragging of the men and the catty remarks of the women. He had very little in common with these people on a social level, and still found that after four years his command of the Dutch language left a little to be desired, feeling more comfortable when those that could, made the effort to speak to him in English. After the sumptuous meal, Johan was taking every opportunity to flatter his more important guests, and made sure that a never ending supply of alcohol was available via a stream of liveried waiters, who were ably assisted in the background by a few serving girls stationed at the periphery of the room, filling glasses. One of the girls had caught Johan's eye, and he began making whispered comments about her behind the back of his hand to one of his guests, a very overweight man in his late forties. Johan and his guest started to slowly and discreetly inch their way closer to the edge of the room where the very pretty young girl stood awaiting instructions from the waiters. Standing beside her Johan started to fondle the girl's buttocks as the other man pressed himself against her pinning her to the wall. The girl stood motionless, too terrified to move. Thaddeus, looking around the room in boredom, caught sight of what was happening just as Johan took the girl's elbow and marched her through a side door closely followed by his guest. Thaddeus put down his glass, and making an excuse to Catharina, made for the door. It opened into a smaller drawing room and at the far end Johan was holding the serving girls outstretched arms above her head as she lay on her back across a card table. The fat merchant had pushed up the girl's skirts and was standing between her knees unfastening his breeches.

'Johan! Leave the girl alone,' Thaddeus stormed across the room and pulled the startled fat man to the floor.

'Mind your business, Cleaver, you're just hired help around here, leave us.' Johan wrestled with the girl's arms as now, with her legs free, she was twisting her body to pull loose from his grip. Thaddeus, raising and turning his leg, stamped his stack-heeled shoe hard down into the side of Johan's knee, causing him to drop to the ground, at the same time releasing the girl's arms. As the big man lay on the floor moaning, Thaddeus scooped the girl up from the table onto her feet and led her out into the corridor and through to the garden.

'Are you all right, lass?' The girl was in shock, her eyes staring blankly. Thaddeus took her by the shoulders, pulling her round so that she faced him, and raised her chin gently with his thumb and index finger so that she was looking directly into his eyes.

'Listen, I promise they will not harm you, do you understand. As much as I would like them to be punished, they are rich and important, and you would not be believed. Say nothing to anyone. I will see to it that you still have a job within the family if you wish to stay, and I can only assure you that this will never ever happen again as long as I am here. Now go to your quarters, get your things and wait for me by the carriages.' The girl nodded and then gathered up her long skirt and ran back into the house sobbing.

Thaddeus walked back into the building to be confronted in the hallway by an enraged Johan, hobbling toward him clutching a sword and looking the worse for drink.

'You have dishonoured my guest, Cleaver, and probably lost us business. You are a puritan fool with no understanding of how things work around here; she was to be a present to sweeten a deal; she's just a serving girl.' At that he lurched forward and took a wild swing with the sword. Thaddeus side-stepped, grabbed Johan's raised sword arm, and turning the big man around stepped behind him placing his forearm under his chin putting pressure on his throat. The Dutchman's face started to turn even redder than its usual florid state as slowly he lost consciousness and slid to the ground. Thaddeus left the man in a heap on the floor as he composed himself and re-entered the main reception. He quickly sought out Catharina and whispered a précised account of the incident to her before walking her out into the warm night air. There they found the frightened serving girl waiting; they helped her quickly into their carriage, and then set off for their own house in the city.

Having arranged with their housekeeper for the girl to share a room with one of the other servants, Thaddeus and Catharina retired to their own bedroom. Catharina had been enjoying the evening up to the point of their swift exit, but was now feeling unusually tired. She lay beside Thaddeus unable to sleep.

'My father will not tolerate Johan's actions of this evening. He is a hard businessman but a good Christian, and would not condone the girl being molested in that fashion; Johan will be severely dealt with.'

'I have made an enemy in your cousin; that was never my intention, but I could not stand by and let him use the poor girl. I despise those that take anything by force, I witnessed too much of it in England during the civil war, and I'll be damned if I will bend knee to your father's clients who expect to be given use of innocents in return for their patronage.'

'You did right by the girl, Thaddeus, and you make me proud. I realise now that I could never have run the company the way my father wanted, but I know in my heart that he would never have stepped to the base level of depravity that Johan exhibited tonight in the name of business.'

'Johan is young, with a young man's appetite for all things of the flesh, and I fear that he will bring your father by association into disrepute unless he is checked.'

'I will speak with my father tomorrow and acquaint him with tonight's events, but now I must try to sleep for I am so tired, yet the heat is keeping me awake.' Thaddeus rolled over and put his arm around his wife, nuzzling his face into the back of her neck. The room to him did not feel extraordinarily warm but as he touched her, she seemed to be on fire.

The next morning Thaddeus was the first to awaken. He sat up and swung his legs over the edge of the bed and cleared the sleep from his eyes before turning to see if Catharina was awake. His heart seemed to jump in his chest as he saw her face covered in perspiration and the early signs of a black bubo on her neck. She looked deathly pale, and as he reached out to touch her she rolled away from him, held her head over the side of the bed and vomited.

'I'm afraid it seems to be the plague.' The doctor pressed the linen scarf tightly to his face as he spoke. He had not touched Catharina with his hands, but had prodded her and lifted her arms with a white stick to examine her for buboes.

'There have been a small number of reported cases down near the quays.'

'What can you do for her, Doctor?' Thaddeus was distraught; he held Catharina's clammy hand as if to let it go would allow the very life to drain from her body.

'I will of course bleed her and light scented candles, and if you would instruct your servants to leave a bowl of milk in the room, that may draw the poison from the air. Sadly, Mr Cleaver, I have witnessed this before and I am not hopeful for her survival. As you must understand, you and the servants must not leave the house for two weeks; as soon as I have carried out the aforesaid procedures I must go and report this. God have mercy on you and your household.'

For two days Thaddeus stayed by Catharina's side and comforted her as his wife writhed in agony and took on the appearance of a living, decaying corpse. The long elegant fingers he had so often lovingly kissed were now blackened by gangrene, and the flesh was lifting from her once beautiful face. The servants had fled, all except the serving girl whom he had rescued, who brought them food and left it at the door. Thaddeus had given up on trying to get Catharina to eat, and instead tried his best to get her to drink a little fresh water. After four long days he now lay silently holding her, having re-lived every minute of their lives together in a constant monologue, delivered to hold her spirit back here on earth, back by the side of the man that truly worshipped her.

The bearers opened the bedroom door, called by the serving girl who realised that Catharina had lost her fight. Thaddeus opened his eyes as he heard them enter, but was too weak to speak. He saw them as if in a haze lift her white linen clad body and shuffle out of the room. The bedroom door was still open as he tried to make out the conversation emanating from the landing.

'Might as well take him too he hasn't got long by the look of him.'

'Nah, give him another couple of days, the pox hasn't come out on his neck yet, anyway we get paid by the visit remember.' He could hear the men laugh as his confused mind succumbed to sleep.

The sound of carriages passing by in the street acted as a stimulus to Thaddeus, he wasn't sure if they were part of a dream or whether he was actually awake. He rolled onto his back, and the effort momentarily made his head swim and he felt nauseous. A cool breeze blew through the window and instinctively he pulled the damp sheets up around his neck. He realised that the fever had broken. His mind immediately conjured an image of a body dressed in white, floating above him; then the reality of the vision hit him, as he understood the terrible truth that Catharina was dead and her body was no longer beside him.

In attempting to get up and extricate himself from the filthy soiled bedclothes he fell heavily to the floor, where he lay momentarily collecting his thoughts. He heard the intrusive creak of the door as it slowly opened, revealing the face of the serving girl who immediately pulled a face of disgust as the stench from the room hit her nostrils.

'You're alive, sir, yet it smells like death in here. I

thought you were going to die like the lady.' The words hit him like a kick in the stomach.

'She is dead then?'

'Yes, sir, sorry, sir, they took her away two days ago, I'm the only one left now, except for you sir of course; I didn't think you would wake up.' The girl started to cry.

'Help me up please; I need to get out of this room. And, what *is* your name?'

'Hannah, sir.'

'Well, Hannah, dry your eyes and draw me a bath, I stink. I need to find out where they have taken my wife.' Despite now having one arm around the girls shoulders Thaddeus's knees started to buckle and she grabbed him tighter around the waist to support him and prevent him from dragging them both to the floor. She guided him towards an upholstered chair in the corner of the room and helped him into it, then wrapped a blanket around him that she found on the floor at the foot of the bed.

'Your lady would have been taken for burial, sir, probably to St Michael's churchyard. You're too weak to go there now, sir, let me draw you that bath and get you some soup. You need to regain your strength before you go anywhere. You are a lucky man, sir, sorry, sir, I know your lady has died, but you, sir, you have survived the plague.'

10 THE FRUIT OF LIFE

London – April 1665

Revelling in his nakedness, the man stood over the girl's lifeless body. He had violated her in every conceivable way before strangling her with a short plaited leather strap, its heavy crisscross pattern biting into her pale white throat like a serpent.

Her crumpled skirts, blouse and bodice, lay by her side on the flat marble slab of the churchyard memorial. On the ground below, lay a starched white apron, delicately edged with lace, slowly absorbing the blood which had flowed to the floor from the gaping hole in her breast where once had been contained her warm beating heart, the heart which a moment ago, he had voraciously devoured. The man drew his finger across his blood-smeared cheek and dropping to his knees wrote upon the girl's forehead the numbers *930*. Standing up, he plucked from amongst his own scattered clothes, a large red apple, which he proceeded to place inside the now vacant cavity from where he had cut the girl's heart. Sally Fletcher would be missed at the chocolate house tomorrow.

'Mrs Fitz-Herbert, may I introduce to you, Mr Johan Evertsen, a business acquaintance of mine from Amsterdam. He is here in London for a while, and insisted on meeting the most beautiful woman in this fair city.' Andrew Carlise bowed with a great flourish as he presented the big Dutchman to the preening woman.

'Are you in fact a Dutchman, Mr Evertsen, or do

you just work in Amsterdam; you see my husband is about to take up arms against the Dutch and I would not want to be seen fraternising with the enemy.' Mrs Fitz-Herbert cocked her head to one side as she spoke and slightly raised one eyebrow as she smiled coquettishly at Johan.

'I am indeed Dutch, Madam, but I do not consider myself an enemy, especially to one of such great beauty. I am sure that your husband would take up arms against any man that so much as looked at you no matter what be their nationality.' Mrs Fitz-Herbert and the small group of admirers standing around her laughed at the man's witty repost.

Johan bandied a few more pleasantries with the woman, but his eyes were elsewhere, watching the coming and going of the chocolate girls. He liked their simplicity, their youthful fresh faces, and the way their bodies moved as they appeared to perform an elegant dance passing between tables and side stepping between the groups of standing customers, occasionally brushing their soft young bodies against the men as they swept past with their trays of food and beverages.

'My dear, Evertsen, I see that you have an interest in more than just chocolate.' Carlisle winked knowingly at the Dutchman as they stood together to one side of the seated Mrs Fitz-Herbert, speaking in low whispers.

'I like simple beauty, my friend, delicate and untouched.'

'Do you not consider our Mrs Fitz-Herbert here a rare beauty?'

'She is without doubt, but I would have no time for her games, I am a busy man and take my pleasures on the run so to speak, and besides I prefer my delicacies to have an air of innocence about them, something that your Mrs Fitz-Herbert definitely does not.'

'A shame, my good fellow, as this establishment offers many delights for a connoisseur, and some of them can involve games at which I assure you Mrs Fitz-Herbert excels. Now I say too much, so let's partake of the simple delicacies openly on offer in this charming salon.' As he spoke, Carlisle raised his voice to its normal volume and spread his arms to emphasise his comments, but in doing so, brought one hand up under a tray of sweetmeats being carried by one of the chocolate girls, the contents of which readily showered over the seated Mrs Fitz-Herbert.

Johan observed the ensuing mêlée, and indeed took some delight in watching as the young girl received a beating from the older woman. When the rumpus had died down and Mrs Fitz-Herbert had stormed off with her entourage, including the vacuous Carlisle, he stood alone amongst the remaining customers as the cliques began to discuss with amusement the plight and temper of the colonel's wife.

'Please forgive that unfortunate display as it is not a common occurrence in this establishment, nor a typical example of the behaviour of London's elite society; Richard Valletort at your service, sir.' Johan turned to see the slim figure of Valletort standing behind him.

'I have seen worse, but usually in the quayside taverns in Amsterdam; Johan Evertsen, your servant, sir.' The two men politely bowed toward each other and Valletort indicated an empty table to which they moved and sat down.

'Please forgive me but I heard you say that you were here in London on business, Mr Evertsen, if I may make so bold, what is your line of work?'

'Shipping, Mr Valletort, I own a shipping company which I inherited from my uncle who unfortunately, died last year of the plague, along with his daughter.'

'A sad business, Mr Evertsen, I read that many thousands in your country lost their lives to it, but thank God you survived eh.'

'God had little to do with it, sir, my uncle had sent me to the Americas to oversee some business, as I fear he believed me to be a rake and thought me in need of isolation from the fair sex after a misunderstanding with a servant girl if you take my meaning. In fact the old fool saved my life and made me rich, so I bear him no hard feelings.'

'You are very forthright and honest about your circumstance, sir, and I find that quite refreshing.' Johan smiled at Valletort's comment and clicked his fingers to summon service from a passing chocolate girl.

'I am a man of appetites, sir, I can hide the fact and starve, or be honest and open about it, which puts me often in the company of those that share my desires and with whom I can hunt.' As he finished speaking he turned to the waiting chocolate girl.

'What's your name, girl?'

'Emily, sir, can I get you chocolate?'

'Yes, and whatever my new friend, Mr Valletort, desires.' The girl looked dreamily into the eyes of Richard Valletort, and then blushed.

'Nothing for me thank you, young Emily, but if you see your unfortunate friend Lizzie, tell her that I have spoken on her behalf to Monsieur Coultier and she has no cause for concern.'

'Yes, sir, thank you, sir.' The girl gave a bobbed curtsey and left to fulfil the order.

'Could she whet your appetite Mr Evertsen?' Johan's eyes followed the girl as she left the salon.

'Most certainly sir, and are you of a similar mind?'

'Alas, sir, no, although like any man I enjoy the gifts of Venus, I prefer to expand my mind in preference to my portion and find that this house offers other delights more in keeping with my interests. If you frequent this establishment on a regular basis, and in the right company, you may at some point be invited to partake of a more extensive menu.' Johan looked at Valletort with increasing curiosity, as he was the second person that afternoon to refer to other activities within *Le Puits de Chocolat*.

Lizzie Jephson tried in vain to wrest herself free from the grip of the man Harper. He had pressed her against the closed door of the now empty green salon, and was fumbling with her skirts whilst attempting to kiss her full on the mouth. She moved her head frantically from side to side to avoid his lips as she let out a loud scream. The door pushed hard into her back as someone tried to come in. It opened a few inches then slammed shut again as Harper threw his full weight against her. Lizzie brought her knee up into the man's groin and he immediately doubled up and fell backwards as someone successfully shouldering the door forced her into him.

Harper looked up into the face of Richard Valletort.

'Get out!' Valletort's words seemed to strike fear into the fallen man as Harper scrambled to his feet, then, bent double and clutching his throbbing groin, slid past him and out into the hallway. Lizzie threw herself at Richard Valletort, sobbing.

'It's alright, my dear, he will not harm you; you are safe now.'

'Mr Valletort, he tried to........'

'I know, my dear; he will be taught a lesson I assure you. It seems that I am destined to be your saviour today.' With that, he kissed Lizzie gently on the forehead.

11 LOST

London – April 1665

After the death of Catharina, Thaddeus's fortunes had gone into decline. His father-in-law Frederik had also succumbed to the plague, and upon his death, Johan had inherited the shipping business. One of Johan's first decisions was to get rid of the Englishman whom he saw as a threat, not to his business, as that was now totally within his control, but to his hedonistic lifestyle, which Thaddeus despised.

Once the plague in Holland had subsided, leaving in its wake fifty thousand dead, Johan returned from the relative safety of America, and promptly settled the soldier's back pay. Catharina had no property as the house she had lived in with her husband was owned by her father, the title of which now fell to Johan; therefore Thaddeus, with few assets and nothing to keep him in Amsterdam, decided to return to England.

He had considered going back to his old life of soldiering, but with the New Model Army now disbanded, he was not sure who to seek out, as technically he was a deserter. He found himself drifting from one casual job to another to supplement his diminishing pay-off from Johan. He had no trade, and therefore relied on selling his services as hired muscle, a risky profession at the best of times, and a line of work that did not give regular employment.

By the end of April, Thaddeus found himself virtually destitute and spending his last few coins on a simple meal in a cheap tavern near Fleet Street. It had been a hard winter, so cold that the Thames had frozen over, and with little work and poor accommodation Thaddeus was at his lowest ebb. Although spring was making its presence felt to most, it was not lifting his spirits. He sat at a corner table in the busy establishment watching the customers come and go, biding his time until the owner would no doubt ask him to buy another drink or leave. He looked up from his near empty ale jug as the tavern door opened; all eyes turned and the banter momentarily ceased as a very tall, thin man entered, wrapped in a clerical cloak. The man looked around the busy room for somewhere to sit, and seeing an empty chair at Thaddeus's table walked across the room towards him.

'Is there room here for a man of the cloth, sir?' The man's height gave him a phenomenal presence and his grey eyes seemed to look right into Thaddeus's soul. He looked back at the man almost transfixed and after a moment responded to his question.

'Please, sir, be seated, God's disciples are always welcome to this poor man's company.' The innkeeper had by now walked across from behind the counter and took the man's order for food making a point to gesture towards the empty ale jug in front of Thaddeus.

'If you're not drinking on your way and make space for them that are.' The priest looked at Thaddeus and then at the innkeeper.

'Another jug of ale for my friend here, and bring him another serving of pie if he has the stomach for it; on my bill if you please.' The innkeeper looked again at Thaddeus as he wiped his hands on his dirty apron, and then looking back at the priest nodded.

'Right you are, Father, right away.' Thaddeus watched the man make his way back to the counter, parting the way between the standing customers with an outstretched forearm.

'Sir, you are very kind, my pride would have me decline your offer but my empty stomach speaks so loud as to drown it out; Thaddeus Cleaver at your service.' He extended his hand to the priest who accepted his gesture with an iron grip.

'Father Josiah Turnbull, new of St Bride's. Tell me, Thaddeus, what brings you to this lowly establishment?'

The conversation came easily as the two men very quickly established a rapport. Thaddeus told the priest a little about his military background and found himself opening up to the man about recent events more than he would have to any other stranger, possibly because of the man's calling, or maybe because he could no longer keep inside the pain he felt at the loss of Catharina and his despair relating to his now reduced circumstances.

The priest it seems had come recently to London, and was at St Bride's to be near local printers with whom he hoped to enter into dialogue and possible collaboration concerning the production of a book that he was writing. He believed that the subject matter was of such importance to mankind that these tradesman would happily donate their services free to save their fellow men, the very thought of which made Thaddeus almost laugh out loud.

'The world has always been a wicked place, Thaddeus, and the Church has done its best to save mankind from itself, but there are now so many factions within the Church pulling in different directions, and more worryingly, there are an increasing amount of sects and societies that purport to do things in the name of God, but whose pure existence is for the gratification of their followers. You told me of your experiences in Amsterdam and the suffering brought about by the plague, I believe that it was a punishment sent from God.'

'But my wife was a good Christian, why did she deserve to die?' Thaddeus had listened patiently to the priest, but was now feeling angered by the direction of the man's philosophy.

'She didn't, Thaddeus, she was killed by the evil of mankind evoking the wrath of God. Unfortunately, as when God sent the many plagues to Egypt, innocents suffered; direct your anger at the sinners not at God.'

'I'm sorry, Father, my bitterness is out of frustration. She died and I survived; she was an innocent, and I carry the guilt of a soldier. As I lay sick with the plague I did think that it was justice for my sins, but then I recovered...'

'You recovered? I'm sorry I did not understand before, I know you said that your wife was taken, but had not realised that you had contracted the disease and survived it. That makes you a very special person in these times; in many ways God has given you the gift of life.'

'Look at me, Father, is this life?'

The priest leaned forward across the table and lowered his voice to a whisper. 'The horror that you saw in Amsterdam could soon be with us here; already the plague is here in London, a few cases officially, but they only enter in the parish records deaths of people of position, many of the dead are poor and are seen to be of no consequence. Before long there will be panic I assure you. It is rumoured already that soon, places such as this will be ordered closed. Think, Thaddeus, you will be able to walk amongst the dead and dying without fear of infection, as you see, having already survived the plague, you are now immune to the disease.' The priest's words were bringing back pictures to Thaddeus of the horrors that he had seen in Holland and the ale was making him maudlin.

'I might as well be dead, I can't go through that again.'

'Think, man, to be able to walk untouched through hell; think of the good that you could do for others. I can see you being of great service to the church, would that not be payback for your sins as a soldier. Look, come with me now, to the church, I will find you somewhere to sleep and we can prepare for what is to come.'

'Immune you say, so I may yet live out my God promised three score and ten years as it says in the Bible.'

'Possibly so, or maybe even longer; did you know that the good book says that Adam survived for nine hundred and thirty?'

Over the next few weeks, the driven priest employed Thaddeus in all manner of ways, and in return he received spartan accommodation and meals within the building of the church. He listened with interest as the man read to him extracts from his writing. Thaddeus was intrigued by the vast array of new religious denominations and related political groups that had sprung up due to radical changes and divisions brought about by the civil war. The priest spoke of Quakers, Ranters, Muggletonians, Seekers and Levellers, even Diggers, each with their own interpretation of the Bible and subsequent code of living. He was intrigued by the beliefs of the Fifth Monarchists. Especially concerning the looming year of 1666 and how the number 666 had been described in the book of Revelations as being significant in the end of mankind's rule of the earth. The more he listened the more confused he was in his own beliefs. As a child things had been so simple, his parents were Church going people, and he accepted their standards of morality and their religious conviction; now as a man, having lived through war and pestilence, witnessing so many horrors as well as feeling the pain of losing Catharina, he found himself questioning his own faith.

By the middle of May more and more plague dead were being buried at St Bride's, and as Father Turnbull had predicted, taverns, theatres and any establishment where the public met in numbers enough to spread the disease were ordered to be closed. With the coming of June it was apparent that the bitterly cold winter had given way to an exceptionally hot summer and the death toll was rising daily. Father Turnbull walked purposefully towards Thaddeus who was filling in one of many new graves in the churchyard. It was midday and the sun was making the toil very hard indeed.

'Thaddeus, leave that, I need to speak with you.' The tall priest draped an arm around Thaddeus's shoulder and walked him slowly from the grave to the gravel path as he spoke.

'I have some news that may be to your benefit. It has been agreed that the parish is to hire bearers to transport the dead from quarantined houses. As most doctors have fled the city, we are also employing searchers from amongst those that we think may have the skills to diagnose the disease, mainly old woman with rough experience of basic nursing; not ideal I know but they will make a few groats from the victims families for their trouble. As for the bearers, the Parish is offering a wage, indeed a good wage as it is felt their life expectancy will be short as they walk amongst the dead and dying risking contamination. I think this could be an opportunity for you to restore your circumstances, for as you told me you have had the disease and are thus immune. The worst you could die from is hard work, are you game for it?' Thaddeus wiped together his soil-grimed hands and laughed.

'If I can survive the plague, Father, then I have no fear of hard work. When do I start?'

'Right away, a horse and cart for transporting the bodies will be here shortly, together with someone to assist you in your labours; a man called Perks, a bit of a rogue so be careful; he was bound for prison for a very long time, but they gave him the option of prison or the plague cart.'

'And you're telling me he chose the plague cart? He must have been convicted of something bloody bad. Sorry, Father.'

'Battering his wife and child I believe, so no more than he deserves. As I always say, God punishes sinners in many ways.'

The work was not so much hard as pitiful.

Thaddeus and his unsavoury helper were given accommodation within the church grounds in a hastily constructed tarred canvas shack, as the other clerics, fearing infection, no longer wanted Thaddeus within the building. By July the death toll for the month was over two thousand, and the King had left the city. The man Perks developed the sickness and died painfully within three days, and Father Turnbull insisted that it was God's justice for his crimes as he introduced Thaddeus to his new helper.

'This is the replacement for Perks. He has a strong back and is totally aware of the risks that come with the position, which he sees as worth taking for the rewards. You see he is very ambitious as I'm sure he will tell you.'

The young man had a beaming smile and an attitude that made him instantly likeable. He put out a hand in greeting to Thaddeus.

'Mr Cleaver, Father Turnbull speaks very kindly of you, sir. My name is William.'

12 ONE DOOR CLOSES

London - August 1665

Captain Abraham stood at the top of the ship's gangway shouting down to the man at the bottom.

'Cleaver, you say. Well, Mr Cleaver, as you have no documentation giving you title to the consignment I must assume that it belongs to those that have. If you have a dispute over ownership with those parties then I suggest that you resolve it using the process of law. In the meantime I shall continue to load the goods and prepare to set sail.'

'Tell me then, Captain, where is the man Bennet who delivered the consignment?' Thaddeus was trying to stay calm, but he could feel his anger rising as the ship's captain was appearing in his eyes to be intentionally obstructive.

'Mr Bennet and his associates have booked passage on this ship to the Americas, and having a certificate of health is now onboard.'

'I need to come on board and speak with him.' Thaddeus clenched his fists, and try as he might, his expression gave away his motive.

'I'm afraid that would be impossible, Mr Cleaver, no one boards this ship without a certificate of health, and even then it is at my discretion. If you attempt to set foot on this gangway I will have you shot.'

Thaddeus did not give a verbal response to the captain's last remark, instead he turned on his heels and stormed off back to the waiting cart where he climbed up onto the driver's seat next to William.

'The bastard has skinned us good and proper;

there was no name on that title, it just read to the bearer. Bennet is on the ship bound for the Americas with my money, William, and there is nothing legal that I can do about it.'

'Can't we just go on board and drag him off?'

'No, William; the Captain has made it perfectly clear that he will defend his passenger's right to be on board with force if necessary. There is nothing we can do; Bennet has buggered me again. But I vow, William, that if ever I see the man again, I will kill him.'

William flicked the whip, and the horses jolted the cart forward. Thaddeus looked back up at the deck of the *Crimson Star* as they drove out of Addison's quay, and he could see two cloaked men standing beside the captain shaking his hand. Never before in his life had he wanted so much to feel a trigger against his finger. He had killed many men as a soldier, but that was war; this time if he had had a musket it would have been personal.

The two men were tired, not only from lack of sleep, but also fatigued from the frustration and disappointment of having their dreams of a good life taken from them. William still looked somewhat under the weather from his heavy drinking bout the previous day, and he declined the offer of food as Thaddeus sat in the churchyard prodding into a bowl of pottage.

'You look really rough, lad, drinking definitely does not agree with you; I suggest a life of temperance from now on, not that you or I can afford to pay the inflated prices of ale from the back doors of taverns for much longer.' William didn't reply, he just sat with glazed eyes and then, he suddenly vomited.

'It's definitely the plague, Mr Cleaver.' Mary the searcher held out her hand as Thaddeus placed a single groat into her grubby palm. 'Shame, he was a nice lad; are you going to tend to him till he goes?'

'Yes, Mary, as much as I can. He has some money put by for his butchers shop, best we use that for the doctor, not that I think he can do much for him now.'

The doctor arrived some hours later, and having first secured his payment, proceeded to carry out his pointless rituals. Thaddeus sat in the sunshine outside of the hovel, and despite his sadness at William's plight, couldn't help but smile at the ridiculous spectre of the beak hooded man stepping out into the sunlight from the canvass shack, causing the churchyard crows to take off in fright.

'I have done all I can but I do not hold out much hope. He obviously knew the risks when he decided to accept the position as I'm sure do you; a foolhardy occupation.'

Thaddeus did not comment on the irony of the statement as the doctor himself took profit from risk, for even the elaborate protective garb that he wore could not guarantee his safety.

William's passing was not easy; the young man was strong and his body tried to fight the disease which extended his torment, but inevitably he succumbed. Thaddeus could no longer bear to enter the hovel, not just because of the putrid stench of death, but because he had formed a bond with the lad, and his painful end had brought back too many memories of his last days with Catharina. Within hours Father Turnbull had found a replacement for William as well as for the absconded gravediggers, all recruited from the endless supply of convicts willing to risk their lives for the opportunity to stand in the open air and once again feel the sun on their faces.

It was now September, and the plague deaths were nearing seven thousand per week. Thaddeus had fallen into a state of extreme melancholy, exacerbated by lack of sleep and a growing dependence on whatever alcohol he could forage. He needed to clear from his mind the constant visions of death and sounds of torment. He needed to feel clean, for it was as if the mal odours of decay had permeated his skin making him feel as if he was a living corpse. Thaddeus found himself in a dirty alley behind a closed tavern; he had been drinking all afternoon with three of the new gravediggers, and their supply of cheap gin was now exhausted. In their drunken state it had been decided that it was now his turn to acquire more drink, and he had started to hammer noisily on the back door of the tavern.

'Open up, you bastard, there are good men here dying of thirst while you feed your face and count your profits.' The three gravediggers laughed and noisily cheered him on as they fell about and indulged in rough horseplay. A casement window opened and a stocky balding man leaned out and shouted down at them.

'Piss off, we're not serving, especially to you pox ridden rabble; now get away from here and go and play with the dead before the watch come and give you a pounding.' Thaddeus swayed slowly from side to side as he looked up at the man.

'Look, bastard, we just want a drink; be nice to us or we'll drop you when we carry you out to the cart.' At this, the four men in the street started to fall about laughing, but their hilarity was cut short by the sight of a troop from the trained band appearing from around the corner. Without any form of challenge the watchmen started to pile in to the inebriated foursome with heavy wooden staves. Thaddeus brought his forearm up across his face to protect himself and received a crashing blow to his wrist which made him spin around only to receive a second blow across his shoulders which felled him to the ground. Through half closed eyes he could see the gravediggers suffering similar treatment as the watchmen beat them to the floor and proceeded to kick them into unconsciousness.

'Why are these here?' The petty constable stood at the doorway of the brick built lockup and nodded to a member of the watch, who took it as instruction to throw cold water from a leather bucket over the four men laying prone on the floor.

'Causing an affray, sir, we caught 'em trying to break down the door of the Unicorn in Mill Street. They put up a fight so we gave 'em a seeing to.'

'I hope you didn't touch them with your bare hands, they could be infected.' The watchman looked at the Petty Constable and smirked.

'No, sir, we kept them all at a stick's distance you might say.'

The cold water drained off between the gaps in the paving slabs and the soaking wet quartet looked up at the watchman through half closed and bleary eyes, squinting as a shaft of early evening sunlight illuminated their bedraggled faces.

Thaddeus could not make out the face of the Petty Constable as the man was silhouetted in the door frame, but something about his voice sounded familiar.

'Captain Henderson, sir?'

'Who wants to know?'

'Sergeant Thaddeus Cleaver. Well I was.'

'Cleaver? Sergeant Cleaver. We had you down as a deserter. Stand up, man, so I can see you properly.'

Thaddeus pulled himself to his feet, nursing his throbbing wrist and wincing at the pain coming from his bruised ribs.

'Well good Lord it is you, Cleaver, look at the state of you, man. You used to be a bloody good soldier; what the hell has happened to you since you buggered off with the Dutchman's daughter?'

'Long story, sir.'

'Well I've got the time, follow me.' Thaddeus raised an eyebrow and gave a half smile to the three gravediggers as he followed the Petty Constable out of the lockup and into a small dark panelled room that the man was using as an office.

'Take a seat, Cleaver, and give me the gory details.' Thaddeus began to relate the tale of the theft of the gold from Fredrik Evertsen, but the ex Captain interrupted him.

'I know about the theft, Jephson told me; do you remember him, John wasn't it. He took a blade in the ribs, but fortunately he survived; he's back working as a cobbler now. Since the New Model Army disbanded we've either all had to go back to our previous lives and occupations or seek out new ones; but do carry on. I want to know why you didn't come back with Jephson. Too late to hang you now, but I'm just bloody curious.' Thaddeus took a deep slow breath then carried on with his story, explaining how he had woken up on the ship bound for Amsterdam and how he had realised that there was no way back after killing the robbers. Henderson listened intently as Thaddeus told how he had lost Catharina and how his fortunes had gone into decline, bringing him ultimately to the parish lock up.

'You've had a rough journey, Cleaver, you were a good soldier in your day and deserve better than this.' Henderson went quiet for a moment and gazed at his clasped hands, leaving Thaddeus to sit looking at him in embarrassed silence.

'Are you still a man that sees an opportunity for what it is? I know you used to be.' Thaddeus thought for a moment, still trying to clear his head from the alcohol and beating.

'Yes, sir, I am.' He knew as a soldier not to reply 'I think so.' Because experience had taught him that you only progressed in the army if you were sure of yourself.

'I need good men in the watch, men that can think first and then act; not like the idiots you met this afternoon. I want things to change Cleaver, I want London to be a safe place to live now that the King is back on the throne, despite us both fighting to keep him off of it. We have to accept what has happened and live with it, but not in a city where wives and children are terrified of going out in daylight let alone at night. The plague has made London lawless, and people are profiteering from the chaos. At the moment our job is only to get up in front of the magistrates those that are pointed out to us as being criminals by the victims and enraged citizens. It is not our job to say who a criminal is, or to find and stop those that repeatedly rob, rape and murder, not unless someone else points the finger, do you understand?'

'Yes, sir.' Thaddeus could sense the way that this was going; he was being recruited.

'Cleaver, as you may know it's every citizen's duty to act as a constable or to be in the watch voluntarily for at least a year; so you are in fact obliged to work for the parish for nothing. However certain good citizens are rich enough to pay others to do their duty for them, which is why I've been a Petty Constable for a few years now. It's not great pay, but there are perks; I need someone like you, someone that I can trust. I know you screwed up with the Dutchman's gold, but from what Jephson told me, I don't think that was your fault; I think you could be a thief taker.'

'Like those thugs of yours outside you mean?' Thaddeus was still trying to see the opportunity that Henderson mentioned.

'No they are just thugs as you say. I need someone that can use their brain to determine who a criminal is, not just grab someone in a hue and cry. There are people that will pay good money to know who the real villains are, and get them onto a gallows; that's the real art of being a thief taker. Are you interested?'

'Do I have a choice?' Thaddeus was still not convinced that this was a real opportunity for him; it seemed that Henderson would be the one to benefit by having more people on the streets.

'Think about it, Cleaver, do you want to go back to carting corpses, or do you want a chance to grab bastards like your Ned Bennet and make sure that he swings.'

'And you say there's pay involved?'

'You won't get rich but neither will you starve, are you in?'

'Yes, sir, I'm in. When do I start?'

13 SECRET PASSIONS

London-October- 1665

The priest knelt down beside the mutilated body of the naked girl, and picking up her discarded coif cap used it to wipe the blood from his hands as he gazed at the numbers nine three zero which had been traced across her forehead. The central churchyard was shrouded in early morning mist and smoke from the burning braziers, but other than for him was empty, as the gravediggers, having finished their night's work, had left for their beds in their makeshift hovels at its perimeter.

Gathering up her clothes from around her, he bundled them on top of her body, before placing his arms under her shoulders and knees he lifted her from the marble grave slab where she had been butchered. Father Turnbull carried the girl's body down to the plague pit, and gently dropped it into a freshly dug space before taking a spade and covering it with lime and soil, a ritual he had witnessed the grave diggers perform daily since the pits were dug earlier in the summer. The death toll from the plague was now decreasing daily, but that said, he knew that the corpse would be covered by more bodies that night and hidden forever.

The closure order on inns and taverns was now in the main being ignored, and slowly *Le Puits de Chocolat* was seeing the return of its old clientele. Some faces were conspicuously absent, including a few of the chocolate girls, and the assumption was that the plague had claimed them. Monsieur Coultier as ever played the convivial host to his guests both upstairs and down, and as he entered the elite blue salon he was approached by the man Harper.

'Coultier, you and others have made mention many times of the availability within this establishment of, how shall we say, additional delights, no doubt to those that can afford your exorbitant prices. Well I, having been left a legacy by my uncle who was foolish enough to catch the pox and die, am now in a position to partake of such pleasures; so tell me man, what do you have to excite me?' Monsieur Coultier disliked Harper intensely, but he regularly spent good money in the establishment and was becoming more and more well connected.

'Dreams turned to reality and fired by your own imagination, Mr Harper, mixed with physical pleasure brought about and shared by like minded individuals; all as you say, at a price.'

'Coultier, I am intrigued; the price whatever it is I am sure I can now afford, so presume that I am now a customer for these services.'

'Very well, Mr Harper, come back here at seven this evening, and I will get one of the chocolate girls to bring you a very special beverage and spiced confection. Consume them both and I will collect you from this salon two hours later, a necessary delay but one worth waiting for I assure you. After that you will enter the room of delights where your mind will be the architect of your experience.'

At nine o'clock precisely, Monsieur Coultier entered the blue salon and discreetly beckoned to Harper to follow him. They walked out and along the hallway to the door at the very end, above which on its surround, a lion's head was carved. Monsieur Coultier grasped the heavy brass doorknob and opened it, and with a flourish of his arm, gestured to Harper to enter.

The room at first appeared to be in almost total darkness, except for a dim candle flickering within a glass holder. Very quickly his eyes grew accustomed to the weak light.

'How are you feeling, Mr Harper?'

'Strangely exhilarated; my heart is pounding in my chest, and your voice sounds slightly distant; what is this room?'

'This is the gateway to the room of delights, Mr Harper, please remove your clothes and put these on.' He handed Harper a crimson silk robe together with a white Venetian half mask from which hung ribbons for it to be tied at the back.

'When you are appropriately attired you may enter the room through this door.'

Opposite the entrance from which they had entered, Monsier Coultier now stood before a white door that was framed with a very ornate surround. Centred in the door, about a quarter of the way down, Harper could make out in the candlelight a carving of what appeared to be an apple tree.

'I will leave you now, Mr Harper, enjoy your experience; you may feel somewhat remote for a day or two afterwards but that can be part of the pleasure, so please enjoy.'

The little Frenchman walked past Harper and left the room by the main door out into the hallway. Harper stood alone in the half-light, and self-consciously began to undress. He picked up the long crimson robe and slipped it over his head. As it fell against his body the silk initially felt cold against his skin, but its softness and sensual touch combined with an anticipation of what was to come triggered him into a state of arousal. He placed the mask so as to disguise his upper face, and tying the ribbons immediately felt disembodied; it was as if he were a spirit observing the world without he himself being seen. Empowered by the anonymity of the mask he slowly turned the doorknob and pushed open the door into the room of delights. The windowless chamber was a quarter of the size of the blue salon, and slightly brighter than the previous with a strange glow, as the candles around the room were in red stained cut glasses which produced moving shadows on the walls as they flickered. He was aware of others in the room who, similarly dressed, paid him no initial attention. Two men sat close together in a corner on a padded bench and seemed at first to be in quiet conversation but he soon realised that they were intimately caressing each other, as were a man and a woman on an embroidered chaise against the far wall. The door from which he had entered began to open and a robed and masked figure entered. Harper felt his heart jump at the sight of crimson silk pulled tightly across feminine curves; the half mask sat above a sensuous mouth to the right of which was a small crescent shaped beauty patch. He felt no shame in staring blatantly as his mask seemed to provide his voyeurism sanctuary.

The woman moved trance-like towards him, and placing a hand upon his chest, walked him slowly backwards to a vacant chaise where she ran her hands over his silk clad torso before pushing him down onto the upholstered seat where she sat down beside him. Her dark hair hung loosely in ringlets over her covered shoulders, appearing to Harper to take on a life of its own, twisting and turning like Medusa's helm, and now brushing against his exposed face as she leaned in close to him to stroke a finger across his lips which parted as he playfully bit it. His head was swimming now from the effects of the hallucinogenic beverage prepared for him by Monsieur Coultier, and any inhibitions that he may have felt had flown as he cupped the woman's ample breast through the silk robe, feeling her nipples harden at the touch of his fingers. The woman's hand was now raking across his covered thigh, tantalisingly getting closer and closer to his straining silk covered erection which she suddenly took in her hand, gently stroking it through its sensual covering.

The woman rolled across his thighs now straddling him, and sitting bolt upright slipped her loose robe over her head as Harper let out a small gasp at the sight of her voluptuous body, milk white, firm and flawless except for two small moles spaced like a viper's bite at her throat. She pulled at his robe exposing his manhood, which she voraciously mounted. He momentarily closed his eyes in pleasure and on opening them again could actually see snakes upon her head, which then started to bite into his flesh, each bite producing an agonising ecstasy. The chaise appeared to have become the back of a Minotaur, which bucked and arched violently, forcing him against her thrusting pelvis. Harper had always been a sexual predator but now he had become the hunted, and the experience was overwhelming as the woman began to pound his chest with her fists, and then slap his face from side to side as she screamed obscenities at him.

Two figures appeared as if from nowhere and stood either side of the dark haired woman; both were naked except for their half masks. One, a man stood behind her as she violently rode Harper and fondled her breasts as the other, a woman, took her face in her hands and kissed her passionately on her open mouth. Harper was now in a weak and confused state, his body was covered in a million red ants as birds swooped through the rising mist towards his eyes. He was spinning along the dark hallway then stumbling down stairs, before being pushed up onto a golden chariot and flying across the night sky to fall face down onto new mown hay.

Harper woke in his own bed at around ten o'clock the following morning. He lay on his back looking at the cracked ceiling, feeling completely drained yet satisfied. He could hear the noise of the usual daily activities coming up from the street, but they sounded more distant than usual. He could remember the beautiful masked woman and her voracity as she made love to him, and the pain coming from his face and torso brought back the violent nature of her passionate assault upon him. He swung his legs from off the bed and tried to stand, but it was as if he was drunk and his knees gave way sending him crashing to the floor. He felt as if something was crawling across his chest and in a panic he tried to brush off the red ants that his confused mind had placed there, before pulling himself back onto the bed and falling once again into a deep sleep.

'Ah, Mr Harper, I trust you are well and have no ill effects from your visit to our room of delights.'

'Coultier, I have never experienced anything like that before in my life. For the last two days I have been hearing and seeing things that nightmares are made of, as well as remembering physical experiences of such an erotic nature that I desperately need again to sate my lust.' The little Frenchman smiled as he moved in closer and placed a hand on Harper's elbow.

'Well, Mr Harper, the room exists for the pleasure of my special customers, although from what they tell me I cannot guarantee that the exact events they encountered the first time can be repeated; for as I say, your imagination determines your experience, therefore your next visit may be entirely different. It could take you to a new higher level of awareness and gratification or deliver you to a hell of your own making, Mr Harper, that is what makes it so exciting is it not?' Harper smiled at Monsieur Coultier and lowered his head in line with the little man's ear.

'When can I visit the room again?'

'Not for a few days yet as your mind needs to recover from the effects of your last revelation; for that is how I see it, in that room your true self is revealed to you in all its shame or glory. Meanwhile, Mr Harper, enjoy the company of your fellows and the delicious, if not more traditional beverages available to you here in our two upstairs salons.' Harper gave a small nod of his head and wandered off to be amongst the laughing and preening guests already in the blue salon. He waved politely at one or two individuals that he recognised around the room and spoke momentarily to others as he flitted from clique to clique before finally standing in front of the seated Mrs Fitz-Herbert, who as usual, was surrounded by an entourage of admirers.

'Madam, your servant, I trust that you are well?'

'Extremely thank you, Harper, you know most of these gentlemen I am sure. We were discussing how, since the onset of the plague, it is difficult to get good servants now in London. I desperately need a new groom since my last had the bad manners to die, and I do so miss a good ride; do you ride, Mr Harper?'

Harper was about to reply when his eyes were drawn down to the sparkling necklace adorning Mrs Fitz-Herbert's throat, above which, were two small moles, spaced like a viper's bite.

14 THE WATCH

London October 1665

'Cleaver, I want you to go down to Pargeters warehouse in Lower Thames Street, they've just had another break in. Some bastard's made off with a small fortune in tobacco.' Thaddeus had just entered the watch room and had barely had a chance to shake off the rain from his cloak before Petty Constable Henderson addressed him.

'What about the man they found murdered on London Bridge, sir? I'm going to need some time to find out who the victim is, let alone who killed the poor sod.'

'There's no profit for us in solving murders, not unless the victims family can cough up a decent fee. But theft from a merchant, that's a different story; they've got money and are prepared to pay to get the villains locked away, and pay even more to get their goods back. So no argument; get down there now and crack a few heads to see who's offering a cheap smoke around the taverns.'

Thaddeus reined in his horse outside Pargeter's warehouse; a grim, lapped wooden façade belied the wealth in goods stored within. The owner, a wigged portly man in his fifties, opened the side door to let him in.

'I want these bastards strung up, do you hear me? I'll be ruined if they keep bleeding me dry like this. Two bales of the finest Virginia tobacco, do you have any idea what that's worth? They hacked their way in through the wall like rats, killed the dogs and pissed off into the night to shred and sell the stuff no doubt.'

'Did anyone see them?' Thaddeus kneeled down and picked up a splintered piece of timber from the floor.

'The boot maker across the street saw them make off with the stuff in a small handcart, but he didn't give chase; cowardly bastard. So what are you going to do about it? I've offered the Petty Constable a tidy sum to catch the vermin with a bonus if he gets the tobacco back, although I think there's thin chance of that.'

'I'll speak to the boot maker and see if he can give me a description, then I'll spread the word amongst the tavern informers; they'll turn in their own Grandmothers for the price of a jug of ale. Anyway not much I can do here, sir. I suggest that you consider some iron bars against the inside walls, it's the only thing that will stop them breaking in. I'll come back again as soon as I have any information.'

With that Thaddeus made his way out into the street. It was still raining as he patted the steaming flank of his miserable looking horse which he had tethered to a post. He walked across the filthy street, the mud splashing up over his boots, and he shuddered as the cold rain bit into his cheeks. He opened the door of the boot maker's shop and stepped into the small workshop. It was warmed by an open fire, which gave the room a pleasing amber glow and a homely atmosphere compared to the stark expanse of the warehouse. He could see a man coming towards him from a back room in response to the tinkling of the small bell triggered by his entry through the front door.

'How can I help you, sir?' The man had obviously been eating, as he discreetly brushed away crumbs from the side of his mouth.

'Bless my soul, John, John Jephson, it is you isn't it?'

'Thaddeus, Thaddeus Cleaver, I thought you to be dead. Thank the Lord you're not of course. Come, come into the back and eat with us, you're a sight for sore eyes.' John led Thaddeus through to a back kitchen where a woman was sitting eating from a plate of cold meat at a square wooden table.

'Martha, this is, Thaddeus Cleaver, who you have heard me speak of as dead; well as you can see he isn't. Thaddeus this is my wife, Martha.' Thaddeus gently took the woman's extended hand.

'Please sit down, Mr Cleaver I will get you some food and ale.' Martha scurried around the small kitchen preparing a plate for Thaddeus as he told John of his life in Holland and the story of his subsequent return to England.

'You have done well for yourself, John, a good business, and if I may say so, a lovely wife.' Martha blushed as she poured more ale for the men.

'And a beautiful daughter too, Thaddeus, Lizzie, she is working at the moment; she pays her way as a chocolate girl as they call them, serving the well-to-do at a chocolate house. We are very proud of her. But what brings you here to my shop; were you seeking me out?'

'Not by name, John, I was investigating a theft from Pargeter's warehouse across the street. He told me that you may have seen the robbers, is that so?' John let out a sigh as he stared at his clasped hands on the table.

'I saw them, Thaddeus, and I feel ashamed.'

'Ashamed, John, why?' John looked up as he hammered his hand down onto the table.

'Ashamed that I did nothing; There was a time, as you well know, Thaddeus, that I would have given chase and cracked their heads; I was a soldier with little to live for, up for the fight as were we all; you remember? But now, since I took that blade trying to protect the Dutchman, I feel that I have come too close to death, and that God for some reason on that occasion spared me. Now as you can see I have much to live for, and something on that night held me back from doing my duty as a citizen, and for that I am ashamed.'

'Then don't be, John, you were right not to challenge them, as you say you have much to live for and now family responsibilities, I'm sure that in your position I would have done the same. But tell me, did you notice anything about them that may be of help to me?'

'Notice anything? Thaddeus I know who it was; it was Ned Bennet.' Thaddeus felt a burst of adrenaline burn into his stomach like fire.

'Bennet; he's back then. The Americas must have spat him out like the bad taste he is.'

'The last time I saw him was that day with you, when he stuck me like a pig, I don't remember much after that, but last night he had that baby-faced henchman with him too. Other than that, sadly, I can't help you; they made off up the street with a hand cart, making for who knows where.'

'John, you have helped me more than you know; I have vowed to kill that man and now that I know he's back in England I have the opportunity. Martha, thank you for your hospitality and please look after John, he's a good man, but I'm sure you don't need me to tell you that. John, we must not be strangers: now I know where you are we must speak more on old times.'

Thaddeus stood up, shook John firmly by the hand and walked back out into the street. The rain had stopped and the late autumn sunshine had started to break through the clouds. As he mounted his horse he felt a determination that he hadn't experienced for a long time; he would spread the word to the tavern informers and instruct the watch to search every known den of thieves for the man whose description he could now give them. He was determined that this time he would not let Ned Bennet slip through his fingers.

The watch duly went about their task, and faces peered in curiosity through dirty drapes as they marched through the back streets kicking in doors and dragging out anyone who they thought might know the whereabouts of Ned Bennet and his band of followers. Thaddeus felt a strange sense of power as his new position gave him the men and resources to be an effective hunter, whereas previously, it was he that had unwittingly been preyed upon by this evil and devious man. The taverns produced the expected flood of rumours from those more concerned for their next drink than their vulnerable throats, and the watch scoured the city following up on every lead, which were mostly fuelled by malice or revenge; save one. As Thaddeus sat in a crowded inn eating a simple meal of chicken stew, a young woman walked towards him. She was dressed like a prostitute, and with a surly air pushed away the groping hands of some of the inn's rougher customers as she made her way across the room.

'I hear you're looking for a man called Bennet.' The woman sat down uninvited on a stool opposite Thaddeus, and proceeded to help herself to a chunk of bread from the table.

'You know him?' Thaddeus spoke without looking up as he continued to eat the thin stew.

'Yes I know him; I've lived with him for the last year, that is until he took up with another poor cow. He's a cruel bastard; gave me what he called his protection in exchange for most of my earnings, but his protection turned out to be knocking me about and riding me for free whenever he fancied. So what's it worth to know where he is?' Thaddeus took the purse from his belt, untied the drawstring and spread the contents out onto the table. He then pushed four groats towards the woman and pressed two fingers on a golden guinea.

'That for telling me where to find him, and this, when we catch him.'

'A guinea now and another when you get him, and you better be bloody sure that you do get him or he'll do for me.' Thaddeus smiled and pushed the guinea toward her.

'He's been selling knocked off tobacco to the smokers around the inns and taverns, but he says its slow work, and he don't like work does our Ned. Anyway, he reckons he can make more money selling it up market to the coffee and chocolate house owners for them to sell to their fancy customers. He knows this girl who works at a chocolate house, and tonight she is arranging for him to see the owner.'

'Where and when?'

'Eight o'clock at a place called *Le Puits de Chocolat* over by Bishopsgate.'

Thaddeus pulled his cloak tighter around his body. It was still light, but the autumn evenings were getting colder. He stood with six members of the watch in an alleyway across the street from the chocolate house, watching the carriages come and go as the wealthy clientele entered the establishment for an evening's pleasure in a style that he could never afford on his meagre earnings. Small groups of wigged gentlemen and finely dressed ladies disembarked from their vehicles laughing and engaged in animated conversations. Occasionally individuals would also arrive by carriage or sometimes on foot, and meet up with others outside or enter straight away through the front or rear doors of the chocolate house.

It was nearing eight o'clock as a lone figure appeared at the end of the street and started to make his way towards a girl who had stepped out from an alley at the side of *Le Puits de Chocolat*, and was now beckoning to the man. On reaching the girl a conversation ensued, the details of which could not be heard by Thaddeus and the waiting watchmen, but by their body language the man and girl seemed to be arguing. The man turned his head, and the soft lights emanating from inside the building, together with the diminishing daylight, was enough illumination for Thaddeus to recognise the scarred face of Ned Bennet.

The conversation between the girl and Bennet now seemed to be very heated, and Thaddeus watched as the thin figure grabbed the girl by the throat and struck her across the face.

'Right, now. Get him.' Thaddeus and the watchmen moved as one to cross the street, but the noise from their boots on the cobbled street alerted Bennet to the danger, who grabbing the girl by her arm, pulled her back into the alley. The watchmen followed, but there was no sign of the man or girl, and the alley branched off in many directions. They stood still and listened, but could hear nothing.

'We can't lose him now, we are so close; split up and search the alleys, but be careful, he is a vicious bastard and won't think twice about sticking a knife in your guts.' Thaddeus was seething. To have been but a few paces away and to have lost him was inexcusable, but also understandable as the light was now fading fast, and the narrow streets, other than for the dim candle and lamplight now slowly appearing from the inside of houses, were unlit, making the maze of alleyways and entries almost unnavigable in the dark. Ned Bennet had made good his escape, either through local knowledge of the area or by sheer good luck, but Thaddeus was now more determined than ever to hunt down the man that had come to be a plague upon his life.

15 CRY MURDER

London October 1665

The young boy stood frozen to the spot, wide-eyed and unable to speak. He clutched awkwardly to his chest a milk jug which his mother had sent him to get filled, the contents of which now spilled freely down his ragged coat onto the cobbles, the white liquid merging slowly with the dark red pool of blood at his feet. He had never seen a dead body of any description before, and to be confronted here, in a narrow alley, with the horrendously mutilated corpse of a half naked girl would leave a deep psychological scar which would be with the boy for the rest of his life. After what seemed like an age, the jug slipped from his limp arms to the floor and shattered, the crashing sound shaking him from his transfixed state. He turned and ran, and ran, as fast as he could, until he came upon a scene of normality, a flurry of people going about their day-to-day business in a busy street

'Murder, Murder, Murder.' The boy grabbed at passers by who at first tried to shake him loose, but then, through his insistence, listened to his tale and followed him back to the grisly scene.

Petty Constable Henderson looked stressed as he ran his fingers through his hair at the temples before hammering both fists down hard on his desk.

'I've told you before Cleaver, there's no profit for us in murder. Once she's been identified get her body back to her relatives and get on with finding this man Bennet.'

'But, sir, I think the murder is connected to Bennet.'

'How so?' Henderson spat out the words and was obviously losing his patience with Thaddeus. He was under pressure from the city's merchants as more and more warehouse break-ins were being reported.

'The victim appears to be the chocolate girl that Bennet ran off with the night we challenged him at *Le Puits de Chocolat*. I believe he may be her killer, and if we can prove it and put the word about, someone else might come forward and turn him in. So really, sir, by looking into her murder we *are* chasing Bennet and that should keep the merchants happy.'

'Look, go down to this piss and chocolate or whatever it's called, I hate the bloody French almost as much as I hate the Dutch. Find out if anyone working there had seen Bennet before, and find out as much as you can about the girl, where she used to go after work and all that sort of thing. I know you want Bennet as much as I want to keep the merchants happy as paying customers, so what are you waiting for?'

'Yes, sir, but first I need to find out how the girl died, it might help.'

'How's that going to help, she was butchered wasn't she; what more do we need to know?'

'It's just that I believe that the more information we have, the more it will help us to understand Bennet, the way he thinks, the way he reacts.'

'All right just get it done and get it done quickly, and more to the point, just get Bennet.'

Old Mary, the searcher, stood motionless in the backroom of the watch house, looking down at the body of the murdered girl, tears streaming down her lined, grimy face.

'Do you understand what I want you to do, Mary? I need to know how this girl was killed so that I can get an idea of what sort of man Bennet is, how he thinks, what excites him. Then I might be able to track him down through his needs and habits.' Mary wiped her eyes with the corner of her grubby apron.

'What sort of man would do this to the poor girl, Mr Cleaver? He has to be some sort of monster; just look at the poor wretch.'

'I know, Mary, she's not a pleasant sight, but it's important that you tell me everything that you find. I'm depending on you. In the absence of a proper doctor you are the closest I can find to someone experienced in examining the dead and dying, and more to the point, you know what should be right on a woman, you know what I mean. I need to know exactly what this bastard has done to her. Anyway there's a couple of groats in it for you, three if you can tell me all I need to know this morning.'

'Don't worry, Mr Cleaver, I won't let you down, but I'll need water and some rags to clean her up a bit, and I don't suppose I could have a mug of gin to help with the shock like?'

'Whatever you need, Mary, I just need some bloody clues to find this butcher.'

Thaddeus left Mary to her gruesome task and rode down to *Le Puits de Chocolat*. Monsieur Coultier was not pleased to receive this rough looking thief taker in his fine establishment and ushered Thaddeus into a small office.

'I do not have time to talk at length to you; I am a busy man so please ask your questions quickly and then go.' Thaddeus immediately disliked this man's dismissive air and intentionally took his time sitting down before disdainfully looking around the room, and speaking in a low authoritative tone, began to question the man.

'I understand from those working here that the murdered girl was called Annie Taylor; what can you tell me about her and her connection to Ned Bennet?'

'The girl worked here for about six months, she did her job well and was liked by the other girls and customers; of this man you call Bennet, I have no knowledge.'

'I have it on good authority that he had arranged to meet with you the night the girl was dragged off by him.' Thaddeus looked directly at the Frenchman and narrowed his eyes.

'The girl just said to me that a man had approached her wanting to supply us with quality tobacco at a good price; I just inferred to her that I would give him a few minutes to hear him out if she brought him along, but I never got to meet the man or beyond that point see Annie again.'

'You don't seem overly concerned by the death of one of your girls, Monsieur Coultier?'

'I have lost many girls this past year; some I know have definitely fallen victim to the plague, others have just disappeared, and I can only assume that they have run off, away from the city without the courtesy of informing me, or they have ended up being quarantined with relatives or friends and now lie in a pit somewhere. My concern is that I have to find replacements; beyond that, in these times I cannot afford sentiment.'

Thaddeus took details of the girl's address, and having established from the other chocolate girls that Annie had only recently been approached by Bennet and had no real relationship with him he returned to the watch house.

'I've never seen anything like it, Mr Cleaver. Look at this.' Mary pulled back a bloodied cloth, which was covering an object on the table to reveal a blood-streaked apple.

'An apple, Mary, I don't understand?' He looked at her impatiently.

'It was where her heart should have been. Whoever did this cut out her heart and put the apple in its place. Oh and I looked at her privates as you asked, she had been messed with, Mr Cleaver, and roughly too I would say. Poor girl was put through all sorts of indignities.'

'Anything else I should know about?' Thaddeus's brain was racing trying to fathom out why Bennet would substitute an apple for the girl's heart; what significance could it have?

'She's been strangled too by the looks of it, look, here on her throat, something has cut into her skin and left a mark, patterned like. And just one more thing, Mr Cleaver, what do you think this could mean?' Mary pulled aside the girl's long dark matted hair from across her forehead, and there, written in blood were the numbers *930*.

'Does that mean anything to you?'

'Nine three zero. Nothing immediately comes to mind, Mary, what do you think it could mean?'

'I have no idea, Mr Cleaver, I mean numbers could

be anything couldn't they, from the number of bricks in a wall to the number of miles a man travels, or even the number of days till something comes about; it's a mystery, it surely is.'

'Cover her up, Mary. She has told us much, yet nothing at all I fear. Let's hope we never see the like again.'

The tall figure of Father Turnbull almost glided between the tables and standing drinkers in the tavern until he reached the table occupied by Thaddeus, who was eating alone in a quiet corner.

'Still seeking out cheap food and low company I see.' Thaddeus looked up and gave a wry grin as the priest spoke.

'Being a thief taker pays less than carting the dead so that's why *I'm* here, and I do enjoy the simple fayre, it tastes much better without the stink of decay in my nostrils. But what brings you here, Father?' The priest pulled over a chair and sat down.

'Like yourself, Thaddeus, near empty pockets sometimes lead us to places that otherwise we would avoid.'

Father Turnbull ordered some food and ale, and the two men brought each other up to date with the recent events in their lives. He was thankful that the plague deaths were now noticeably decreasing, as like Thaddeus, being constantly surrounded by death and grief his spirits had started to decline. He was now able to spend more time on his writing, and had been investigating rumours of increased activity by the very cults that were the subjects of his books and pamphlets. Thaddeus spoke of his new position and how Ned Bennet had returned to blight his life. He then proceeded to tell the priest about the discovery of Annie Taylor's body. As he described Mary's findings the priest began to grow pale. At first Thaddeus thought that this was due to the horrific nature of the girls mutilated body, but then he could see that something else was troubling the man.

'I'm sorry, Father, I can see that my graphic description of the poor girl's state has upset you. Did you know her by any chance?' The priest remained silent and stared blankly at the table. 'Father Turnbull, are you alright?'

'Yes, Thaddeus, I'm sorry, It's just that what you have described I have seen before. Tell me, was anything written across her forehead, in her blood?'

'Yes there was, Father, numbers, a nine a three and a zero, do you know what it means?'

The priest took a large swig of ale from his mug and then cradled it between his long slender hands.

'Nine three zero happens to be the number of years that according to the Bible, Adam lived. A number which, in itself could be coincidental and insignificant, but add to that the replacing of the girl's heart with an apple, then I am seeing a definite link to Adam and Eve, wouldn't you say? Look, Thaddeus, there's no easy way for me to say this, I have a confession to make. Some time ago I came across the body of a dead girl in the churchyard; she had been laid out across a tabled tombstone. From what you have just described I would say that she had been murdered in an identical manner to Annie Taylor.'

'Did you report this at the time?'

'No, Thaddeus, to my shame I didn't. I believed that

if the word got out that there had been a murder with a secular connection it would cause panic within the community and that, through ignorance, vigilantes would seek out anyone with a connection to any minority religious belief. People want someone or something to blame for the plague, and who better than someone murdering innocents with a perceived religious motive.'

'So what happened to the body?'

'I buried it amongst the plague dead; no one except myself, you and the killer know anything about it.' Thaddeus seemed perplexed; it was looking less and less like the murders had been committed by Bennet, for although he was an evil man, Thaddeus did not consider him to be a fanatic, but then again he could be wrong; what did he really know about him? He knew that he was a thief, motivated by easy money; he knew that he had killed, but killed men whilst in the act of thievery and as part of a gang of thieves, whereas the murder of the girls seemed to be very much a ritual, premeditated act.

'Tell me, Father, do you know who she was?'

'I had never seen her before; there was nothing in her possession that gave clue to her name, although her clothes seemed to be that of a serving girl of some kind.'

'A serving girl; Annie Taylor worked as a chocolate girl, there could be a connection. Tell me more about this Adam and Eve stuff. Why would anyone kill with a reference to the Garden of Eden?'

'Kill I don't know, but I do know that for centuries a cult known as the Adamites have carried out all sorts of excesses proclaiming to have regained Adams's primeval innocence. They believe in the abolition of marriage and practice all sorts of carnal acts whilst holding the belief that sin would not exist had it not been for Eve, therefore lawlessness is a more natural state. So you can understand why I write my literature condemning all cults of this kind; it would bring about the end of society as we know it if they had a broad following.'

'Until you spoke of them I had never even heard of the Adamites so how on earth would I go about tracking them down?'

'A dilemma indeed, Thaddeus, they are in essence a secret society, a society built around hedonism. By its very nature a hedonistic lifestyle does not thrive within poverty, therefore you will need to look amongst the richer classes, the haves rather than the have nots. But even amongst them, those that have not been touched by this cults depravity lead an exclusive life, and those that they exclude are the likes of you and me. So you see, Thaddeus, although we may know where to start looking, how do we get amongst them; they see us as the very dirt beneath their very feet.'

16 HAND OF THE KING

London-November 1665

'You have done well, Richard, and your success in tracking down the absconders that signed my Father's death warrant has been duly noted. You are a good friend to me, and I wish that I could acknowledge the fact publicly, but it serves me better that people just see you as an occasional face at court and not too close to me.' Richard Valletort reached out to take the extended hand, and kissed the royal ring.

'Thank you, Your Majesty, it is, and always will be, an honour and a privilege to serve my King.'

The two men sat inside the large black carriage and continued talking as the driver stood holding the bridles of the two lead horses, speaking softly to calm them. Mounted soldiers, wearing long black cloaks to conceal their uniforms, positioned themselves at a discreet distance from the coach, far enough away not to hear the conversation inside, but close enough to respond should any threat to the King arise. Richard had ridden to the crossroads, tethered his horse to a tree, and waited in the clearing for the king's coach to appear. This was an assignation that he had fulfilled on now so many occasions.

'What of the Dutch shipping owner of whom you spoke at our last meeting, do you think he could be of value to us?' King Charles gazed out of the coach window at the early morning sun shining through the trees as he spoke, then slowly turned his head to prompt Richard's response.

'As a man I deem him to be worthless, crude,

uncultured and driven by base desires. Yet his business gives him access to many ports and many houses where, if suitably persuaded, he could obtain all sorts of information and intelligence should a need arise. I shall groom Johan Evertsen as I have others, to become without their knowing, the eyes and ears of His Majesty.'

'Excellent, Richard, and now of lighter things, what is the latest gossip in the chocolate houses, is the Colonel's wife, what is her name again?'

'Mrs Fitz- Herbert, Your Majesty.'

'Mrs Fitz-Herbert, yes; is she still being tupped in their numbers by the gentry and trade alike?'

'Yes, Your Majesty, a woman of voracious appetite.' The King raised an eyebrow and smiled.

'Tell me, Richard, do you think that I should find some pleasure in her company?'

Richard thought for a moment before answering, not wanting to displease the King but genuinely concerned for his interests.

'I fear that she is not a lady that I would trust. She seems devoid not only of morals but also discretion, and I have been a witness to her outbursts of temper and I'm afraid to say, violence. She uses men as if they are actors in a play, and she writes the plots, placing herself always in the leading role.' The King gave a broad smile as he reached across the carriage and playfully punched Richard on the knee.

'An actress, Richard, now there's a thought, a woman with imagination and beauty, what pleasures could that combination bring eh!'

'Too dangerous a game with her I think, Your Majesty, yet if the thought pleases you I would suggest a visit or two to the theatre to see and meet ladies who are at the top of their profession, very discreet and who would be very, very grateful for, Your Majesty's, patronage.'

'It is a shame that I need you to be faceless, as I believe you would be such good company, Richard, on such an excursion. But for now, use the Dutchman; I need to know what the people in London think of me and to uncover any disloyalty or plots against me. Richard, we are done for now; enjoy your ride back to the city. I will amuse myself on my return journey by thinking about your suggestion regarding the theatre.'

Both men laughed as Richard Valletort opened the carriage door and stepped down onto a blanket of frost-covered leaves; he then nodded to the coachman to release his hold on the horses, and to once again take up his place on the drivers seat. The sound of a sharp tap of a cane against the interior carriage roof signalled to the coachman to gently whip the horses into movement, and Valletort, standing by his mount, watched as the King's coach and escort of outriders made its way along the country road towards Oxford.

Thaddeus Cleaver walked towards the door of the boot maker's shop. Nearly a month had passed since his last visit, and once inside John and Martha Jephson were pleased yet surprised to see him again so soon. John shook him firmly by the hand and led his former Sergeant into the back room where, as before, Martha sat him down and poured him some ale.

'What brings you back so soon, Thaddeus? Not that it's not always good to see you.' Thaddeus took a long drink from the tankard and looked John straight in the eye.

'I must be honest with you, John, I'm here to see your daughter, Lizzie isn't it? Don't worry, she's done nothing wrong, it's just that when I was last here you told me that she was working at a chocolate house, and I think that she may be able to help me catch a killer.' Martha took her husband's arm and pulled herself close to him.

'This won't put her in any danger will it, Mr Cleaver?'

'No, Martha, quite the opposite; I believe that with her help I can protect her and all of the other chocolate girls from a very dangerous man. What I am going to tell you must go no further as I don't want to frighten him off.'

Thaddeus told the couple what he knew so far, leaving out the fine details of the murders, but explaining the coincidence of serving girls clothing. He told them how he needed to get close to those in society, but that to do this, he needed information from Lizzie.

'She's upstairs now, Thaddeus, I'll fetch her down.' Martha disappeared up the narrow wooden staircase while John poured them both another tankard of ale. Within a few minutes Martha came back down the stairs, closely followed by Lizzie, who through embarrassment was straightening her dress and fussing with her hair.

'This is our Lizzie, Mr Cleaver, she's a good girl, and a hard worker; ain't that right, John?'

John nodded as he pulled out a chair for his daughter to sit down opposite Thaddeus at the table. He was immediately struck by the look of the girl who was not commonly pretty, but something more. She had elegantly delicate features, and her face radiated a warmth that made Thaddeus feel that, although they had just met, he had known her all his life.

'Lizzie, my name is Thaddeus Cleaver; your father and I served together in the army before I became an officer of the watch. I'm sure that your mother has given you an idea of why I need to speak with you?'

'Yes, sir.' Lizzie dipped her head shyly, and then slowly looked back up at Thaddeus.

'Lizzie, I need to know if you have any knowledge of any of the customers at the chocolate house being involved in…, how shall I put this? Excesses.' He realised once the words left his lips that he hadn't explained himself properly.

'Excesses, Mr Cleaver? I work in a chocolate house, all of the customers one way or another indulge in excess, either too much wine, too much bad language or too much grabbing at our skirts sir.'

'Yes I'm sorry, Lizzie.' For some reason Thaddeus's face started to flush; the girl was having an effect on him and he had to stop himself staring at her.

'By excesses I mean anything beyond that, in secret with others maybe, sort of religious perhaps?' Thaddeus realised that in the girl's presence he was getting almost tongue tied and unable to articulate his true meaning.

'If it's in secret, sir, then I wouldn't know about it. Yet saying that of course, there is the room of delights, but I never hear any hymn singing coming from it.' Lizzie laughed as Thaddeus's brain immediately cleared and began to focus on the reason for his visit.

'The room of delights, what's that all about?'

'Well, sir, I've never been in it, and Monsieur Coultier only lets his special customers use it.' Thaddeus was getting impatient now to know more; could he have homed in on the Adamites so quickly?

'Tell me about his special customers; who are they, and why are they special?'

'Money, sir; from what I hear and can make out, the room of delights costs money, I mean rich people's money. None of us really knows what goes on in there, but people come and go up and down the back stairs, and you can tell from their clothes that they've got money, sir. I've seen Mrs Fitz-Herbert go in quite a few times, and recently the big Dutchman.'

'Dutchman? What's his name?

'I don't know, sir, I don't like him very much, he looks at you funny like; all the chocolate girls try to keep away from him, too free with his hands he is. He's something to do with ships I've heard say, but please, Mr Cleaver, I'm telling you all this as you are a friend of my fathers; I could get into terrible trouble with Monsieur Coultier for telling tales.' Thaddeus could see the worry in her eyes and needed to reassure her. He leaned across the table and placed his hand over hers; it was as if touching her skin released a fire in his loins, a feeling that he thought had died along with Catharina.

'Don't worry, Lizzie, anything you say to me is in the strictest confidence, and if I have to act on it, you will not be implicated in any way. The Dutchman, is he a frequent customer?'

'He first came around spring time. He was often there after that, then he would disappear for a few weeks before, once again, becoming a regular. I think the breaks were to do with his business. He became friendly with Mr Valletort; strange really because he's nice, and I wouldn't have thought that the Dutchman would have been a man that he would have kept company with.'

'Valletort, who is he?'

'Some say he mixes with royalty, well, before the plague I suppose. He's a nice man, very kind; seems in the main to keep himself to himself, that is until the Dutchman arrived. Mr Valletort saved me from Mr Harper and he hasn't bothered me since.' Thaddeus was trying to mentally note the names and their association, and realised that he was still holding Lizzie's hand, which with embarrassment, he released.

'Harper? Tell me more?'

'He's not a nice man, sir, he thinks he is all things to the ladies if you understand me, but he just takes liberties with us chocolate girls. Monsieur Coultier has his measure, and Mr Valletort saved my honour when Mr Harper trapped me in an empty room; terrified of Mr Valletort he was, sir, as if there was history between them.'

Thaddeus realised that this was the first that John and Martha had heard of these stories, and sensed their concern for Lizzie.

'John, I intend to keep an eye on the chocolate house, but I will need Lizzie to feed me information from time to time. As long as she continues to work the public rooms she will be fine, and with your permission, I will ensure that she is escorted home at night by one of my men, or when possible by myself.'

At this Lizzie shot Thaddeus a look and smiled.

17 THE DUTCHMAN

London November 1665

The following night, and for some nights thereafter, Thaddeus escorted Lizzie back to the boot makers shop where he delivered her safe and sound to John and Martha. On their walk back home Lizzie would tell Thaddeus of the days coming and goings, of any new faces at *Le Puits de Chocolat*, and of any snippets of overheard conversations between the clientele, particularly relating to extremes of drinking, carousing or any other form of excess. But alas, events retold in their stories were very tame, and bore no clues towards helping Thaddeus uncover or confirm the existence of Adamites associated with this particular chocolate house or its customers.

December was approaching fast; the night air was bitterly cold and numbed his face as Thaddeus waited as usual for Lizzie to finish work. It was around ten o'clock at night when a small carriage pulled up outside the chocolate house and a large man alighted, pulled his cloak tighter around his body, and paid the driver. There was something familiar about the physicality of the man, and then Thaddeus heard him speak.

'I want you back here at midnight, and it will be the worse for you if you are late my friend.' The thick Dutch accent brought back fleeting pictures of his time with Catharina, as he immediately recognised the voice of Johan Evertsen.

Seeing him standing there, arrogantly dismissing the coach driver, reminded him how much he hated this man and all that he stood for. Having seen Johan's conduct with young women previously, he began to feel concerned for Lizzie's safety. His first thoughts were to go and warn Evertsen off, but something told him that this man's presence here could be an opportunity. He began to realise that this could be his chance to infiltrate the society of the chocolate houses, but he needed to give a lot of thought as to how he could use his knowledge of this man to persuade Evertsen to introduce him into this circle as a gentleman of means, instead of the lowly officer of the watch that he was.

Evertsen walked through the front door of *Le Puits de Chocolat*, roughly brushing past Lizzie without a glance as she was leaving. Thaddeus crossed the road, and gently took Lizzie's arm as they began the relatively short walk back to the boot maker's shop.

'That man who went in as you were leaving; is that the big Dutchman that you were telling me about?' Lizzie nodded as she held tightly onto his arm.

'Yes, Thaddeus, he usually arrives at this time if he is going into the room of delights, sometimes by way of the back stairs, or if he is meeting others first, then through the front door as he did tonight; do you know him?'

'Oh yes, Lizzie, I know him all right, I was married to his cousin before, two years ago in Amsterdam, the plague took her from me. I mean to speak with him tonight, and so need to return here at midnight when his carriage will arrive to pick him up. But first, let me get you safely back home.' Lizzie went quiet for a moment then spoke.

'I didn't know that you were once married,

Thaddeus, you must miss her; what was her name?'
Thaddeus stared straight ahead as they walked briskly.

'Catharina, and yes I miss her every day.' Lizzie's
spirits were deflated as she had become very fond of
her protector, and now realised that she must rival
with a ghost for his affections. She placed her right
hand upon his as he held her arm and they continued
the homeward journey in silence.

Johan Evertsen lay spent on a couch within the
room of delights. His head was still foggy from the
nutmeg potion he had consumed earlier, and his hand
carelessly ran slowly up and down the back of the
masked naked young woman, lying exhausted on top
of his large frame. He stood up quickly, causing the
woman to fall heavily onto the floor where she rolled
over and then lay motionless. Johan walked unsteadily
to the door, and turning the door knob, entered the
dimly lit anti room where he proceeded to dress
himself, after which he made his way down the back
stairs. Once outside in the narrow street, the cold night
air revived him, and his head began to clear as he
walked around to the front of the chocolate house
where his carriage was waiting. The driver opened the
door for him, and Johan put one foot onto the small
step before pulling himself up into the comparative
warmth of the carriage interior. As he slumped back
into the leather upholstery he was surprised by a
familiar voice.

'You look as if you have had a good night, Johan.'
He turned his head sharply to see the outline of a
figure sitting in the opposite corner of the dimly lit
carriage.

'Who are you, what do you want?' Johan still slightly dazed from his earlier experience peered into the gloom, trying to see the face that belonged to this voice that he felt he should know.

'Come now, Johan, has it been so long since we last met that you don't recognise your late cousin's husband?'

'Cleaver, what are you doing here?' Johan relaxed slightly and rubbed his hand over his eyes and face in an attempt to further clear his head.

'Through choice, Johan I would be nowhere near you, but it falls upon me to seek your assistance.'

'Assistance; why should I help you? You're just a puritan meddler; I thought that I was well rid of you and your interference. Yet as it happens, your meddling probably saved my life, as being sent away by Frederik to the Americas kept me free of the plague; on top of which I now own his business. So on second thoughts, Cleaver, you have made me the rich man that I am today, whereas you, what are you these days? Still a soldier fighting other people's battles for pennies?' Johan was now feeling quite smug as he pulled himself upright on the carriage seat and smirked at Thaddeus.

'Not a soldier any longer, Johan, but an officer of the law, with certain official powers that mean I could make your visits to this country quite difficult if I wished.'

'Your threats mean nothing to me, Cleaver, I have friends in this country in high places, and you are still the little man that you always were; so state your business and go.' Thaddeus took a slow deep breath to control his anger and obvious dislike of this obnoxious man.

'I want you to introduce me to chocolate house society, Johan, nothing more. I need to get amongst those with time on their hands and money to dirty them in places like this.' Johan looked at him contemptuously.

'You, in society; look at you. You wear rags and smell of the gutters; people would see you for what you are as soon as you entered a room, a nobody; it can't be done.'

'It must be done and will be, Johan. Something is happening in London that needs to be stopped before it goes any further; as the plague has destroyed so many bodies, this thing if left unchecked, could destroy people's very souls.'

'It sounds like you are intent on meddling again, Cleaver, whose fun are you intent on spoiling this time?' Thaddeus was getting irritated with the Dutchman's attitude.

'If you do not assist me, Johan, your fun will be the first to be stopped. I don't think your smart friends in the chocolate houses would look very kindly on a common rapist and molester of young women, at least not in public. No matter what they get up to in private these people still like to convey an air of respectability, and a word or two from me in the right quarters would make you an outcast, and it wouldn't be long before your business in this country at least, started to suffer for it.' Johan sat in silence for a moment, brooding over Thaddeus's words. He knew that his public image needed to be exemplary, particularly now that he was working for Richard Valletort whom, if rumours of his royal connections were to be believed, could be his passport into an even more exclusive level of society.

'What do you want me to do, Cleaver?' The words left his lips begrudgingly.

'As you say, Johan, my current appearance would betray me, so I thought that initially you would sponsor me to new clothes, something that you can well afford to do. Then I want you to introduce me around the chocolate houses and at any other opportunity that would get me amongst the elite and privileged.' Johan threw back his head onto the leather upholstery, casting his eyes up to the roof of the carriage as he drew a long breath through his wide nostrils.

'You have me by the balls, Cleaver. Give me your address and I will get my tailor to visit you tomorrow at the hovel no doubt live in, and begrudgingly I will pay for you to be suitably attired as a gentleman. After that I will make arrangements for you to accompany me to the most fashionable establishments in London until I believe that you can stand on your own two feet amongst such company; then, you are on your own, and I never want to see you again.'

'There's been another one.' Petty Constable Henderson beckoned for Thaddeus to follow him into the backroom of the watch house where, on the table, lay a corpse covered by a dirty sheet. The Petty Constable pulled back the sheet to reveal the grey face of a dead girl. On closer inspection Thaddeus could see the familiar *930* written across her forehead as well as the pattern around her throat from a braided ligature.

'Where was she found?' Thaddeus pulled the sheet

lower down the girls body as he spoke to reveal a bloody hole where her heart had once been, and he knew what he would find in its place had he the stomach to look further.

'Face down in a crumpled heap in a street by St Paul's. Some kids found her; it seems that she might have been thrown out of a carriage as they heard one clattering off in the distance and there was fresh horse shit close by the body. The word's out now, Thaddeus, and people are getting nervous. You can imagine that with every re-telling of the news the body gets more mutilated and the murderer more satanic; had to smack one of the kids round the ear when I heard him telling some passers by that he had seen cloven hoof prints in the mud. I know there's no profit for us in finding the bastard that did this, but I'm getting pressure from the magistrates to catch him as they're afraid the mob will start hanging anyone that looks at their daughters sideways.'

'I don't think the killer is one of the masses, sir; I have a theory that it may be one of the gentry.' Henderson shot Thaddeus a worried glance.

'Don't start upsetting the money or we will all find ourselves with a begging bowl.'

Thaddeus related the conversation that he had had with Father Turnbull and how he planned to infiltrate elite society to try to uncover the Adamites, but his intentions were not well received.

'You can't go swanning off playing the bloody lord of the manor just like that, wouldn't we all like such an opportunity? I think you're getting way above yourself, Cleaver, don't forget you're a thief taker, that's how we make our money. No one pays us for catching killers unless it's the victims family, and these girls look like they're from the masses like you and me.'

'Yes but just think, sir, if we can catch this bastard our credibility will be raised incredibly. As you say the people think the killer is a demon, if we can flush him out they get their streets made safe again. The merchants will think that if we can catch someone like him then we can catch anybody, and then they'll give us more business. Maybe even the magistrates will use us more and may even petition for public funds for us. I have a way in, sir, a way to get amongst these people, and I need to protect someone close to me. It won't cost you, but you will get the glory if I succeed.' Henderson stroked his chin as he thought for a moment; he was a man of action not a man of strategy, and the tale of the Adamites seemed too fanciful for him to grasp its implications for society, but the prospect of personal glory in many ways moved him more than gold.

'Cleaver, do it. But if the world falls down on your head you're on your own, I've never heard of you.'

The tailor had excelled in his craft, and Thaddeus, catching sight of himself in a full length hall mirror, could not believe the transformation. Instead of his usual leather jerkin worn over an open necked grubby shirt, a style that was a throwback to his civil war soldiering days, he now stood admiring his finely tailored knee length blue frock coat. Brass buttons fastened it from neck to lower hip with the rest left fashionably undone to the hem to expose glimpses of his black velvet breeches. Underneath he wore white silk hose, tied with a ribbon just below the knee.

Instead of his old boots, he now stood in fine black leather stacked heel shoes with a high tongue and brass buckle. The most noticeable transformation was the dark brown periwig, fashioned so that its curls framed his now clean-shaven face making him totally unrecognisable as the ex soldier, now thief taker, who two weeks previously, had coerced Johan Evertsen into introducing him to this elevated level of society.

Thaddeus walked slowly behind Johan toward the sound of the chamber music. The strains of two violins and a harpsichord gave the occasion a sophistication that brought home to Thaddeus the fact that for him, this was a different world. More and more of the influential and wealthy were beginning to return to London as deaths from the plague had decreased significantly. Acquaintances were being renewed, and all had their own tales about their lives in exile during the height of the outbreak. They were at the Westminster home of a titled lady and Johan began to take on airs and graces that Thaddeus had never seen him exhibit before. He watched as Johan fawned over the woman and her entourage, and he felt uncomfortable as he was introduced to them as the son of an emigrant plantation owner in the West Indies. It dawned on him the enormity of the task that he had set himself in trying to uncover a nest of Adamites that may not even exist. What if the killer had no connection at all to this sect, in which case he was wasting precious time socialising with these people that, if he was honest, he found superficial, vain and somewhat boring. Maybe he should be looking closer to home.

It struck Thaddeus that in his eagerness to be introduced to the elite he had seen Johan as a means to an end; what if Johan was in fact the killer. Evertsen now frequented the coffee and chocolate houses where the victims had worked. He had displayed his penchant for young serving girls back in Amsterdam, and watching him now soaking up the luxury of their present surroundings, Thaddeus could easily believe him to be a hedonist. Seizing a break in the conversation he took Johan's arm and lead him to one side.

'Is this all that these people do, drink and talk?' Johan seemed surprised by Thaddeus 's impatience.

'What do you expect of them, Cleaver, they are human like you and me; look closely, when they talk, they flirt. See, look there; watch how the woman in the green dress occasionally strokes the hand of the man she is talking to; he's not her husband. It would not surprise me if they arrange an assignation for another time far away from this place. You are supposed to be the clever one, the thief taker; use your eyes because the extremes that you seek are not always overt, they are very often dressed in subtlety. Now I must circulate; unlike you I have learnt to watch, and most importantly to listen, and for that I expect to reap great rewards.' At that Johan drifted off into the crowded room.

Johan's words had touched a nerve in Thaddeus, he had been distracted by the opulence of his surroundings and of course should have been using his eyes and ears like the professional he professed to be. Looking around the room he could see an obvious hierarchy with the hostess, who he had ascertained was a Lady Cunningham, being the centre of attention. An inner circle of curtseying women surrounded her, each with their hand-kissing escort. On the periphery of this were smaller groups of men with their escorts or wives, who were obviously waiting for an opportunity of inclusion into this inner circle. This would be either by way of introduction, or by calculated chess-like manoeuvres, which would place them in close enough proximity to their hostess to enable them to react positively to any jovial or amusing comment that she may make. At the very least these people would endevour to just catch her eye with an acknowledging bow of the head.

'It's as if you are watching a ballet isn't it? The dance of the sycophants.' Thaddeus turned towards the voice to look into the face of a tallish young man who Thaddeus estimated to be somewhere in his late twenties.

'Do forgive me, we haven't been introduced; Andrew Carlisle at your service. I saw you come in with a business acquaintance of mine, Johan Evertsen, so I thought I would take the liberty of introducing myself to you as he seems otherwise preoccupied.' Carlisle nodded towards Johan who was trying to engage a pretty young waitress in conversation as she nervously endeavoured to extricate herself and go about her duties.

'Johan has still not quite lost his taste for the help, but I'm sure that you have realised that already if you know him well.'

'Let us say, Mr Carlisle, that you have a history together where I have had cause to rein in his enthusiasm.' Carlisle smiled at Thaddeus's remark and took a sip from his wine glass.

'Do you share his passion, Mr Carlisle?' Thaddeus saw this conversation as an opportunity to explore Johan's possible involvement with the murders, but he had to be subtle.

'I like women of course, but I set my sights higher than serving girls. I have no interest in forcing that which is not given freely, and must confess that I do like a fiery woman of experience. I have recently taken it upon myself to wean Johan from his predilection, and have introduced him to more mature pursuits best befitting a man of his social stature and undeniable appetite. But, sir, you haven't told me your name if I may be so bold?' Thaddeus took the man's proffered hand.

'Thaddeus Cleaver; your servant, sir. My father owns a plantation in the West Indies, and we use Evertsen's ships. Although born in this country I have been away for many years, and ironically it has befallen this Dutchman to introduce me to the elite society of my own country of birth.' Carlisle laughed at this and took another glass of wine from the tray of a passing serving girl.

'Tell me, Mr Carlisle, you speak in riddles of the more mature pursuits to which you have introduced our mutual friend, may I be so bold as to press you further?' Carlisle looked from side to side somewhat conspiratorially before answering.

'It is no real secret amongst men of means that there are establishments in this city that, how shall we say, cater for the more sensual needs of discerning gentlemen.'

'Brothels you mean?' Carlisle shook his head.

'No, no, Mr Cleaver, nothing so base. You can buy a whore's body but never her mind, and at best she is still a whore. The establishments of which I speak act as host for gentlemen and ladies who mutually wish to abandon the inhibitions of polite society, and indulge in activities that free their minds and satisfy, in every carnal way, their bodies, whilst still allowing them total anonymity.' Thaddeus had to take a chance now and ask the question that was uppermost in his mind in a way that was direct whilst not wishing to appear disapproving.

'Is this some form of religious cult, Mr Carlisle?'

'A cult? No definitely not; religion is the last thing on the minds of the people that meet up in this way believe me.' Thaddeus forced a knowing smile, as he did not want to alienate the forthright Carlisle.

'And our friend Johan, are his needs satisfied by these places?'

'Totally. Although through habit he may still occasionally make a lascivious comment to a serving girl, his physical needs are served at a much higher level, which not only satisfies him, but challenges the hunter within him as these ladies of whom I speak are as much players in the game as the gentlemen.' Thaddeus was sure that Carlisle was making reference to the room of delights at *Le Puits de Chocolat*, but needed confirmation. If it was true, then was the activity there just the tip of the iceberg, he needed to be sure. He decided to infer knowledge of the place as if Johan had told him.

'I believe I know one of the establishments of which you speak; Johan has mentioned extraordinary pleasure taken at *Le Puits de Chocolat*. He has not related to me the finer details, but I believe that they have activities for special customers in a room of delights; am I correct?'

'You are, Mr Cleaver, and I am sure that all in good time Johan will, as part of your introduction to the hidden treasures of this city, take you there, where hopefully we will meet again in a more relaxed environment.' With that Carlisle bowed his head, turned and began to circulate with others in the room.

18 THE COLONEL'S WIFE

London December 1665

The chestnut mare had been ridden hard, and it now stood in the courtyard panting warm breath which, upon leaving its nostrils, rose like steam as it touched the early morning frosted air. The groom held the bridle and offered a hand of support as Mrs Fitz-Herbert slid from the sidesaddle onto the mounting step. The biting cold air had reddened her face giving her a healthy glow, and her tailored riding jacket accentuated her trim waist, which made her waiting husband realise how much he had missed her whilst he had been overseas serving his country.

The previous evening had witnessed not the happiest of reunions as he had expected his wife to be more pleased to see him, but instead she had appeared cold and off hand. This had developed into an argument where he had accused her of philandering, and she had stormed off to her own room leaving him standing in front of the mantle watching the dying embers of the fire whilst clutching a half filled brandy glass. He hoped that her early morning ride would have given her an opportunity to think upon his words, and make her realise that his anger and accusations were merely disappointment at her lack of warmth towards him.

Lydia Fitz-Herbert stormed past her husband without a word and left him standing watching her make her way noisily over the gravel towards the front door of their opulent Westminster home. He followed her inside and into the breakfast room, where she stood gazing silently out of the window.

'Lydia, I'm sorry. It was wrong of me to make unfounded accusations last night, but you seemed so cold towards me when I arrived home; it made me think that there must be someone else.'

'Someone else? If only there was. I have no one, nothing, whereas you, you have another life. You are continually in other countries with your greatest love, my rival, the bloody army.'

'You knew the life I had chosen before we were married, you seemed to accept it then, so what has changed between us?' Colonel Fitz-Herbert grabbed his wife's wrist as he spoke, and spun her around to face him.

'I am bored, Cedric, I feel that I am withering away inside this mausoleum, wasting my remaining youth, while you play soldiers in foreign lands like a little boy. You are leaving me locked up here like a discarded toy, and the pent up frustrations I feel inside are slowly killing me; I hate you for it, Cedric, I hate you, I hate you.' Lydia raised her free hand, and brought the riding crop that she was still holding hard down across the side of her husband's neck causing him to immediately place his hand over the source of the pain. He raised his hand to strike his wife, but she struck him again and again with the crop before throwing her full weight against his chest knocking him to the ground. As he lay dazed on the floor she raised her riding skirt and straddled him, ripping open the buttons on his breeches and grabbing his manhood with one hand whilst slapping his face hard with the other. He found himself in a confused state; the burning pain on his face from the continued assault and the soft stroking sensation of his wife's hand on his penis was bringing him to erection, and although he was physically capable of doing so, he refrained from pushing her away. Instead Colonel Fitz-Herbert allowed himself to be mounted by his wife. He felt himself slip inside her as she slapped his face continuously, raising her hips up and down whilst screaming obscenities at him, the like of which he had never heard from the lips of a woman. She fumbled with the buttons of his long waistcoat, and tore at the ties of his linen shirt exposing his chest, which she clawed with her well-manicured nails. He was now reaching orgasm and his body was controlling his mind as his wife reached to the side of her and picked up a sharp pointed knife which had been knocked to the floor as a consequence of her husband's backwards fall. His eyes were closed with pleasure as she placed the point of the knife on the exposed skin over his heart and began to push on the blade; not hard enough to deeply penetrate his chest, but sufficient to draw blood. His eyes immediately shot open and his head fell back as he looked into his wife's contorting face, ecstatic with pleasure. She then looked down at him to catch sight of the injuries that she had caused to his neck; there they were, bright red welts in a crisscross pattern, caused by the braided leather whip at the end of her riding crop.

Lydia Fitz-Herbert was woken the next morning by the sound of iron-hooped wheels driving across gravel. She leapt from her bed and ran to the window just in time to see their small carriage trundling through the front gates. On its roof was strapped the luggage that her husband had arrived with two days previously. She ran across the hall to her husband's empty room where the servants had not as yet lit the fire, but she was oblivious to the cold as she stared momentarily at the small patch of blood on the bed sheet from the wound that she had inflicted upon him the night before. On his pillow was a letter, which she snatched up and began to read.

My Darling Lydia,

I have decided to return to my regiment as your actions last night have left me not only confused, but also concerned for my life. As a soldier I have faced many enemies that have tried to end my days, but I have always felt that it was an even playing field; it was not only acceptable, but also my duty to try to take their lives in return. Your assault on me was that of a woman possessed, and I have great concern for your sanity. The truth is Lydia I love you, and would never harm you, and I feel that if I stay, I may be forced in defence of my life to retaliate in some way that may cause you injury. I intend to speak in confidence with Doctor Llewelyn and ask him to attend you until such times as you return to being the woman that I know and love. This decision may seem to have been made in haste, but my purpose in returning home was to seek a brief respite from the stresses of military life, but I have not found the calm and love that I had anticipated and even expected from our reunion, I have instead, within two days been pushed to the brink of despair.
Yours truly,
Cedric.

Mrs Fitz-Herbert stood motionless, her eyes unfocused, holding the letter out in front of her; then, as if triggered by an instance of revelation, she tore the letter into pieces and scattered it upon her husband's bed before storming back to her room to start her morning dressing ritual.

'My dear, Mrs Fitz-Herbert, may I introduce to you, Mr Thaddeus Cleaver, who has recently returned home after spending many years in the Americas.' Johan Evertsen bowed politely to Mrs Fitz-Herbert continuing the sweep of his hand to gesture towards Thaddeus.

'Your Servant, Madam.' Thaddeus took and kissed her extended hand.

'Tell me, Mr Cleaver, what line of business are you engaged in that you have been able to leave it for such a time to honour us with your company?' Thaddeus hated the pretence of his assumed new persona, but needed to sound convincing to maintain his place among the company in which he now found himself.

'Family business, Madam, my father owns a tobacco plantation and has given me leave to widen my horizons, yet at the same time forge new contacts for the business here in England and its neighbouring countries.' Mrs Fitz-Herbert eyed Thaddeus up and down from her seated position.

'I presume then that that is how you met the good Mr Evertsen'

'It was, Madam, and now we use his shipping company extensively to our mutual benefit.'

'Tell me, Mr Cleaver, what do you think of *Le Puits de Chocolat*? Do you have chocolate houses in the Americas?' Thaddeus improvised a response:

'We have chocolate of course, but we definitely do not have the sophistication of such surroundings in which to drink it, or the exquisite company such as your good self with whom to enjoy it.' Johan shot Thaddeus a glance and raised his eyebrows at the eloquence that seemed to come so naturally from the lips of this rough ex soldier. He had brought Thaddeus here at his request in order to enable him to try to get Monsieur Coultier to extend an invitation to the room of delights, hoping that The Frenchman did not recognise him from their previous encounter.

'Tell me, Mrs Fitz-Herbert, I understand that chocolate is not the only delicacy on offer here but that there are more cerebral if not spiritual pleasures to be had if one knows who to speak to?' Johan rolled his eyes in despair.

'I know not of which you speak, Mr Cleaver, but I detect that your interests may be of a nature not appropriate for conversation with a lady; I wish you good day, sir.' On that she turned her head and joined in the conversation of her ever-present entourage.

'Thaddeus, you fool, you can't just mention things like that directly to a lady of Mrs Fitz-Herbert's standing; you sounded as if you were propositioning a common punk. Although there may be some rumours of her whoring, the company that you mix with here live by the law of discretion; you could very well find yourself snubbed from now on.'

'I don't think so, Johan, you recently told me to use my eyes and ears to understand the true nature of those in a crowded room. Look casually towards Mrs Fitz-Herbert, yes any second now.' Hardly had the words left his lips when Johan caught sight of Lydia Fitz-Herbert looking coquettishly at Thaddeus and giving him a knowing smile before quickly turning her head to rejoin her group's conversation as the two men turned and slowly walked away to seek out Monsieur Coultier.

'So, Mr Cleaver, as you are a good friend of our Mr Evertsen and he has vouched for your character in such things, I will expect you back here this evening to experience our room of delights. It only befalls upon me now to seek the necessary advance payment from you.'

The little Frenchman sniffed as he turned his head away slightly and held out his hand as Thaddeus spoke:

'My good friend, Mr Evertsen, has been kind enough to gift me the experience that I look forward to with relish tonight, and it will be he that pays you now; won't you, my dear Johan?' Johan opened his mouth to protest, but Thaddeus looked him straight in the eye and raised one eyebrow as if to say, refuse and you know what will happen.

Lydia Fitz-Herbert fumbled to remove her clothes in the anti chamber as under normal circumstance she would have had the assistance of her maid. She slipped on the long crimson silk robe that had been placed there for her, and immediately it clung to her body defining her womanly figure as she ran her hands slowly over her hips, delighting in the sensuous feel of the silk against her firm flesh. She put on her Venetian mask, and at once became emboldened by the anonymity it gave her as she proceeded to enter the room of delights.

Thaddeus had been forewarned of the potency of the nutmeg brew that would be given to him by Monsieur Coultier, and switched it for a glass of chocolate carelessly put down by a less privileged unsuspecting customer, and whilst doing so, he could not help but imagine the outcome for this poor soul as he drank it and took leave of his senses amongst society in such a public place. Thaddeus sat on a chaise in the room of delights, and now that his eyes had become accustomed to the dim light he was able to take in the view of his surroundings and observe those around him. He was amazed at how openly couples were indulging their sexual appetites. He noted with amusement that many of the players in this theatre of lust were neither young nor physically attractive, and had to stop him self from laughing aloud at the sight of the wobbling stomachs of a naked mature couple as they engaged in sexual athletics that would more than likely see them both confined for weeks to a sick bed. He had been embarrassed by Johan's recent criticism of his lack of observational skills as it had wounded his professional pride, but had convinced himself that it had been down to him being in awe of the society in which he had found himself. Tonight his eyes took in the smallest detail as he scanned the room looking for any sign that this orgy was being carried out for any purpose other than just plain lust. He observed that the proceedings were not being led as he would have expected had there been a religious purpose for them, and that there was no sign of any cult paraphernalia; all in all this was just an elite bawdy house.

Thaddeus still wore his crimson robe, and the Venetian mask made him feel less embarrassed as he stared openly at those around him. A tall young man who had been standing behind a voluptuous slightly older woman whilst running his hands over her silk clad body and caressing her breasts, suddenly pulled his robe over his head and let it drop to the floor, exposing his hard naked body. Thaddeus felt slightly uncomfortable watching as the woman took the man's erection in her hand, but then he noticed that the man had a small gold chain around his neck from which hung some form of charm. In itself there was nothing strange about this, but as Thaddeus looked about the room, he noticed that two or three other men also wore a similar pendant. One of the men was by now lying in a stupor on a chaise, and this enabled Thaddeus to move across the room and, avoiding the naked woman at the man's feet, sit next to him, from which position he could now see the pendant in greater detail. The charm was in the form of a tiny open hand on which rested, as if being offered, a golden apple.

Lydia Fitz-Herbert looked purposefully around the room of delights and almost immediately, her eyes fell upon her prey. She had heard Thaddeus arranging his visit with Monsieur Coultier, and decided that this newcomer had the look of experience. Unlike the pale-skinned fops that surrounded her in the main salon, this man had a face that had been sculpted by life and the elements, and his rough manner of speech excited her. Lydia swept past the others in the room who paid her no attention, as they were either fulfiling their own physical needs or their drug-intoxicated minds had taken them to a different plane. She stood behind the chaise on which Thaddeus sat and began to caress his shoulders through the silk robe. He sat for a moment enjoying her touch, then closed his eyes as the exquisite sensation of Lydia softly biting his neck began to arouse him. She slipped around the chaise and straddled his knees thrusting her hips closer and closer to his groin whilst kissing him passionately full on the mouth. Thaddeus temporarily lost all sense of why he was in the room and gave himself up to the moment, only to be brought back to reality by Lydia slapping his face in an uncontrolled frenzy. He heaved himself up and in doing so cast Lydia backwards, hard onto the floor, where dazed, she looked up at him and began spitting out a torrent of obscenities. Thaddeus reached beside him and snatched the pendant from the unconscious man on the chaise, at the same time pulling off the man's mask to confirm his suspicion that this was the man Carlisle, the man that he had met some weeks earlier at the home of Lady Cunningham. Thaddeus stepped over the screaming woman on the floor and began to walk out of the room hearing her cry after him.

'You bastard, nobody casts aside Lydia Fitz-Herbert.'

19 HUE AND CRY

London - January 1666

'So, Cleaver, what have you found out while you have been enjoying yourself in the company of your new society friends?' Petty Constable Henderson had a sarcastic tone in his voice as he leaned back in his chair, impatiently drumming his fingers on its scratched wooden arms.

'*Le Puits de Chocolat* is a society brothel, no more no less. But that said, some of its male clients share some form of brotherhood, signified by the wearing of pendants such as this.'

Thaddeus threw the broken gold chain with its hand and apple trinket onto Henderson's desk, and watched as the Petty Constable picked it up and examined it closely.

'So what am I supposed to be seeing here, they all belong to an apple grower's lodge?'

Thaddeus chuckled at Henderson's lack of imagination, he was truly a soldier through and through.

'No, sir, I believe the apple to be symbolic of the Adamites, the sect that I told you about before I undertook this line of investigation. I firmly believe that the killing of the chocolate girls is somehow tied in with these people, but I still need to understand how and then get proof. I've identified one of the members, the man from whom I took this pendant, and I intend to get the truth from him, but I need to go carefully just in case I frighten off the real killer; assuming that is, that it is one man and not the whole cult; who knows?'

'You need to know, Cleaver, that's your job. Its all well and good you playing the gentleman in your fine new clothes, but I need results and quickly. The Magistrates are on my back, and spending time on these murders is not making us money, do you understand?'

Before Thaddeus could reply the door of Henderson's office flew open and a member of the night watch stood framed in the doorway.

'They've got him, the Satan killer. There's a hue and cry going on a couple of streets away. They've got him trapped in an old warehouse.'

Thaddeus and the Petty Constable arrived at the warehouse on foot within minutes of being told the news, and were confronted by an unruly mob armed with swords and wooden clubs trying to smash open the heavy doors of the old wooden grain store. As the crowd threw their collective weight against the aged timbers a pistol shot rang out from inside the warehouse, and the heavy thud of a lead ball was heard as it embedded itself on the interior of the oak door.

'How do we know that this is the killer?' Thaddeus looked at the leader of the hue and cry for an answer.

'He picked the wrong one to tangle with this time that's for sure. He tried to kill Welsh Sally over at the Anchor. She served him a meal then took him upstairs for something to help his digestion, if you know what I mean, and the bastard cuts her with a knife, and then tries to strangle her. Sally's a strong girl and does no more than breaks a bottle over his head. We all heard the commotion and went upstairs, just in time to see his arse disappearing out the window, down the ivy and into the back alleys; we gave chase and got him holed up here.'

'What makes you think he's the one that's been killing the chocolate girls?' The man looked around at the others in the crowd to back him up.

'Well he's got to be the one ain't he? I mean Sally is a serving girl; he cut her and tried to strangle her, just like the others; makes sense don't it.' Those closest to him in the mob nodded and loudly voiced their agreement. Thaddeus looked the heavy doors up and down.

'Alright, we need to get in there. He obviously has a pistol so we need to be careful. You men find something with which we can break down this door.' Within minutes a group of men returned carrying between them a small anvil from a nearby blacksmith's shop, and under Thaddeus's direction they began to pound the rusty iron hinges on the side of one of the big doors. It didn't take long for the rotting timbers and rusting bolts to give way, and the hinged side of the door lurched inwards still secured by its lock to its twin, but opening enough to allow men to pass between it and its broken frame. As the crowd entered another pistol shot rang out, and one of the pursuers fell to the ground clutching his chest, a pool of blood forming on the floor along one side of his body like a crimson shadow.

Thaddeus had seen the direction from where the pistol flash had emanated, and sword in hand, led the others towards it. A shadowy figure stood up from behind a pile of grain sacks and began slashing wildly with a sword. Many of the crowd now stepped back afraid that like a cornered dog, this man would try to take down as many of his pursuers as possible. Thaddeus parried the man's awkward thrusts, and getting in close brought the basket of his sword handle up sharply under the man's chin, knocking him senseless. Within seconds those behind Thaddeus had grabbed the now unconscious form and were dragging him out into the street, which was almost as bright as day, lit up by the multitude of lanterns being carried by the crowd. The man lay face down in the muddy street and groaned as Thaddeus rolled him over with his boot. Even with the mud smeared across his face and encrusting his hair Thaddeus would have recognised this man anywhere, but even if he had been unsure, the old scars from powder burns around his right eye and temple confirmed that at last Thaddeus had captured Ned Bennet.

'Your nemesis, Cleaver, how many people has this bastard killed that you know of?' Henderson sat behind his desk as Thaddeus sat perched on its corner, looking at the semi conscious Bennet tied securely to a chair in front of him.

'Assuming that the man that he just shot at the warehouse survives, three, possibly four, sir. Hawkins, Tom Wright and Potter for definite when we were escorting the merchant, and we never saw Simon Wainwright again after Bennet said that he had been asked to stand in for him. I think he killed him too. Then there's the money; I could be a rich man now if this piece of shit hadn't made off with my warehouse full of nutmeg, for all the good it did him; look at him.'

'He'll hang for the three you witnessed that's for

sure, but we need to find out just how many of the chocolate girls he's killed, and why for God's sake. Wake him up.'

Thaddeus got up and took a pitcher of ice-cold water from the washstand in the corner of the room, then he took great delight in pouring it slowly over Bennets head. Some of the water splashed onto the burning logs in the small fire grate and made them smoke and flicker, giving the room, already bathed in a red glow from the fire and tallow candles, an even more hell like appearance. Thaddeus spoke as the last of the icy water dripped onto the flagstone floor:

'Can you hear me, Bennet? Wake up, you bastard, how many more, we need to know?'

The man rolled his head back grinning, his eyes still shut. The water had washed away some of the mud that had been caked on the side of his face, and created rivulets through the rest as it dripped from his long filthy hair.

'I know that voice, Thaddeus Cleaver, if I'm not mistaken. I thought the plague had done for you last year, and that you'd taken a last ride in your own cart.' With the memory of William's dying face brought to mind by Bennet's words Thaddeus struck him full in the face, almost knocking the chair over to which he was tied.

'How many, Bennet, how many of those innocent girls have you butchered?' Even as the words fell from his lips he realised that he didn't believe that Bennet was responsible for the deaths of the chocolate girls, but he knew that he would not be allowed to continue his search for the Adamites if Henderson believed that he was guilty

'Welsh Sally, her innocent? She's about as innocent as a fox in a chicken coup. I only cut her 'cause she stole my purse, the cow.'

Thaddeus looked across at Henderson who raised his eyebrows then gestured with his hand for him to continue.

'We're not talking about Welsh bloody Sally, we're talking about the serving girls from the chocolate houses; how many of them have you butchered?'

'I've had nothing to do with that, I mean, where's the profit in it?' He sniggered before Thaddeus struck him again, deeply cutting the man's lip. Henderson moved across the room and stood warming his hands in front of the fire, looking deeply into the flames.

'I think we should hand him over now to the boys in the Tower, these murders have religious implications and the church will want to get involved, Cleaver. That takes it out of our hands; they will insist that the king employs any means available. The Crown have their own means and professionals when it comes to getting the truth out of scum like this.'

'I think you're right, sir, what they do ain't pretty, but it's effective.' Bennet visibly shivered. Whether it was the January cold in the bleak watch house, or the thought of being tortured in the Tower of London Thaddeus wasn't sure, but Bennet suddenly started to be more cooperative.

'OK, Cleaver, I know I've caused you some grief in the past, but I don't butcher young girls. I've heard about these killings; people are saying it's the Devil himself that's carving up serving girls, but that's not me. Look I'm no devil, I admit I've done bad things in my time but not that.'

'Hawkins, Wright, Potter all dead by your hand when you robbed the Evertsens at London Bridge'. Thaddeus stood accusingly over Bennet, resisting the desire to strike him again.

'Not by my hand, Cleaver, it was the others, they did for your men.' Thaddeus could control his anger no longer and struck Bennet hard across the face causing his already cut lip to explode, producing a stream of blood which glistened in the firelight as it poured down the man's face.

'I witnessed you personally shoot and kill Tom Wright, and then thrust your sword into the ribs of John Jephson. Fortunately he survived. I also believe that you killed Simon Wainwright in order to take his place within the escort.'

'Tom Wright got in the way of my bullet. I was only trying to startle the horses into moving off, and as you say Jephson didn't die did he? As for Simon Wainwright, it was as I told you, he asked me to cover for him; I never saw him again; did you?' Thaddeus knew that this man would not confess even by his coercion to murder; he knew that he was a killer, but still felt sure that he had nothing to do with the deaths of the chocolate girls.

'Tell me one thing, Bennet, the nutmeg; how is it that you are by all appearances, not a rich man?' Bennet started to laugh quietly to himself.

'Do you read, Cleaver? The newspapers I mean, *The London Gazette*. I have it on good authority that the sinking of the *Crimson Star* got a mention somewhere in that illustrious paper. Captain Abraham was not the seaman he claimed to be. He holed the ship before we reached open sea on wreckage from *HMS London*, which had blown up weeks before in the Thames estuary, but convinced everyone that it was possible to complete the journey without repairs. Well to his cost he was proved wrong; the fool drowned and I spent four days in an open boat before being picked up by a Dutch merchantman. I lost it all, Cleaver, the gold, the nutmeg, all at the bottom of the ocean.' He looked at Thaddeus and smirked which cost him yet another blow across his face.

Thaddeus walked across to Henderson and they both gazed into the fire as he spoke in lowered tones so as not to be heard by Bennet.

'I firmly believe that he has nothing to do with the chocolate girl murders. You can make him a scapegoat if you wish, but we will all look fools if more girls are killed while we have him in chains. Let him hang for killing my men and God knows how many others, but let me continue to seek out the Adamites and find the true killer of these girls.' Henderson thought for a moment then looked across at Thaddeus and nodded.

'Find them and prove they did it so we can hang them. In the meantime get this miserable excuse for a human being out of my sight.'

20 THE ADAMITES

London – February 1666

London society was buzzing with excitement at the news that the King had returned to the city. Once again Thaddeus found himself at the home of Lady Cunningham, this time, although His Majesty was not in attendance, attending a soiree to celebrate the King's return. Thaddeus was able to move in such quarters now without the company of Johan Evertsen, and he had made enough acquaintances within these circles to afford him not only invitations, but also continued dialogue at such events.

Thaddeus needed to challenge Andrew Carlisle regarding the significance of the apple pendant, but in such a way that he did not expose himself as the thief taker that he was. He knew that as a frequent face at such events Carlisle would be here, and it was a case of waiting for an appropriate opportunity to arise that would enable Thaddeus to broach the subject with him.

Andrew Carlisle stood holding court with a group of finely dressed ladies and could be seen openly flattering them as they coyly laughed and hung upon his every word. In his privileged position as the son of a wealthy banker he had many opportunities to practice the art of genteel conversation, and develop a persona pleasing to the company that he chose to keep. Thaddeus kept one eye on Carlisle as he himself conversed politely with a tall gentleman who had a very military bearing, and who insisted on re living, to Thaddeus's now tired ears, every battle that he had ever been in.

Thaddeus excused himself from the man's company as he had seen Carlisle move towards the door of the opulent music room and walk out into the hall. He followed him and caught up with him as he began to descend the wide staircase.

'My dear, Mr Carlisle, so good to see you again; in fact I must confess that I was hoping that we would meet at this fine event.' Carlisle stopped in mid step holding onto the polished banister rail as he turned his head slightly to see Thaddeus approach from behind.

'Mr Cleaver, how good to see you; I was about to take some air, well at least for as long as I can stand the cold; would you care to join me?' Thaddeus smiled and confirmed that he would as the two men walked down the stairs, along a hall and out onto the terrace of a large garden still sleeping from the cold winter. The night was clear and the stars filled the heavens as the two men stood by an ornamental balustrade, and having just come from the warmth of the house, accustomised themselves to the relative chill.

'Any excuse for a celebration eh, Cleaver, the return of the King is being seen as the rising of the sun on a London too long in the cold and darkness of pestilence and misery.'

'A sun still unsure as to whether it is healthy to walk amongst us though, my dear Carlisle, don't you think? Although I am sure that he celebrates his return with others that he deems safe, as they have journeyed at a distance from the plague with him. Anyway, I am glad that I have met up with you this evening as I have something that I wish to return to you.' Carlisle looked puzzled as Thaddeus thrust his hand deeply into one of the large side pockets of his frock coat and then holding out a closed fist, gestured with his eyes for Carlisle to take that which was held within. Carlisle held out a cupped hand into which Thaddeus let slide the broken chain from which still hung the apple pendant.

'My dear Cleaver, where did you find this? I thought that it was lost to me forever.' Thaddeus smiled.

'I found it by your feet in the room of delights at *Le Puits de Chocolat*. Unfortunately you were not in a condition for me to hand it back to you, and your state of dress afforded you no pockets into which I could place it. So, I have carried it with me since, with a view to returning it to you.' At this the two men began to laugh, partly from embarrassment at being reminded of their naked vulnerability at the chocolate house.

'Tell me, Carlisle, it is a fine pendant, but I did observe that it is not an original piece as I noticed others in the room on that occasion wearing similar; does it have a fraternity significance?' Carlisle looked momentarily embarrassed; he looked up at the stars for a moment as if considering how he should reply then, clearing his throat, he looked almost apologetically at Thaddeus.

'You appear to me as a man of the world, Cleaver, if you weren't you wouldn't have been in a position to find my pendant eh? Well it's like this; a year or so ago I was introduced to a group of people who, like myself, were bored. We all have money, we are all relatively young, and if for some only through our father's eyes, we had all seen the horrors of a country split in two by war. We wanted excitement, we wanted adventure, but our religious beliefs drummed into us from birth held us back from experiencing these things and filled us with guilt, that is until individually we stumbled upon a group known as the Adamites. Until then I had followed the way of the protestant church as directed by my parents, but suddenly I was confronted with a religious doctrine that said it was permissible to have all the things that I desired as a young man but without the guilt that the church puts upon us. You see the Adamites believe that sin didn't exist until Eve tempted Adam with the apple, and that the carnal desires that we all indeed have are there to be openly sated. They call their Church paradise, and to me it was. Sexual pleasure, my dear Cleaver, free from the bonds of marriage. For most of us that's all it was; we rarely spoke of God, we just revelled in excess without guilt.'

'And these excesses, are these all that you indulge in at *Le Puits de Chocolat*, or are there other much darker practices carried on elsewhere?' Thaddeus hoped that he was not pushing Carlisle too far with his questions, but the young man seemed only too happy to talk about his experiences.

'Since the room of delights became available to us, most of us have used it to quench our thirst for the physical pleasures of life, and it has also introduced us to substances that, how shall I put this, make paradise a little more real. But there are those, or should I say one, that has taken the beliefs of the original Adamites to a dangerous level, Cleaver, a true fanatic who has caused the rest of us to disassociate ourselves from the cult. We continue to wear the pendants purely to remind us that we should feel no guilt in the pleasures that we seek, but no longer as a symbol of fraternity to the brotherhood that has been taken to diabolical extremes by this one man who seeks to use the doctrine of the cult to achieve ultimate power.'

'And who is this man? You have intrigued me immensely, Carlisle, please do not let your tale leave me in suspense.'

'I can tell you no more, Cleaver, other than to say that he is a man that already has great power and influence in this city, and for that reason alone he is dangerous. Should his beliefs be founded in truth then he could become as the very Devil himself.' Thaddeus needed this man to give him the name but to push too hard would expose him as being more than just curious and arouse a suspicion in Carlisle that he had a further motive.

'No I completely understand your reluctance to speak further, but for my own safety tell me, is this man known to me, for if so I must avoid him surely?'

'Let me say this in parting, Cleaver, I do not believe him to be within your immediate circle, but I have observed that he is known to, and appears quite regularly in the company of, your business associate Johan Evertsen; now please excuse me, I must return to the soiree before I freeze to death.' At that Carlisle turned and made his way back into the house leaving Thaddeus to ponder on the known circle of associates of Johan.

Thaddeus hated the expense, but thought it appropriate to hire a small carriage to take him to the newly acquired house of Johan Evertsen. It was still important that he maintained his new persona as a wealthy plantation owner, and arriving on horseback would not be in keeping with the fine clothes that he wore in order to keep up the charade. Johan had done well for himself, and his house in Long Acre had all the trappings of success. Once it had come to a standstill on the cobbled forecourt, Thaddeus was courteously helped from his carriage by one of Evertsen's man servants, after which he was led into the house and to a finely furnished sitting room to await the arrival of Johan.

'Cleaver, I thought that you were now able to conduct your snooping without me having to hold your hand; what do you want from me this time, more money I suppose?' Thaddeus despised the fact that he was dependant on this arrogant bully to enable him to continue his pursuit of the killer, but as he looked at the man's flat puffy face he took delight in the fact that once this task was complete he had the means to destroy Johan's social standing in London.

'Johan, once again as much as it pains me to ask for it, I need your help. I know that you now move in very high places, and I need the assistance of someone from your circle that has extreme influence within this city on a matter that, should it not be resolved as I have inferred to you before, could be injurious to this society, the church and possibly the crown.' Johan now stood by the window looking out at the bright morning sunshine and spoke without turning.

'If this matter is so important then why aren't you speaking of it through official channels to the King?'

'Evidence, Johan, until we have substantial evidence on this matter our suspicions would seem fanciful and we would not be believed. I wish that I was in a position to tell you more, but from what I now believe to be true, if I did so it could put you at risk, and as wide as the differences are between us I would not see you harmed.' Thaddeus bit the inside of his lip as he uttered this lie.

'So who is it that you wish to help you?' Johan turned from the window now to look Thaddeus straight in the eye.

'This is the problem, Johan, I don't know. I need to approach someone that has the highest possible connections in this city, but I do not know them by name; I only know them to have extreme influence and power and that they are known to you.' Johan began to shake his large wigged head.

'You talk in riddles, Cleaver, like some parlour game for ladies. Since I have established myself in London I know many men of influence and power, and I will not risk my relationship with them by letting you meddle in their affairs.'

'Johan, I have no interest in meddling; for God's sake man, this matter is of the utmost importance. All I ask from you is a list in order of importance of the most influential men in your circle; I have no need at this stage to approach them or to mention your name, but if you are not prepared to give these names freely, then you know full well that I have the means to break you in this city.' Johan's face started to flush with anger, but he knew that he had no choice, as should rumour of his past indiscretions be spread then his standing in society would be destroyed.

'Reluctantly I shall prepare for you a list, but let this be the end of it, Cleaver. You are trying my patience, and your threat towards me diminishes by the day with the influence that I now have within this city. So be warned, or very soon it will be you that is destroyed and dropped back into the gutter from which you came.'

21 A MAN OF INFLUENCE

London February 1666

'A list you say; you did well to tell me about this, Evertsen, and you were right to include my name.' Richard Valletort half folded his arms as he stroked his chin in contemplation. 'I am not familiar with this man Cleaver; should I be concerned in any way?' Without even giving it a moments thought, Johan Evertsen sycophantically blurted out his reply:

'Not at all, Mr Valletort, he is a nobody, an ex soldier turned thief taker, and his reason for the list, as I said, is to seek assistance not to condemn.' Valletort now stroked the aged wood of the backrest of the church pew behind which they sat. The church was empty save for the two men and their conversation was delivered in whispers, as if in prayer.

'You say he has knowledge of a plot against the King?'

'I don't know if it is a plot exactly; he just mentioned a matter that could be injurious to society, the church and possibly the Crown. Those were his very words. He wants help from someone with the highest influence; other than that I know no more.'

'And what are you hearing in other circles, Evertsen? Does Cleaver's request add weight to any mumblings of malcontent amongst those with whom you trade and debauch?' Johan raised his head and looked up at the timber-vaulted ceiling.

'God would condemn them for their greed and self-obsession, but the King would not have cause. It seems that now that the plague has subsided, the people are happy once again to be able to pose and preen in public, and rather than criticise His Majesty, most would seek his favour.'

'And you, Evertsen, would you seek the King's favour? I know you to be ambitious in business, but do you seek power?' Johan considered his words carefully before replying as he observed Richard Valletort to be continually sounding him out, and although he sought the patronage of this powerful man, he also suspected that he could be dangerous.

'Power, Mr Valletort, I believe comes with wealth. I do not seek it for its own sake, but if it comes as a companion to a heavy purse then I will not snub its presence.' Valletort smiled, stood up and slowly walked toward the alter, where he picked up a chalice and spoke at volume so that his words echoed off the cold stone walls.

'The Church has power, my dear Evertsen, and even now that we are broken with Rome it still has wealth, but it has taken time to gain both. We as mere mortals are not given the luxury of enough time, enough time to learn, build, position and finally place ourselves above and in control of our fellow men. The Crown has time; generation after generation of kings and queens moulding and shaping the people into subservient followers, a pattern that not even Cromwell could ultimately break, and a king at birth inherits the time served by his forefathers. How many years would it take for an ordinary man to gain such power, a hundred, two hundred, three hundred years, and at what cost? Friendship, love, sanity. What would you sacrifice, Eversten, for enough time to become all powerful?' Johan was surprised by the passion of

Valletort's outburst, and he replied in lowered tones as he watched the man staring, as if transfixed by the light reflecting from the chalice.

'I am a realist, Mr Valletort, I do not hunger for that which I know to be impossible for me to achieve. With God's grace I will live my three score and ten, and rather than sacrifice, I will endeavour to take the things that I desire within my allotted time span and sleep easy, as I assume no guilt, and do not desire the heavy burden that must come with ultimate power.'

Valletort let out a long sigh at Johan's words, and seemed to snap back to the moment.

'A heavy burden indeed, not that I would know of course eh, Evertsen, ultimate power is beyond the likes of you and I. Enough said. I believe that I will take this man Cleaver off guard and approach him. If he genuinely seeks my assistance and has news of threats against the King then we share a cause. If his motives in seeking me out are otherwise, then I shall deal with him accordingly.'

The early morning mist was starting to clear and the sky held the promise of a bright clear day as the cart trundled towards the triple tree at Tyburn. Already a large throng had gathered, and far from sombre the atmosphere was slowly taking on that of a carnival, with street sellers from the city, having made their short journey along the Oxford Road, now selling their pies and trinkets to the accompaniment of busking musicians, all endeavouring to make what they could from the crowd attending this, one of London's eight regular hanging days.

Members of the watch who had been seconded for

the day to provide escort, and now on horseback, rode close to the cart, their long pikes acting as deterrent to any that would try to either rescue the condemned men or attempt to mete out their own justice. The prisoners tied in pairs, sat with their backs to the horses on the wooden floor of the simple cart, each dressed in their own clothes over which had been pulled a loose, white linen smock. Every prisoner wore an ill-fitting, oversized deep white linen cap which made the men cock and twist their heads pathetically in an attempt to see out from under the excess of material that had been hurriedly rolled up just above their eyes.

Thaddeus worked his way closer to the cart in an attempt to confirm that amongst its wretched cargo was Ned Bennet. At first, dressed as they were, it was hard to tell, but then one of the men turned his head, slightly exposing the scar around his eye and temple which Thaddeus's pistol shot had given to him, and he now felt a warm glow knowing that justice was about to be delivered to this worthless low life. The three main posts of the gallows had many years ago been driven into the ground with connecting timbers erected on top, so that if viewed from above they would appear as a triangle, hence them being known as the triple tree. Beneath one of the cross-timbers stood a long flat-bedded cart, forming a stage. One by one the prisoners were transferred from their original conveyance to stand upon it; the hangman then roughly placed ropes around their necks before rolling down the linen caps to cover their faces as a chaplain prayed for their souls.

'There is comfort in seeing justice delivered, don't

you think?' Thaddeus turned his head towards the speaker to see a very distinguished looking gentleman of similar age to himself, dressed in fine clothes and dark periwig. He was immediately drawn in by the man's steely blue eyes, and for some reason at once felt at ease with this stranger.

'Some good men of my acquaintance will rest easier in their graves tonight knowing that one up there has performed his final dance beneath the deadly never green.' Thaddeus kept his eyes on the triple tree as he spoke, watching as the chaplain continued with his prayers.

'Yes I've heard it called that, the dead tree which bears fruit all year, even if the fruit is rotten to the core eh!' The man extended his hand to Thaddeus. 'Richard Valletort, a pleasure to meet you, Mr Cleaver'. Thaddeus looked puzzled.

'How do you know me, sir?'

'Forgive me, Mr Cleaver, but I understood that it was you that wished to know me, or so our mutual friend Johan Evertsen tells me.' Thaddeus was caught unawares. Here stood the man that could possibly be the most evil creature in London, but he had no evidence, just suspicion; how should he proceed with this conversation? Suddenly, a whip cracked and a roar went up from the crowd as a team of horses pulled the stage away from beneath the feet of the prisoners, leaving the six men to begin their macabre dance of death. Thaddeus looked at the twitching form of Ned Bennet and felt not an ounce of pity, not even as Bennet, in common with his dangling companions, pissed himself. Thaddeus knew that as a convicted murderer Bennet would now be gibbeted. The hair from his lifeless head would be shaved, and then like the rest of his body, covered in tar before being bound in iron hoops and hung from a gibbet at the scene of his crime, which in this case would be London Bridge, where it would rot away to dust.

'So, Mr Cleaver, which of your desires has been the most sated, justice or revenge?'

'Oh definitely justice, Mr Valletort. As great as my desire was for revenge it would have had me dancing up there beside five of those wretches.' Richard Valletort smiled.

'You are a rare specimen, Mr Cleaver, an honest, and I would hazard a guess, a moral man.' Thaddeus now saw his opportunity to take back control of the conversation that Valletort had instigated and that in doing so had caught him unprepared.

'I try to work for the common good, which is the very reason that I was seeking you out via our acquaintance Evertsen. You see it was not you by name that I sought, but someone with influence and connection to His Majesty, as I believe I have knowledge of something that could be detrimental to him but of which alas, I have no proof.'

Thaddeus was suddenly aware that as they had been speaking a group of four large men had sidled up quite close to them. Valletort had also picked up on their presence, which by now, due to their size and very close proximity, felt quite threatening.

Without a word, one of the men made a grab for Valletort's purse as another slipped behind him and placed a muscular arm across his throat. Thaddeus felt a sickening blow to his right temple as a massive fist struck him, felling him to the ground. He could feel hands tugging at his own purse and rifling through the inner pocket of his cloak. A scream pierced the air as the thug holding Valletort released his grip and clutched his side from which now ran a stream of blood, drawn by the blade of Valletort's dagger. Thaddeus had recovered sufficiently from being punched to seize an opportunity to upend one of his assailants by grabbing his ankle and forcing him backwards before himself rising to his feet.

With one of their number lying mortally wounded on the ground, the two upright opportunists pulled swords from their cloaks and faced Thaddeus and Valletort who now, with their swords drawn, stood side by side, cautiously shuffling and crouching low as they feinted with their weapons. Both were now very aware of the third man, who previously felled by Thaddeus, was slowly rising to his feet drawing his sword. One of the men lunged his weapon at Richard Valletort who without effort, parried the blade and reposted, piercing the man's chest. Both of the remaining thugs ran at Thaddeus, wildly swinging their swords overhead without any show of formal swordsmanship. Simultaneously he blocked both blades with his own and kicked one of the assailants hard in the groin, dropping him to his knees in agony as he caught the second across the chest with a downward sweep of his sword opening up a fatal wound which, with wide eyed surprise, the man clutched before falling stone dead to the ground.

'You handle yourself well, Mr Cleaver, a soldiers training no doubt.'

'As do you, Mr Valletort, but I detect a style of swordsmanship more in keeping with expensive private tutorage than parade ground exercises. These scum were attracted by your fine clothes and rings, normally easy pickings on a hanging day when the gentry come down to amuse themselves, but they certainly misjudged the man inside; a mistake that has cost three of them their lives this day and this wretch a pair of aching balls and a return visit to Tyburn as the main attraction.'

By now the mounted men of the watch who had been escorting the prison cart had ridden up to investigate the commotion. Thaddeus spoke with them and they led away the surviving robber and made preparation to cart away the dead. Valletort having wiped his sword on the coat of one of the dead, slid it back into its scabbard and stood straightening his cloak.

'I consider us now comrades in arms, Mr Cleaver. Please, my carriage is nearby; let's continue our interrupted conversation over a good breakfast. I know a local coffee house with a pleasant private room which normally has a roaring fire in the grate, please join me as my guest.'

The coffee house was somewhat austere in comparison to *Le Puits de Chocolat*, but the aroma on entering, although different, was just as welcoming. The comforting smell of ground coffee mingling with pipe tobacco had a relaxing effect on Thaddeus who, though used to violence, was still tense from his encounter with the robbers. Valletort caught the eye of the proprietor and pointed towards the narrow wooden staircase. The man obviously knew Valletort and reciprocated with a nod of his head and made a welcoming hand gesture for him to go up to the upper floor. They entered a small room at the top of the stairs in which a roaring fire was already burning in the grate. After warming themselves by the fire the two men sat down on the hard wooden chairs placed either side of one of four small empty tables, just as the proprietor entered the room.

'Good morning, gentlemen, what may I get for you?' Unlike Monsieur Coultier the man was of English stock, had tied back medium length greying hair, and wore a white apron over his long sleeveless waistcoat with more of the air of an innkeeper than that of an owner of a fashionable coffee house.

'Good morning, Jack, two of your finest breakfasts served with ample coffee. Is that acceptable to you, Mr Cleaver?' Thaddeus nodded and the proprietor smiled, turned and made his way back down the creaking stairs.

'So tell me, Mr Cleaver, what is it that you have knowledge of that you feel may harm His Majesty?' This was Thaddeus's opportunity to draw Valletort out. He needed to choose his words carefully and look for and gauge the man's reaction to see if indeed, he was at least capable or at worst culpable of committing these atrocious murders.

'A delicate matter, Mr Valletort. It has come to my attention that there may be one, a man already with power and influence in this country, who has taken the practices of a religious cult too far in an attempt to gain supreme power. If this is the case, and at the moment my findings are based on conjecture, he may be not only a threat to the Church, but also the King. I am but a humble thief taker, but loyal to His Majesty, and therefore I approached our mutual friend Johan Evertsen for a list of names of people that he knew and could trust who had the influence in this city and at court to delicately seek out this individual and assist me in gaining evidence enough to condemn him. Your name was on that list and it was my intention to approach you accordingly, but you have turned the table and approached me first.' Thaddeus could see no look of surprise in Valletort's expression at any of the things that he had just said. He just watched him sit expressionless considering his words. After an embarrassingly long silence Valletort spoke.

'Forgive my silence, Mr Cleaver. I have been considering your words relative to the people in my circle, and I must say that unfortunately not one name comes to mind. What is it exactly that this person has done to give you such concern?'

'Murder, or should I say murders. You must be aware of the recent killings that the superstitious citizens of London are attributing to Satan. Someone is butchering, in the most horrific and ritualistic way, innocent serving girls. I believe that this is connected to the core beliefs of a cult called the Adamites, but they have been taken to extremes by one man, and it is that man that I seek.' Once again Richard Valletort's expression gave nothing away.

'Adamites? Not a name that means anything to me, Mr Cleaver, but now that you have brought it to my attention I shall be vigilant in looking for any signs of their existence among those close to me or His Majesty. How do these people manifest themselves, what are their practices? You have intrigued me, Mr Cleaver, so please tell me more.' Thaddeus had nothing to lose in telling Valletort all that he knew. If he were innocent then he would hopefully become an ally. If guilty then maybe now knowing that Thaddeus was aware of the cult and the murderer's connection, Valletort may be panicked into making a mistake that could expose him. Somehow though, Thaddeus did not feel that Richard Valletort was a man that could be panicked. He had just fought alongside him and the man had a calm head on his shoulders. He proceeded to tell him all that he knew about the Adamites and the condition that the murdered girls had been found in. The two men talked into the late morning as they ate a hearty breakfast of cold cuts, and warmed themselves with strong coffee until the fire in the grate became no more than ashes, speckled with a few glowing embers.

Thaddeus could not perceive anything suspicious about this man, and in fact, in the short time of their acquaintance, had grown to like him. They paid the proprietor of the coffee house and walked out into the bright yet cold February morning, shook hands, and each went their own way.

22 BLOOD ON THE STREETS

London February 1666

Having finished her evening's work serving at Mason's chocolate house, the girl left by the back door. Mason's was fast becoming a contender for the patronage of the fashionable in London, but still had quite a way to go before it could ever think of attracting the elite clientele of *Le Puits de Chocolat*. She walked quickly along the back alley, and out into the dimly lit cobbled street pulling her hooded cape tightly around herself as protection from the cold driving rain. At midnight the street was empty save for the odd drunk sprawled in the gutter, to whom she gave a wide berth. She couldn't wait to reach home some three quarters of a mile away where she knew that there would still be the last remains of a fire in the grate, and hopefully, a modest supper on the table that her mother would have prepared before retiring to her bed.

She could hear, slowly approaching behind her, the iron hooped wheels of a carriage, and without looking around she stepped aside, close to the wall of a timber-framed house to enable it to pass. However, instead of doing so, the carriage drew up alongside her and a woman's voice spoke to her from its dark interior:

'You, girl, you look soaked through, and much too young to be walking these streets at this time of night. Where are you bound for?' The girl could see the woman as a silhouette, backlit by a dim light coming through the far window of the carriage from the house alongside which it had stopped.

'Pardon me, Ma'am, I'm on my way home. Its not too far from here, some ten minutes or so.'

The woman placed a gloved hand on the bottom edge of the window surround and pushed the carriage door open.

'Quickly, girl, get in. The weather is foul, and the streets too dangerous for even such a short journey. I would not be performing my Christian duty if I let you continue in these conditions. We shall take you home.' The girl was amazed at such a kindness being extended to her, a serving girl, and from someone that was obviously gentry and to whom she would usually be invisible. She stepped up into the coach and immediately realised that the woman was not alone. In the opposite corner of the carriage sat a man. In the dim light it was difficult to make out his features, but her initial impression was that like the woman, he was not very old, but older than herself. The girl sat next to the woman and felt slightly embarrassed by the situation, mainly due to the class divide. The wet smell from her cape mingled with the woman's perfume only making her feel more embarrassed. She was thankful as the carriage moved off that it was dark inside, and that they were unable to clearly see each other faces.

'Where have you been on such a dreadful night without an escort?' The woman's tone was kindly and the girl felt more at ease now in telling her that she had been serving customers at the chocolate house. The man remained silent but the girl felt that he was staring at her through the gloom.

'It is good that you serve. Many women feel that it is beneath them to fetch and carry for men, but after all, we owe them that at least, don't you agree?' The girl didn't understand the woman's train of thought, but thought that to question her would be impolite.

'It's an honest living, Ma'am, and feeds my mother and me.' She heard the woman breathe in sharply.

'But to serve men should not be purely for profit, it should be the duty of every woman. If it were not for our deceit there would be no sin and our lifespan would be tenfold.' The girl was now confused.

'I'm sorry, Ma'am, I don't understand.'

'I don't expect you to.' The woman drew her face close to the girl who could now see in close proximity that the woman's eyes were wide and fixed, and she started to feel a little afraid.

'Your innocence, girl, is in that you serve. You have started already to pay back for that which she, the first woman, took from all of mankind. But now you have an opportunity to make it right.' As she spoke the man lit the internal lamp and pulled down the blind on his side of the carriage. Similarly the woman reached across the girl and did likewise on her side, now cutting off the outside world. In the flickering yellow glow of the lamplight the girl could see that the man's face had a stony expression as if devoid of any feeling. The woman suddenly thrust her arm behind the girl's neck, and with her other hand pulled across her throat a plaited leather strap that was attached to a riding crop that she was holding. She proceeded to pull the girl down so that she was half lying across the seat of the carriage, as the man dropped to his knees in front of her and lifted the girl's skirts.

The girl flailed the air with her arms, and tried to scream, but the strap across her throat cut off any sound that she attempted to make. She clutched desperately at the strap, and raised her eyes to see the inverted face of the woman, manic eyes cast heavenward, and teeth bared. The man had forced himself into the girl, and was tearing at the rest of her clothes as the woman, tightly securing the strap with one hand, stroked and caressed the girls now exposed breasts with the other. The man let out a wild primeval scream as he reached orgasm. Then without pause, he took a long knife from beneath the carriage seat and thrust it into the girls chest, wildly hacking at her ribs until he exposed, cut out, and then veraciously devoured her still beating heart. When he had finished, he wiped the blood from around his mouth with his forefinger. He then stroked it across the woman's lips before tracing in blood the numbers nine, three, zero across the girl's forehead. Finally he placed a shiny red apple into the girl's chest cavity, where once had beaten her innocent heart.

The body fell with a thud, pushed from the carriage doorway onto the wet cobblestones, rolling twice before ending its trajectory in a heap resembling a grotesque broken doll. The rivulets of rainwater running down the street swirled around and through the dead girl's hair, giving it movement and life. This was a paradox to her now plaster white face, with wide startled eyes that stared at, but were unable to see, the approaching feet of the patrolling night watch, who soon would raise a hue and cry.

Later that night the carriage once again came to a halt in a quiet dark street in Westminster. The horses stood motionless as the driver stared straight ahead waiting for someone to alight or to be given the signal to move on. Inside the now unlit carriage the two passengers sat unspeaking, both feeling a glow of contentment as if oblivious to the smell of death that now pervaded the enclosed space. It was the man that first broke the silence.

'You have done well, my dear. I have decided that the time is almost right for you to partake of the fruit of life; the next heart is yours.'

'Thank you, my Lord, I am truly grateful for the great honour that you bestow on me.' As she spoke the clouds broke in their passing of the moon, and for a moment she could, in the resulting light, see the man's eyes staring upward, as if he was in great contemplation.

'It is destined that my life will be long, my dear, and I will need a constant. For I will see the passing of so many over time, and my greatest pain could be loneliness. You are my match in both lust and ambition, therefore I have chosen you to be my companion. But you need to earn my trust; one careless word or deed could expose me, and although I believe to have mastered longevity, I have not found immortality. Those that in time I plan to usurp would have my head on a pike.' The woman slid from the carriage seat onto her knees and rested her cheek on the man's lap.

'I would never deceive you, I am not Eve. Is it not me that now leaves the mark of the serpent on these betrayers of mankind? I want to be by your side, always.' He caressed her hair as she spoke.

'Come, the hour is late, and the mute needs to drive me home before daybreak and clean the carriage.'

The woman stepped down into the night, and disappeared into the shadows as the driver responding to the tap on the roof from within whipped the horses into motion.

'Lizzie, I don't want to frighten you, but I have concerns for your safety working at the chocolate house. Last night another serving girl was murdered.' Lizzie gasped at Thaddeus's words.

'From *Le Puits de Chocolat*?'

'No, she was from Mason's chocolate house, near Blackfriars bridge. Her body was found by the night watch; just left in the street. From what I saw of it last night, she was killed in the same ritualistic way as the others.'

'Thaddeus, I'm scared; is it the Devil?' She pulled him close to her as they stood in the warmth of the boot maker's kitchen. He wrapped his arms tightly around her and kissed her hair.

'Not the true Devil, Lizzie, but one I believe that aspires to be. You will come to no harm for I will always protect you, but I think the time has come for you to leave the chocolate house and find a position elsewhere.'

'But you need me to listen out for clues. If I go how will you ever catch him, and besides, the boot makers is taking too long to recover its trade since the plague, and my father has debts.'

'Lizzie, I need to ask you something.' The girl stood back slightly holding on to his hands, but looking anxious.

'Don't look so concerned, girl, I've been meaning to speak about this for some time. I am very much older than you, Lizzie, almost twice your age, and I know that you must have so many men much younger than me fighting for your affection, but I truly love you, Lizzie. I never thought that I could love anyone after Catharina, but you have put purpose back into my life. It's as if a grey veil has been peeled from my eyes, and by telling you this I know that I risk disappointment but.......' Lizzie reach up and placed her finger on Thaddeus's lips.

'I would never disappoint you, Thaddeus, I love you, and why would I be interested in silly boys?'

Thaddeus grasped her finger and kissed it.

'Lizzie Jephson, will you marry me?

'Yes, Thaddeus, yes.' Her face beamed as she pulled him close. Thaddeus stroked her hair and looked serious for a moment.

'All I have to do now is ask for John's permission.'

'What has taken you so long, Thaddeus?' He turned to see John and Martha smiling broadly, standing in the doorway leading from the shop. 'Welcome to the family, Martha, close the shop and fetch some ale.' John took Thaddeus's hand and shook it vigorously as Martha walked over and gave him a warm hug.

'You take care of our Lizzie, Thaddeus, I heard your conversation. Catch this killer, be he a man or the Devil; it's a worrying time for mothers. And of course you keep safe too; you're family now, or soon will be. Now Lizzie and I have a wedding to plan.' Martha poured the men some ale, and whisked the giggling Lizzie away upstairs.

'Is she in danger, Thaddeus?' John looked grave as he tightly clutched his mug of ale with both hands.

'I would give my life for her, John, you know that, but until this murderer is caught and hanged she will always be in danger whilst working at the chocolate house, which as you know she insists on doing despite both our arguments. Why he picks on the serving girls is a mystery to us all, but a reassurance for the moment at least to other girls in the city that are otherwise employed. I no longer want her to feed me information from that place, but she's stubborn, John, and I have probably made it worse by assuring her of my protection. I thought I knew who he was, but I have no proof and having spent time with the man I am now having my doubts.' John slammed his mug down onto the oak dining table in frustration.

'But, Thaddeus, you have to do something. Can't you just go in and arrest all of those that debauch there; at least they would be behind bars.'

'*Le Puits de Chocolat* is but one of many chocolate houses. Who is to say that the murderer will be there when we arrive? The latest girl worked at Mason's. It may only serve to alert him to our suspicions and drive him underground. Please, John, talk again to Lizzie about working elsewhere. I know the family is short of money, but I will contribute to the household finances now that we are to marry. I know now that I have made a mistake in asking her to be watchful of anything suspicious, but I am afraid that she feels she would be letting me down by leaving, despite me trying to convince her to the contrary.'

Petty Constable Henderson rocked back in his chair. He looked at his booted feet resting on the desktop as the flickering fire in the grate cast sprite like shadows across their leather toe tops. He was being pressurised more and more by the magistrates to find the murderer of these girls, and all he had to show for the time and effort his now dandified thief taker had put in, was a gold pendant, stories of a room of delights and the name of someone with so many high connections that without solid proof was untouchable. He decided to take action. If not convinced of its efficacy, he at least believed that it would show the magistrates that he could be decisive and was not idle.

The front door of *Le Puits de Chocolat* burst open as fifteen men of the night watch swarmed into the downstairs salon. Chairs and settles overturned as the clients took to their feet in shock and confusion. Monsier Coultier placed his open palms on both cheeks and opened his mouth as if to scream, but no sound was forthcoming other than that of a very long, slow intake of breath. Ten men of the watch led by Petty Constable Henderson charged upstairs, leaving the remaining five to guard the lower salon, permitting no one to leave. Once upstairs they burst into the blue salon, and amidst screams from the ladies present, proceeded to corral the younger male clients into a corner where they were made to unbutton their shirts, or if refusing, had them ripped open by the watch who searched as instructed, for signs of golden apple pendants. Three men including Nathaniel Harper were found to be wearing the symbolic jewellery, and were subsequently manhandled down the stairs into a waiting cart just as Thaddeus rode up. He instantly dismounted, and passing the reins of his horse to one of the watch, ran stormy faced into the chocolate house and up the stairs into the blue salon.

'You grace us with your presence at last, Cleaver.' Henderson look pleased with himself as his men searched more of the clientele that had been brought through from the other salons. Some to shame them, in a state of nudity, and obviously not wearing pendants were pushed in and paraded from the room of delights.

'What have you done, sir' Thaddeus spoke in low tones, holding back his anger. 'If the killer was here, and I can see that my main suspect is not, he will surely now be alerted, and either vanish or be very much on his guard.'

'I had to do something, Cleaver. The Magistrates are at my throat. Anyway if he vanishes, problem solved, no more murders, and we can go back to paid work rounding up warehouse thieves.'

As Henderson finished speaking a commotion began in a corner of the salon. Two watchmen were unsuccessfully trying to restrain an opulently dressed woman who, with flailing arms and clawing nails, was succeeding in tearing their rough faces to shreds. She caught sight of Thaddeus and flew across the room like a windmill in a hurricane screaming at the top of her voice.

'You bastard, Cleaver, I knew you were no gentleman, but a common thief taker.' Thaddeus fended off her blows then caught her wrists and bending them backwards forced her to her knees. The woman seemed to be in an intoxicated frenzy.

'Mrs Fitz-Herbert, calm yourself or we will be forced to take you into custody.' The ensuing tirade of obscenity shocked even the Petty Constable as he looked down on the screaming, squirming beauty at their feet.

'I curse you for eternity, Cleaver.' She spat out the

words through clenched teeth and then tried to bite his hands as they held her like iron manacles. 'When Richard Valletort finds out that you have touched me he will destroy you, and we will both watch you age and wither as we, forever young, grow stronger and more powerful.'

'What is she on about, Cleaver?' Henderson looked quizzically at Thaddeus.

'I think, sir, that she has just given me all that I need to now confront the man I believe to be responsible for the chocolate girl killings.'

23 THE DEMON UNMASKED

London-February 1666

'What exactly do you want me to say to this man?' Father Turnbull sat in the carriage opposite Thaddeus as they traveled on their way to meet with Richard Valletort at the same coffee house where the two had previously breakfasted after the hanging of Ned Bennet.

'I don't know exactly, Father. I need you to provoke him into an argument about his beliefs in the hope that he will give himself away. Lydia Fitz-Herbert has condemned him from her own mouth and, under expert persuasion, the rakes arrested at the chocolate house gave him up as a member of the Adamites. But he is too influential to be thrown into a cell and tortured into a confession.'

The two men clattered up the wooden staircase and entered the room, now familiar to Thaddeus, in the coffee house. The warmth from the open fire was welcome, as the carriage, despite being enclosed, had been cold.

'My dear Cleaver, so good to see you again.' Richard Valletort gave a gentle bow as he invited the two men to sit down by gesturing towards a table. 'And who may this gentleman be?'

'Richard Valletort, may I introduce to you a good friend of mine, Father Turnbull. When I sent you the note suggesting that we meet again, I eluded to the fact that we have made progress in uncovering the activities that I believe may be of danger to the crown.' Thaddeus stopped speaking as the coffee shop owner entered the room with a serving girl, and lay before the men a breakfast of cold cuts and coffee. Thaddeus watched Valletort, as the food was served, for any sign of anxiety, but the man was the very model of calm. After the owner had left the room Thaddeus continued.

'I mentioned to you when we last met the existence of a religious sect known as the Adamites. Father Turnbull, is an expert in these matters, and I thought you should know that we have arrested and questioned some of its members who were regularly meeting at an establishment known to us both, *Le Puits de Chocolat.*' At the mention of the chocolate house Thaddeus observed Valletort give an involuntary sniff.

'I have never seen any religious activity in that establishment, quite the opposite. As I'm sure you already know it is notorious in certain society for its worldly pleasures, definitely not those of a spiritual nature.' Father Turnbull set down his coffee glass.

'It is those very worldly pleasures that are the fundamental doctrine of the Adamites. Sin without guilt, depravity without remorse, carnal knowledge without the sanctity of marriage.'

'Yet your Church, Father Turnbull, uses the concept of sin as a cudgel with which it beats its miserable followers until, as a submissive flock, they die, never having had experience of the joys that freedom from guilt can bring.' Valletorts's repost surprised Thaddeus as he thought it would take much more than this to goad this otherwise calm and controlled man into an impassioned outburst.

'So you endorse sin, Mr Valletort?'

'My dear Father Turnbull, the concept of sin is the

creation of man not God. Its suppression suffices to keep in check the masses, that otherwise, with their meagre intelligence would become unruly. *We* are not of the common herd, we are entitled, as is our station, and as thinking people, and being mindful of consequence, we are able to enjoy the pleasures of this world.'

'I disagree, Mr Valletort. Man's disobedience was seen by God to be a sin. The breaking of his rules *he* denounced, using *his* terminology.' Valletort considered his reply carefully before speaking calmly, and smiling as he spoke.

'You refer to the Garden of Eden no doubt. You would have me as one of your Adamites, Father Turnbull. I simply imply that there is a level of society that is better equipped intellectually to enjoy life than others. We have all in recent times experienced extremes of torment, the horrors of war, the plague, and personal loss. Are we not then entitled to gain some comfort from more pleasurable activities, I must confess, I do. As an unmarried man I savour a willing woman and the gifts of Bacchus, as I'm sure does our good, Mr Cleaver, here.' Thaddeus smiled as he lowered his gaze to his lap.

'Forgive me, Mr Valletort, I do not suggest for one moment that you are an Adamite, but you do seem to share some of their beliefs. Thaddeus invited me here to answer any questions that you may have had about the sect, yet I observe that I may have offended you.' Thaddeus realised that Valletort was back in control after his brief outburst, and that the only option now open to him was to confront him directly.

'I need to be honest with you, Mr Valletort, you

have been named as an Adamite by three men that we have recently arrested. Respecting your position, I needed to make you aware of this.'

'How interesting. Was my name put to these men under torture or did they individually offer it willingly?'

'I admit yours was amongst many names on a list of influential people put to them.'

'Ah a list. I often wonder how, why, and by whom such lists are compiled. We all have enemies, Mr Cleaver. The war set brother against brother, neighbour against neighbour, and as a consequence, so very few of us now are totally surrounded by loyal friends, if by any friends at all. And, as I asked, were they tortured?'

'They were encouraged to offer information by physical means, a process that I'm sure you have ordered others to employ during the war.'

'Then honestly, why should I be worried? My name appears on a list of those accused of belonging to a ridiculous religious sect, and is then verified by the testimony of tortured rakes from a bawdy house. How is this of concern to the crown, after all, this is why we are meeting is it not?'

'Power, Mr Valletort, extreme power that could challenge the throne, gained through deviant cult religious practices. We believe that the killing of the serving girls from the chocolate houses in London is linked to someone trying to achieve that power. Father Turnbull, here has a theory linked to beliefs of the Adamites.' Father Turnbull pushed away his now empty trencher and looked solemnly at Valletort

'My theory is this. If a man works hard he can achieve most things but his biggest enemy is time.

However if a man can outlive those standing in his way, then in time, he can become all-powerful. The Bible says that we have three score years and ten, yet Adam lived to be nine hundred and thirty, a number that we have seen written upon the bodies of these pitiful girls, girls that by the very nature of their profession, serve. I conclude that this deluded killer believes that by consuming the hearts of these poor wretches, for that is what we are sure he is doing, he will somehow rectify within his own mind at least the deceit of Eve, and that he will be gifted with the lifespan of Adam. He leaves an apple in place of their hearts as a symbol of Eve's temptation to Adam.' Valletort sat bemused.

'This is surely fanciful nonsense, gentlemen, only a madman could conceive of such an idea.' Thaddeus decided to now play his final card.

'We agree then the killer must be a madman, but he has influenced others. Why, Mr Valletort, would Lydia Fitz-Herbert tell me that you and she would stay forever young, growing stronger and more powerful?'

'The woman is deluded, a fantasist, by reputation a woman of loose virtue. I feel, Mr Cleaver, that you have brought me here not to make me aware of dangers to the crown, but to accuse me of being that threat. I'll have you know sir that my loyalties have and will always be to His Majesty, and that you should seek your maniacal killer elsewhere. Gentleman, our conversation is at an end.' With that, Richard Valletort stood up, noisily pushing back his chair, and left, leaving Thaddeus and Father Turnbull sitting in silence, both contemplating their next course of action.

'Plotters in Holland you say, well I would think so, considering that we are yet again at war with the Dutch. And now that Louis and the Danes have sided with them, I at times suspect that half the world is plotting against us. Why, Richard, are you telling me the obvious?' The King sat back in his carriage seat and glared disparagingly as Richard Valletort continued to deliver his fiction.

'These are exiled Englishmen, Your Majesty.'

'So exactly *who* are they, and what are their intentions?'

'This I have yet to determine, Your Majesty. The Dutch puppet Evertsen has given me to believe that he has heard some mumblings whilst on a recent visit to his homeland. As you know he is not a supporter of the States but an Orangeman. Apparently there is a small group of Englishmen that, having Dutch connections, sought safety in Amsterdam from the plague, and they are now considering returning to England. It appears that it is they who speak as malcontents and critics of the Crown. He has no names, only their haunts. Therefore I intend to sail to Amsterdam tomorrow, and infiltrate their number to see if in fact they genuinely pose a threat, or are just common blowhards who have not had enough to occupy their feeble minds whilst in their self imposed exile.' The lies tripped too easily from Valletort's tongue, and the King, always anxious as to the security of his position, reacted positively to his most trusted agent's plan to travel abroad to seek out the potential danger, and nip it in the bud.

'This war, Richard, is bleeding me dry. I have a nation of rural peasants from whom I cannot raise a mere groat, and the city population that have previously borne the burden of my taxes are now decimated, thanks to the plague. Sources tell me that the Dutch are continuing to build a new fleet, which is easy for them having more urban taxpayers. The last thing this country needs is dissenters and rabble rousers. Seek them out, Richard, seek them out.'

Valletort realised that Thaddeus Cleaver had deduced his guilt, but fortunately for him the thief taker was in too lowly a position to act upon it. By concocting for the King's benefit a story of overseas plotters, he could flee to Holland, retain his credibility with Charles, and wait until the panic amongst the ordinary people of London had subsided. After all, his beliefs that were driving him to commit these crimes meant that he had time on his side. The King gestured from the carriage window to one of the cloaked mounted soldiers, who was strategically positioned close by, that he was ready to leave.

'I will send word, Your Majesty, as soon as I have the measure of these exiles. I bid you a safe return to the city.' With that, Richard Valletort opened the door, climbed down from the carriage and walked purposefully towards his horse. He knew that Johan Evertsen had secured him passage on a ship bound for Amsterdam the next morning, but before he left, he had just one more important thing to do.

The crossing was rough, yet despite this Richard Valletort insisted on being on deck. The heavy spray soaked his face and cloak and somehow, the cold and discomfort seemed to cocoon him from the real world as he contemplated his strategy for the future. As far as he was concerned nothing had really changed, he would always crave the power that he so desperately strived for, and whether his methodology for longevity was carried out in London or Amsterdam was quite irrelevant. His only disappointment was that he would now need to find a new companion to share his ambition and desires. Lydia Fitz-Herbert had betrayed him. He had always known that the woman's volatile nature made her a risk, but he had hoped that she had the intelligence at least to be discreet about their relationship, and definitely not divulge to anyone their ultimate goal. He had chosen her as his consort for the very reason that she *was* dangerous. Her fire and passion not only aroused him but also served to validate his ambition. She understood his dream, and wanted to be part of it, encouraging every necessary deed of his that would eventually have seen them both omnipotent. He could still see her face in the early hours of that morning, the look of shocked surprise as he plunged his dagger up into her heart as she pulled him close to her, imploring him to forgive her for her thoughtless outburst to Cleaver. As the life left her body her face relaxed, and this woman, always in control, always the hunter, now looked lost and confused, and ultimately in death, her face took on an air of serenity and innocence that he had never seen there before.

'I have raised the Dutch flag as we are in our waters now, so unless we come across your navy we are set for a safe passage.' Johan Evertsen stood beside his passenger and mirrored his stance as both men gazed ahead into the grey mist. He was in the unique position of being able to cross to Holland as and when he liked, despite the war. His ship was not out of place in English ports, as many Dutch merchant vessels had been captured and now lay at berth idle, in anticipation of being sold on by the privateers that took them. He had paid his bribes to the authorities before the war to operate in English waters under an English flag, and as an Orange supporter was seen as an ally. He still had the bulk of his business interests in Holland and feigned support to the states, which enabled him to conduct his business in a chameleon like manner.

'You have secured me lodgings befitting my station I trust, Evertsen?'

'My own town house, sir, with full staff who are paid well to be discreet. I myself shall be travelling on business, so please treat my home as your own.' Valletort nodded his approval.

'You understand that you must tell no one in England of my whereabouts. I am on a secret mission for the King to seek out dissenters, and it is of the utmost importance that no one knows where I am, or even that I am absent from the country. You may if you wish perpetuate a rumour that I am ill and have left London for treatment elsewhere.'

'I will be the soul of discretion and keep your presence in England alive with stories of occasional sightings, and reports of your slowly improving health. Speaking of which, come below decks now and I will have us both served a hearty breakfast and hot beverage before we both freeze to death.' Both men smiled as they turned and made their way across the rain soaked deck to the door leading down to the captain's cabin. Meanwhile the city of Amsterdam slowly stirred to life, picking up the momentum of a new day, totally unaware of the deranged fugitive heading for its shore.

Thaddeus stood with the men of the watch looking down at the body in the alley. The fine silk of the women's dress was absorbing the filth from the rain soaked cobbles, giving the appearance of a tide, creeping in slow motion up a beach, as a large crimson stain beneath her breast was simultaneously spreading out slowly to merge with it. The pallid face, eyes wide open, was instantly recognisable to him. The fury that was Lydia Fitz-Herbert was now forever calmed.

On closer examination Thaddeus realised that she had not been killed in the manner of the chocolate girls, as had been suspected by the watchmen. Whether or not she had been killed during a robbery would never be known. The absence of jewellery could be attributed to those that found her body, or even the deft fingers of the first arrivals of the watch. A rich corpse was a gift from God to those with meagre or no income. As others speculated amongst themselves why a woman of her position was walking alone in a back alley late at night, Thaddeus stood up from his crouching stance, realising that Richard Valletort would now be a hard man to find.

24 LIFE GOES ON

London May 1666

The smell of stale beer and tobacco smoke hit the nostrils of the two men as they pulled away the last pieces of wattle and daub from the small section of the inn wall at street level in the alley. One after the other they squeezed through the hole into the main salon, and then, rising to their feet, took a moment to survey the Aladdin's cave from which they would pilfer as much booty as they could load onto a small handcart and carry off between them.

They knew from their recent visits as customers, that the innkeeper and his family were away for a few days attending a funeral outside of the city. They were therefore confident that they would not be challenged, as they started to line up against the breached wall, the more expensive bottles of wines and spirits, together with a small quantity of tobacco that the innkeeper kept on the premises for regular customers.

One of the men, small and rat faced, pulled himself back out through the hole into the alley, as his taller heavier built comrade passed the purloined items through to him to load onto the cart. Once all of the goods were off the premises, the larger man slowly started to emerge headfirst out into the darkness of the night. He had just about squeezed his shoulders through the damaged wall, when a strong hand grabbed his collar and pulled him out in one movement, so that he fell heavily, face down onto the hard cobbles.

'Chain this bastard up with the other one, and get

them both over to the cells where they can wait till the morning for the magistrate to finish his breakfast, and for their sake I hope it doesn't give him indigestion.' Thaddeus smiled as the men of the watch took away the two thieves together with their handcart of stolen goods, and hoped that some of it would still be there as evidence the next day.

At the end of a long night, Captain Henderson sat in his office and poured Thaddeus and himself a glass of red wine.

'Your health, Cleaver, this one's on the innkeeper; it's the least he owes us for catching those thieving bastards. He was right to be suspicious of them and dropping us the nod. We've had a good few months thief taking, and the merchants are paying us well in cash, and kind. I'm glad the panic has settled down, now that the so-called Satan murders have stopped. Nasty business but no profit in it for us.' Thaddeus took a sip from his wine glass.

'I'm still not convinced it's over, sir. I would stake my life that Richard Valletort is the culprit, but he's gone to ground somewhere and can't be challenged.'

'But we had no proof, Cleaver. We couldn't take him off the streets like a common criminal. The man is so well connected that we could have found ourselves on the gallows. I know you were enjoying dipping your toe in the waters of the privileged life, as lived by the elite, but that's not what you get paid for. You're a thief taker and by tonight's result a bloody good one.'

'I'm a soldier, sir, first and foremost, and of late I've been thinking about re-enlisting. We are at war now, not only with the Dutch, but also France, and our country is at threat whilst all I do is chase low life robbers for fat arsed merchants.' Thaddeus had been bottling up these thoughts for some time, and now his frustration could be held back no longer.

'Look, Cleaver, this war will not be won by soldiers. It will be won at sea, not on land, so unless you have hidden skills as a seaman you would be wasting your time, and anyway you are to be married in October. What would young Lizzie think about you deserting her.'

'That's the point, sir, I wouldn't be deserting her, I would be protecting her and our way of life.'

'Where has all this patriotism suddenly come from, Cleaver? It wasn't that long ago that you fled these shores, deserting the army and living in the country with which we are now at war.' Henderson's comments now were visibly frustrating Thaddeus.

'I had little choice in that at the time, if I had stayed in England questions would have been asked that may have led to even you being arrested. I feel that I have paid for that. I buried my wife and sank so low that I had to totally rebuild my life. All I want to do now is protect the life I have found and the woman I now love.' Captain Henderson sat swirling the red wine slowly around in his glass. He didn't want to lose Thaddeus but he knew that the man was very principled, and liked and admired him for that. He took a sip from his glass before cradling it with two hands and lowering it to his lap.

'Don't do anything in haste, Cleaver. I appreciate your motives but there must be a better way to serve your country. I still have a few friends in the army, let me see if there is an opportunity for you to fight for your principles without becoming cannon fodder. Give me a few days. In the meantime finish this excellent wine and get some sleep; you are delivering tonight's catch to the magistrate in the morning.'

The warm May sunshine gave promise of a good summer to come. The harbour made its own rhythm as water lapped as if in harmony to the constant banging of oak timbers, as ships collided with each other, and against the wooden dock, as choirs of gulls sang discordantly overhead.

'Ships, Mr Cleaver, little Dutch ships. Captured merchant vessels mainly, brought here by privateers. These are our gains, but they are not fighting ships. We fear that the Dutch are building a new fleet of heavy ships, which could pose a significant threat to our navy. It is imperative that we win this war, and that the King's nephew William is made Stadholder of the Dutch Republic.' As the man spoke he looked Thaddeus up and down, taking in his tanned weathered features and muscular build. He himself was quite thin, with a gaunt pale face, not used to seeing sunlight, as he was more accustomed to dark offices and secret night time meetings in his role as aide to George Monck, the First Duke of Albermarle.

'Henderson here informs me that you are eager to once again serve your country.' Thaddeus wasn't sure where this was going, as all he had been told by the Petty Constable was that they had an important meeting out of the city on the coast, and that he was to ask no questions.

'Yes, sir, I feel that I should be fighting for my country and way of life instead of chasing petty thieves and robbers.'

'Do you speak Dutch?'

'I understand more than I speak. I definitely would not pass for a Dutchman, but I can make myself understood having lived there for some time.' The man nodded thoughtfully.

'No matter, no matter. Look, Mr Cleaver, I will get to the point. We need to know numbers. How many new ships do they have ready, what size are they, and what is their firepower. Also how are they making these ships so fast? Most importantly we need to know this now. We have received no recent information from our agents in Amsterdam, and fear that they have been exposed. We therefore need to get a new face over there to replace them immediately. I have it on good authority that you could be trusted to be that man. Am I right, Mr Cleaver?' Without a moment's thought Thaddeus's smile gave away his answer.

'I am that man, sir.'

'Good. I was assured that you would be. A ship leaves for Amsterdam tonight. There will be documents onboard with the address of a trusted sympathiser. He will assist you in locating the shipyards and getting you back to England with the information that we need. Needless to say if you are successful, His Majesty will handsomely reward you. If you fail, we could lose this war.'

'I will not let you down; I can be ready to sail by sunset tomorrow. But first there is someone that I need to say goodbye to.'

Lizzie buried her face in his shoulder as he held her closely.

'Why, Thaddeus, why? I thought we were to be married.'

'We are, Lizzie, and nothing will change that, but I have some important work to do that hopefully will help us win this war. I can't stand by and watch as others fight to preserve our way of life. I am after all a soldier, and have been so since I was a boy; your father will understand.'

'But you have fought for this country, if not for this King. Let somebody else take their turn, I need you here, Thaddeus.' Lizzie burst into tears, which made him momentarily regret his decision to go. He stood back, took her face in his hands, and kissed her gently on the lips. She responded passionately hoping that by giving herself to him it would make him stay. They slid to the floor aroused by each other, and emotionally charged by the situation, they made love. Lizzie's tears tasted of salt as he kissed her face, which in a strange way excited him. She pulled him to her tighter and tighter. It was as if she was trying to devour him, pulling him deep inside her, trying to shackle him with her lithe limbs to stop him from leaving.

Once their passion was spent, neither of them spoke as Thaddeus put a few items of clothing into a canvas kit bag. He stroked her face as he stood by the open door of the boot makers shop, knowing that her parents would soon be back from delivering shoes in the city.

'It won't be for long, Lizzie, a few weeks at the most. How could I stay away knowing that you are waiting here for me.'

'Thaddeus, keep safe, I don't know what I would do if you came to any harm.' He kissed her again and took a step backwards. They stood facing each other with their right arms extended, holding each other's hand until their fingers slowly slipped apart as he walked off into the late afternoon.

It had taken two and a half days to sail the two hundred or so miles from London to Amsterdam. The tall masted, square-rigged fluyt, having been captured from the Dutch, attracted no suspicion as it sailed into the port. Typical of its class, it had been built as a merchantman and carried no armaments, which initially had concerned Thaddeus, but he realized that once in Dutch waters, and sailing past their patrolling ships of the line, that it would be seen as a benign vessel and would draw little or no attention.

Once the ship had docked, Thaddeus made his way through the rough dockside streets onto the Prinsengracht Canal, searching for the address given in the papers that had been waiting for him on board. He knew the area relatively well from the few years he had spent in the country whilst married to Catharina, and rather than feeling threatened by the hard accented Dutch language being yelled across the streets from one group of drunken seamen to another, it made him feel nostalgic for the happy moments they had spent together.

He stood outside the five storey, narrow, stepped gabled house, and felt somewhat exposed. In the midmorning sunlight, a constant stream of this overpopulated city's residents passed by, each going about their everyday business, seemingly unaware of the covert mission of this lone stranger. He knocked at the door and was quickly ushered in by a tall, muscular man in his early forties, who looked up and down the canal side street, before closing the door behind them.

'You are, Petrus de Graaf?' Despite the man's powerful build he looked nervous as Thaddeus awaited his reply.

'I am he. You have a letter for me?' Thaddeus handed over a wax-sealed letter, which the man broke open and hastily read.

'You are, Thaddeus Cleaver, yes? You have friends in high places it appears. Come follow me, I will get you something to eat and drink whilst we talk.' He led Thaddeus into a large welcoming kitchen where at one end a bubbling pot was suspended over a fire in a bricked recessed fireplace. Petrus ladled some potatoes, vegetables and a small piece of meat onto a pewter trencher, and beckoned Thaddeus to take a seat at the oak table in the centre of the room. Then, having likewise served himself, he pulled out a sturdy wooden chair and sat opposite his visitor.

'I claim no power to see into your mind, Mr Cleaver, yet I know your thoughts. You are thinking, why would this Dutchman betray his country by aiding you to spy on us? Am I right?'

Thaddeus swallowed the meat he had been chewing, then took a large swig from the mug of ale that had been poured for him before replying.

'The thought is foremost in my mind I must say. You see, I intend to live to a ripe old age, and to do so I need to quickly take stock of all situations. So, as you brought the question to the table, feel free to let the answer join it.'

De Graaf sat back in his chair and smiled.

'I love my country, Mr Cleaver, but it is divided, as

was yours during your civil war. I know not, nor care for which side you fought then, but I would see this country led by its true ruler William. As you may know, The Act of Seclusion, hidden away within The Treaty of Westminster, forbids him, or any member of the House of Orange from becoming Stadtholder of the province of Holland, and thereby any of the other six provinces. Now that your King Charles is on the throne, I believe in common with many others, that he would wish his father's grandson to take his rightful place as head of this country; so now you see where my loyalties lie.'

'Politics, like this ale, if taken in excess give me a headache, Mr De Graaf, so I am moderate with my consumption of both. So, let's to the job in hand. I am told that you will take me to the shipyard and harbour. I am tasked with obtaining information on numbers and firepower, so we may have to get in close. Can this be done?' De Graaf began nodding and gave a wry smile.

'I can get you into the very belly of the *De Zeven Provincien*,' Thaddeus shot him a quizzical look.

'What's that?'

'That, Mr Cleaver, is the world's most powerful ship of the line. Completed last year by Solomon Jansz van den Tempel.'

'Who is?'

'Who is, Mr Cleaver, the world's greatest master shipbuilder, and if it were not for him, you would have no need to be here. Now I need to prepare for our visit to the shipyard tomorrow. There is someone to whom I need to take a little gift, if you understand me. I am sure you are tired after your voyage here, so please treat my home as yours until I return this evening. Then you can sample some more of my ale and politics, both as you say, in moderation.' The tall Dutchman then left the house, and Thaddeus found himself alone with his thoughts.

25 THE SHIP INSPECTORS

Amsterdam May 1666

The morning chill was becoming less biting as the sun appeared, giving promise of a fine day. De Graaf had returned the previous evening with a bundle of clothes, which Thaddeus now wore; a dark brown hip length jacket with matching breeches, a white laced collared undershirt, and white hose making him look less English and more important. He also carried under his left arm, on De Graaf's instructions, a domed wooden writing case. Thaddeus instinctively pulled the wide brim of his hat down to hide his eyes, but De Graaf pushed it back up again, saying it made him look too furtive.

'Today, Mr Cleaver, you are an important man. You are a ship inspector. You must look confident and in control. I will do the talking, as your accent will give you away. I have it on good authority from the shipyard gateman that only minor officials will be present today, as the head of the yard and his team leaders are attending a celebratory banquet on the harbour side. A pat on the back for their hard work perhaps.'

Thaddeus felt strange as he walked through the busy streets towards the shipyard. It felt as if everyone knew he was an impostor, and he expected any minute to be challenged and arrested. Yet he took comfort from the wearing of his disguise, and his adoption of the physical bearing of importance.

After fifteen minutes or so of walking, they approached a long complex of brick built custom houses. Passing between these, they came upon the manned gates of the shipyard. Thaddeus was aware of the sounds of men's toil, constant sawing and hammering, interspersed with the hard cries of gulls and the rough shouts of men at work.

'You have until two o'clock, Petrus.' The gateman swung open the heavy wooden pedestrian door in the main gate to let them through. 'No one with high enough authority to challenge your story is left here this morning. Inspections are quite common these days, and the men never so much as look up from their work. It is only their masters that fear being judged as incompetent, and today the admiralty will get them pissed for being hard taskmasters. If anyone does ask you why you are here, make something up about surveying the site to see if anymore keels can be laid.' De Graaf patted the man's arm, as he and Thaddeus stepped through the doorway into the shipyard.

The ground sloped away towards the waters edge, and like the skeletons of giant sea creatures, the keels and frames of a multitude of ships, in various stages of construction, lay side by side. Their bows pointed towards the sea, awaiting that moment when they would slide, as if in birth, down the slipway, to join the rest of the Dutch fleet in battle against England.

'I have never seen the like.' Thaddeus stood watching the hordes of industrious craftsman in awe. 'Heavy ships, Mr Cleaver, we have learnt our lesson from previous encounters with your navy. Built frame first, and then with double planking. We can build seven ships in the time it takes England to build one. We now have naval superiority.' The two men slowly walked along the line of partially built ships, and encountered not the slightest of interest from the men busy at their labours. Thaddeus tried to gauge the size of the ships from those nearing completion, and estimated them to be around 150 feet long by 40 feet wide. From purely looking at the hulls he could not gauge the ship's potential firepower, so De Graaf would definitely need to get them on board the *De Zeven Provincien* later that day.

Having walked back up the slope, the two men now had an elevated view of the ships, and Thaddeus sat down upon the grassy bank, and opened up the writing box, which he had rested upon his lap. Opening the lid of the inkpot, he took out a quill, and having charged it with ink, began writing rough notes regarding the ships construction. Although no artist, he made crude sketches of the ships, as De Graaf stood behind him, looking over his shoulder. Suddenly a hard loud voice bellowed from behind the men, and the quick release of adrenalin caused a stab of pain in the pit of Thaddeus's stomach.

'What are you doing here? What are you writing?' Both men turned to see a thickset man standing behind them, holding in one hand a large axe. De Graaf responded instantly to the man in Dutch.

'And who may I ask are you, sir?'

'Yard foreman, a man with this axe and a nose for spies, now, who are you?' De Graaf gave the man his most disdainful look before drawing himself up to his full height.

'As yard foreman then, you should know that we are admiralty inspectors. Now about your business and leave us to ours.'

'Papers. You should have papers. Show them to

me.' The man would not be browbeaten, and swung up the head of the axe so that he now held it threateningly in both hands. Thaddeus had by now closed the writing case and had risen to his feet.

'We are not answerable to the likes of you.' continued De Graaf, still trying to intimidate the man with authority. 'Who is your superior? I demand to know your name.' The man tapped the head of the axe slowly and repeatedly into the palm of his large hand.

'This morning this axe is my superior, so show me your papers or he will bite you, you arrogant bureaucrat.' De Graaf turned to Thaddeus and raised his eyebrows, as if to say, "go along with me."

'Show this fool our papers we have wasted enough time.' Thaddeus looked back at De Graaf, cocking his head slightly, and looking initially confused. Then he inspirationally made a show of trying to open up the writing case. This action enticed the man to walk towards Thaddeus, and in doing so, position De Graaf behind him. Thaddeus raised his head to look at the man in time to see De Graaf place a hand around the man's mouth, and plunge a knife into his back. The yard foreman went limp and slid to the ground, where the two men positioned him with his arms behind his head and one knee raised, as if he were sleeping.

'We have seen enough I think, Mr Cleaver, now we must go. The harbour is but a short walk from here.' De Graaf cleaned his knife on the grass, after which they both slowly walked back towards the shipyard gates.

The harbourside was awash with people. Dignitaries from the admiralty mingled with shipyard managers and supervisors. The remains of a banquet could be seen on rows of dressed tables laid out along the cobbled quay, and at this stage in the event, a pompous looking little man, assisted by a trio of subservient underlings, was trying to organise, with a notable lack of success, the gathered mass into manageable groups. Roped to the quay was a great ship, its sails tied up tightly to their spars on all three masts. The guns had been rolled out for display, and pointed threateningly towards the city. Beyond this ship lay anchored out in the harbour six more, gently rising and falling in the swell, as if bizarrely dancing to the constant song of the gulls.

'We have arrived just in time, Mr Cleaver. Now that the meal is over they are intending to show off the *De Zeven Provincien* to the ship builders, so that they can see what happens to their good work once the ships are fully rigged and armed. She was completed a year ago, and most of these people would never have stepped on board an active ship of the line, so they will see it as an honour. All we have to do is join the throng, most of who will have drunk too much to be suspicious. Once again, Mr Cleaver, try not to speak to anyone.'

The two men boldly walked forward, and merged with the noisy groups that were by now being shepherded towards the wooden roped walkway leading up onto the moored ship. At the foot of the walkway, the groups were brought to a halt ceremoniously, the little man, having ascended a few steps so he could be seen by all, began to speak:.

'Gentlemen. Gentlemen, please. It is with great pleasure that I now lead you on board the world's finest ship of the line. This ship was made possible by your hard work, and the efforts of people like you, working for the security of our wonderful country. As you walk around this magnificent vessel, feel proud in knowing that you have played your part in the inevitable defeat of our English enemy. Gentlemen, welcome aboard the *De Zeven Provincien*.' At this, a great cheer rose from the crowd, followed by the sound of their noisy banter and shuffling feet as they made their way up onto the deck.

Thaddeus was conscious that he still clutched the wooden writing case, having not had an opportunity to stow it, and its contents, safely away, but it did not seem to draw attention from the crowd. They were led along the gun decks, where the gun crews stood proudly to attention by their gleaming cannon. Thaddeus counted 12 thirty-six pounders and 16 twenty-four pounders on the lower deck. Some of the ship builders, the worse for drink, tried to joke with the sailors, but were met with disciplined stoney faces, and were ushered along by escorting marines. On the upper deck, Thaddeus counted 14 eighteen pounders and 12 twelve pounders, information that would be well received back in England. As they were guided around the poop deck, forecastle and quarterdeck, he made a note of a further 26 six pounders. He had by now, not trusting his memory, started to log this information, by scratching it into the polished wooden surface on the side of the writing case with the edge of a silver button that was attached to his jacket, Roman numerals for the quantity, and Arabic numbers for the poundage.

De Graaf had started up a conversation with one of the ship builders, and had told him that he and

Thaddeus were admiralty clerks. The man very proudly began talking quite openly about the structure of this class of ship, telling them that it weighed some sixteen hundred tons, and how it only had a draft of fifteen feet, enabling it to come closer to the shoreline for land bombardment. He also told them that he believed it needed some four hundred and twenty men to crew the ship. Thaddeus tried as discreetly as possible to log this information as they continued their tour, but unfortunately, his actions had caught the eye of a nervous looking naval officer, who seemed very uncomfortable at the fact that civilians were swarming all over his ship.

'That man there, you, sir, what are you doing?' The navel officer gestured towards Thaddeus who was busily scratching numbers onto the writing case. De Graaf quickly interceded.

'We are admiralty clerks, sir, just enjoying seeing the things that we write about every day. You have a wonderful ship, sir.' The navel officer ignored De Graaf's attempt at diversion, and walked over to stand square on to Thaddeus.

'I know you, but not as a clerk. Where have we met, sir?' Thaddeus pursed his lips and shook his head to imply he had no idea; he was trying hard not to have to speak to the man.

'Frederik Evertsen. That's it. I met you at the house of the shipping company owner some years ago. I remember him well because he had a beautiful daughter, what was her name? Tell me, man, what was your business there?' Thaddeus's eyes were now flicking around the deck trying to pre-empt a hasty escape. He observed that De Graaf had fallen back obviously realising that their masquerade had been seen through, and he was now melting into the crowd.

'I was his bodyguard at that time' Thaddeus heard his own words and his heart sank as he knew that his pronunciation and underlying English accent would now expose him completely.

'You were the girl's husband. It's all coming back to me now. You are English, a soldier. You are no admiralty clerk, you are a spy.' Before the man could say another word, Thaddeus barged passed him, but ran straight into two burly marines who grabbed his arms and stopped him in his tracks. 'Get him off this ship before Admiral de Ruyter arrives. Take him to the harbour brig. I will attend to his fate later.' Thaddeus knew it was pointless to struggle, and instead yielded to the pushing of the marines as they guided him through the assembled group of amazed shipbuilders, out onto the main deck.

The wooden walkway leading back down to the quayside was crowded with rowdy shipbuilders, who having seen enough, and with no chance of more liquid refreshment on board, were hastily leaving the ship, no doubt to find a local tavern where they could finish off the day. As Thaddeus and his escort approached the walkway, a second group cut in front of them, eager to disembark, and Thaddeus saw this as his opportunity to break free. He thrust back his elbows into the stomachs of the marines, and threw himself forward into the crowd, pushing himself deeper and deeper into the unruly hoard. He was now at the head of the walkway, and the surprised marines were now roughly pulling the shipbuilders aside to follow him. But his surprise escape had gained him too much of a lead on them, as obscured from their view, he barged his way down the wooden structure and onto the quayside, where after running across the width of the quay, he slid in to the nearest alley and made good his escape.

26 FUGITIVE

Amsterdam - May 1666

The sound of seven pairs of studded leather boots, marching in time over cobbles, sounded like the crisp beating of a military snare drum. The six pike men marched at speed, side by side in pairs behind their officer. Their bell shaped armour swayed back and forth, rubbing against their grey coarse breeches as the white plumes on their domed steel brimmed helmets fluttered in the morning breeze. The sound of their progress resounded down the street, to act as a fanfare to their arrival.

'Quickly, in there.' With the secret panel beside the fireplace open, the light from the window flooded into the small hiding place, highlighting a high step, up to what was no more than a deep stone white washed shelf. There was room enough for a man to sit upright with his knees brought up to his chest, and wide enough for him to lie down in a similar position. The panel was now hastily being closed, leaving only a sliver of light from a paper-thin gap left at the top.

The officer banged impatiently on the door of the smart merchant's house with the pommel of his sword, and continued to do so until a startled maid opened it.

'Where is your master?' Before the girl could reply, Johan Evertsen appeared from a side room and addressed the officer.

'What is the meaning of this? By what authority do you disturb the peace of my household?' The officer forced his way inside, followed by the pike men, who were forced to lower their weapons to facilitate entry.

'By the authority of the State. Search this house from top to bottom, he has to be here somewhere.' The body of pike men divided like an amoeba, and flowed into the side rooms, re-emerging quickly to noisily ascend the stairs, and continue their search of the rest of the house.

'I demand that you tell me what is going on.' Johan's face was flushing red with anger as he confronted the officer, who continued to act as if the protesting man was invisible. 'Whom do you seek? For the love of God, man?'

'You open your home to Englishmen, Mr Evertsen, then you cannot expect us to enter with the courtesy of invited dinner guests. These are troubled times and your activities are now under scrutiny. Good day to you, sir.' At that, the officer gestured to his men, and strutted out of the door followed one by one by the armoured soldiers. Outside the men assembled in formation in front of their officer. 'Attention. The English spy must be captured at all costs. We will return to the harbour side from where he made his escape and search every inn, brothel and alley until we find him.' At the prospect of visiting these potential hiding places the pike men grinned and smirked at each other until the officer, glaring at them, gave the order and they marched away.

Back in the house, the panel door slowly opened, and the light momentarily hurt the eyes of the man that had been hiding within.

'You can't stay here. My home will now be watched, I am sure of it. I have tried to help you to the utmost of my ability, but you have gone too far. You now endanger not only yourself, but me also. I have worked too hard to lose it all now.' Johan was visibly shaken as he offered a hand to extricate the incarcerated fugitive from his hiding place.

'Never forget, Evertsen, that I am, and always will be, a powerful man. I reward my friends and smite my enemies, and you must now choose amongst which you wish to be counted.' Richard Valletort stared hard at Johan who would not meet his gaze, and seemed to visibly crumble.

'I am loyal to you, and put much value upon our friendship, but the girls, Mr Valletort, the girls. If I am to keep my sanity I cannot keep bringing these poor wretches to you here in my house. I have not been a good man. I have sated my carnal appetite on the unwilling on many occasions, but all have lived. You pluck the very life from them, showing no more concern than if one would de-stone a cherry.'

It was two months earlier that Johan Evertsen had returned home unannounced from business in England. He hoped that Richard Valletort had been discreet whilst using his house, and had not drawn attention to his presence there. But he was totally unprepared for the spectacle that greeted him, as tired from the sea crossing he entered his own bedchamber. Valletort, naked, his torso smeared with blood, knelt over the mutilated body of a girl. He turned his head abruptly towards Johan as he entered, revealing his wide-eyed frenzied face, the lower half of which, like a child caught gorging from a jam pot, glistened with sticky blood from the still warm heart that he was voraciously consuming. Johan was struck speechless, and fought to control a wave of nausea that rose from the pit of his stomach. Valletort stood up, and grabbing the dumbstruck man's upper lip between his thumb and forefinger twisted it, pulling him down towards the china white face of the dead girl.

'She is yet another temptress, Evertsen. This daughter of Eve under the pretence of serving us, entices men with rich and wonderful delights, wearing us down, until finally, we have no resistance and succumb to her charms as did Adam. But I have the knowledge, the power to take her still beating heart, this true fruit from the tree of life, which will give me the lifespan of Adam himself.' As he spoke Valletort dipped the index finger of his free hand into the girl's blood, and traced upon her forehead the numbers nine, three, zero. 'Time enough for me to become all-powerful, Evertsen. Don't you think?' Releasing Johan's lip, he pushed the man's face, projecting him backwards onto the floor, where afraid to move, he watched as Valletort picked up an apple and pressed it into the girl's open chest.

'Here I return the forbidden fruit, Evertsen. In itself it has no power, it was purely the instrument of a test from God, and the reason we have but so little time to realise our dreams. Once again I have performed my duty, and as long as I do so, I inherit Adam's span. What could you achieve in nine hundred and thirty years. For you, just an opportunity to eat and drink the world dry I would hazard, but for me, as I believe, an opportunity to wait, learn and grow; to become the rightful supreme omnipotent ruler of my country, and even beyond. Now clean this mess up, dispose of this carcass, and when the need next arises, be prepared to furnish me with more of the same so that I may fulfil my destiny.'

Since that time, Johan Evertsen had been forced to entice serving girls from the society chocolate houses at the whim of Richard Valletort. Occasionally they would be lured back to his home, a practice he desperately tried to discourage, or more often, plucked from the streets as they left work, and butchered on the floor of his carriage. Johan often tried to understand the power that this man had over him. Initially he saw him as a means to an end, a conduit for his own ambitions, but now it was something more. This man who could be so charming, and exude a benign magnetism, could within a moment induce fear deep into Johan's very soul, a fear that he had never before experienced or dreamed possible. Now, as the sound of the pike men's boots grew faint as they marched away from the house, Johan knew the additional fear of potentially being exposed as an accomplice. Somehow he had to encourage Valletort to return to England.

Knowing that the military would be looking for a man alone, Thaddeus had paid for the company of a street girl, who although she would never pass for a lady, did with her cloak pulled around her, look relatively respectable. Walking at a normal pace, heads up and trying to appear as inconspicuous as possible, the pair walked slowly alongside the Herengracht canal until they approached the home of Johan Evertsen. Thaddeus holding the girl's arm in a gentlemanly fashion, stepped up to the front door, and hammered the large brass lion's head knocker twice onto its plate. After what seemed an age, the maid opened the door.

She immediately recognised Thaddeus as the husband of Catharina, and beckoned him enter, which after paying off and dismissing the street girl, he did.

'Thank you, Lena, it is good to see you again. Is your master home?' The woman confirmed that he was and led Thaddeus to a well-furnished study to wait while she fetched him. Within minutes the door opened, and a very surprised looking Johan entered.

'Cleaver, what in God's name are you doing here?' Feeling somewhat diminished by his ship inspector disguise, and still clutching the wooden writing case, Thaddeus stood up from the comfortable armchair in which he had been seated to address this contemptible man.

'Once again I need your help, Evertsen. This time not for me personally, but for my country, a country to which I know you hold some allegiance, if not due to your Orange loyalties, then to your purse. I need passage immediately back to England.'

'But what are you doing here in Amsterdam, dressed as a scribe?'

'A long story, but all you need know is that I have important information to get back to London, and I need to leave tonight if possible. Can you arrange that?' Johan looked thoughtful for a moment.

'Wait here, I will be back shortly.' With that he turned, opened the door, and left the room, leaving Thaddeus alone with an opportunity to transpose the information scratched on the wooden writing case to a piece of paper within it.

A short time passed before the door to the study was opened, and Johan re-entered the room. But this time, he was closely followed by Richard Valletort.

'Valletort, what are you doing here? Rumour had it that you were seriously ill, being nursed in secret somewhere in England.'

'As you can see, Mr Cleaver I am in good health, and enjoying the hospitality of our mutual friend, Mr Evertsen. You seem genuinely surprised to see me. You see, after our last meeting, I was under the impression that you had the intention of pursuing me, with a view to convicting me of heinous crimes, of which I am totally innocent.'

'Proof, Mr Valletort, or should I say lack of, made my superiors assign me to other tasks. However, since you decided to vanish from London society, there have been no more occurrences of chocolate girl murders. Strange don't you think?' Johan's eyes flicked involuntarily towards Valletort, an action that didn't go unnoticed by Thaddeus.

'Coincidence: pure coincidence, my dear Cleaver. My business here is of national importance. And excuse me for saying, but not for divulgence to one of your lowly status. I will say however, that it necessitated me to appear to be in England. And, as a man cannot be in two places at the same time, on my behalf by subterfuge, a rumour was spread of my apparent ill health. And you, Mr Cleaver, why are you now in the country of our enemy? Should I now be suspicious of you? I know that through marriage you have sympathies with the Dutch, do you not?'

'My sympathies are, and will always be, with England. I know you have connections in high places therefore I am confident in telling you that I have strategic information vital to the defence of our nation, and I must get it back to England immediately.' Johan was visibly becoming more and more agitated as Valletort replied.

'I am sure, Mr Cleaver that our good friend Evertsen can arrange such passage for you. Isn't that so, Evertsen?' Johan's anxieties were being made worse by the outwardly calm nature of the other two men as they exchanged words. His face had become flushed, and he continually mopped his brow with a large handkerchief.

'You must both go, tonight. I will arrange passage immediately. I can have you in my house no longer, Mr Valletort. All that I have worked for is now at risk. The military will be back I am sure of it. Both of you are drawing unwanted attention upon me. You, Cleaver for your damn patriotism, and you, sir, as much as I fear and respect you...' Johan bit his lower lip and looked to the floor. 'And you, sir, for the girls, those wretched girls. They will soon be traced here, to my house.' As soon as the words left his mouth Johan realised what he had said. Thaddeus's eyes shot from Johan, to meet the eyes of Valletort.

'Girls? You mean you have continued your vile practices here. So I was right after all.' Thaddeus's right hand instinctively crossed his body to grab at his sword but he had forgotten that as part of his disguise he was not wearing it. Valletort seizing the moment drew his, and held its tip at Thaddeus's throat.

'Evertsen, you are a fool. Your loose tongue has brought about the need for our noble, Mr Cleaver to die. A pity, as I really like you, Cleaver, you seem to have honour. But rest assured I will ensure that the one you love the most is well taken care of.' Thaddeus was powerless to respond, and stood stock still, as the sharp point of the sword, pressed lightly against his flesh, brought forth a small trickle of blood. Valletort's eyes widened, and his face took on a manic appearance as he continued to speak:

'You, I have observed, have your own little chocolate girl, and now since the untimely death of Lydia Fitz-Herbert, I am in need of a consort. Your lady will, once she understands the benefits of longevity, take her place by my side, and enjoy my power and protection. You see, beneath her demure and innocent façade, she is a temptress. Ultimately she is a chocolate girl, she serves, and Mr Eversten here knows my opinion on that.' Johan had slowly been edging himself to a position to the side and slightly behind Thaddeus, and had surreptitiously picked up a silver candlestick. Without warning he raised the hand holding it, and brought it down heavily against the side of Thaddeus's head. Thaddeus dropped to his knees, then toppled over to lie face down on the floor, unconscious.

'In the name of God forgive me, Mr Valletort, but I will see no more murder here. Not for love of Cleaver you understand, but for fear of discovery, the risks are now too great. I will keep him here until you are safely at sea, bound for England. Please help me tie him and I will then get you to a ship. If you stay in this country any longer you will be exposed.'

27 THE RETURN

London-Early June 1666

The initial reaction of panic had passed. Now calm, noises and smells filtered through the thick material of the cloak that had been used as a makeshift hood. The sensation of movement, and the sound of horse's hooves, confirmed that the hard floor beneath was within a carriage, bumping over cobbled streets. Every so often, the shouts and laughter of people hurrying home to their beds could be heard, their voices no doubt amplified by gin and ale consumed in the taverns that they were leaving. She had been grabbed from behind, and lifted into the air as the cloak was thrown over her head and hastily tied around her body, inducing a rush of adrenalin that had heightened her senses. Her instinct for survival had now replaced her fear, making her slow down her breathing and relax her body. This enabled her to best use the oxygen diffusing into the now uncomfortably warm and moist small space created by the fabric around her head.

Occasionally the carriage would slow down, and then feel as if it was turning. She could also sense the silent presence of someone sitting above her. Finally the carriage came to a halt, and she heard the driver jump down from his seat and take a few steps before hearing what sounded like two heavy gates being swung open. The carriage leaned slightly at the driver's weight, as he pulled himself back up into his seat before whipping up the horses to presumably pass through the gates. It then abruptly came to a halt. The smell of horses was now much stronger than before, and pervaded the interior of the carriage as the door was opened. Someone on the ground grabbed her feet, as from behind her, the passenger took her arms, between them lifting her out where they stood her upright. Someone then placed an arm behind her knees and scooped her up into their arms like a child before carrying her inside.

Her heart was now racing as she was placed in a chair, and she felt the binding around the cloak being untied. Her anxiety had returned, but she was too afraid now to struggle, and sat there finding it difficult, other than in short irregular gasps, to breathe. The heavy garment was then gently, and somewhat ceremoniously, lifted from her head, like the unveiling of a work of art. It took a few moments for her eyes to adjust from the total blackness of the makeshift hood to the dim yellow light emitting from a single candle, and the glow from a small fire positioned to one side of the room, burning low in a grate. As they did, she could make out the figure of a man leaving through the doorway, and another standing with his back to her a few feet away. Slowly the figure turned, and went down onto his haunches in front of her.

'I can only apologise, Lizzie, for the manner in which I had to bring you here. I hope you will forgive me.' Lizzie Jephson was speechless, as she gazed into the steely blue eyes of Richard Valletort, the man that had previously been so kind to her. Although now slightly reassured by this familiar, and up until now, friendly face, Lizzie was confused by the circumstances that had reunited them. Missing Thaddeus immensely she had continued to work at *Le Puits de Chocolat*, and had felt more secure in doing so since the cessation of the murders in London. With Thaddeus not around to escort her home, the duty had fallen to her father, but that night he was delayed by a last minute awkward customer at the boot maker's. Having left the chocolate house, Lizzie had been on the street for less than a minute before she was taken.

'Firstly, Lizzie, there is no need for you to be afraid. Come, sit over here by the fire with me and take a glass of wine.' Valletort raised her from the chair by her hand and led her across the room to a rustically made settle next to the grate. In front of it was a small table, on which was placed a jug of wine and two heavy glasses. He sat Lizzie down and proceeded to pour the wine before sitting down beside her.

'I don't understand, Mr Valletort. Why have you brought me here? Where is this place?' Lizzie looked around at the room. Its furnishings had seen better days, and although not small, it had more the appearance of commercial premises than a home. A large desk in one corner was piled high with dusty ledgers, and on the floor in a corner, was a pile of leather tack, not of a kind used by gentlemen for riding, but more associated with carriage livery.

'All will become clear, Lizzie, all will become clear. Firstly, this is my home. Not what you would have expected of me I'm sure, but my home for all that.' Having drunk deeply, the initial glow from the wine was surging through her body and had started to relax her. But she could not contain her surprise.

'But, Mr Valletort, you are a gentleman. I had imagined you living in a big fashionable house.'

'Once upon a time, Lizzie, but circumstances

brought me to this. Mainly having a father with an appetite for both gambling and avaricious women meant that I had no inheritance other than his debts. I salvaged this livery business from what remained of his estate, and the money I have made by my own efforts and connections has been enough for me to outwardly maintain the appearance of a gentleman. But that is to change, Lizzie, and that is why you are here. I believe that you have the qualities necessary to be my consort. Together we can achieve power, such that in time, with you by my side, we will have riches beyond your imagination. You, Lizzie, could be a queen. We will live ten fold the lives of mortal men, and all you need to do, Lizzie, is trust me, obey me and be true to me.'

'But I am to marry Thaddeus, Mr Valletort. He is a good man and I love him.' Valletort took a slow deep breath and gazed towards the fire.

'I hate having to be the one to tell you, Lizzie, but Thaddeus is dead.' Lizzie dropped her glass and slumped back in the settle. She suddenly felt cold, and a pain filled her throat so that it felt as if it would burst. Unable to speak she raised her tear filled eyes towards Valletort.

'He died in Amsterdam. Serving his country. You should be proud of him, he was a good soldier. I promised him that I would take care of you, and he was comforted that I should do so.' Lizzie started to find her voice.

'How, Mr Valletort? How?'

'He was, I understand, gathering information that could help us to win this war. Sadly he was discovered, shot and left for dead. I happened upon him at the quayside where I found a mutual friend tending to him. I was with him at the end. So you see, Lizzie, I had to bring you here to carry out Thaddeus's wishes. I could not tell you in front of your parents as I am also undertaking important work for the King, and need, for the time being, to keep my whereabouts in this country a secret. It is important that no one knows that you are here. Your connection to Thaddeus could put you in danger from our country's enemies. It is complicated, Lizzie, so please do not press me for further explanation; just be assured that I will care for you from now on.'

Valletort sat down beside her and placed an arm around her shoulders as she began to sob, burying her face in his chest as he softly stroked and kissed her hair.

Richard Valletort had become both the master of seduction and abduction. It was therefore a simple task for him, the next day, to pluck from the street yet another chocolate girl as she left work at *Le Puits de Chocolat*. Katy Tyler recognised Valletort from his earlier visits to the establishment, and felt flattered that this charming man should stop his coach for her, and honour her with the opportunity to serve that evening, at a private soiree for himself and a lady friend. She paid no attention to the route of their journey, as all she could see, was the handsome face of the man that had become legend amongst her co-workers, the object of their youthful fantasies. Katy could not believe that this man had chosen her from all the others to serve him, and coyly asked after his health, as rumour was that he had left the city to recover from an illness.

Two hours earlier Valletort had encouraged Lizzie to imbibe a spiced concoction, telling her that it would help to calm her, and ease the pain she was feeling at the loss of Thaddeus. Reluctantly she agreed, but was initially unsure of the taste, which although new to her, somehow had an essence of things familiar, a taste and aroma that vaguely brought to mind *Le Puits de Chocolat*.

'What *is* this, sir?'

'Firstly, Lizzie, you are to call me Richard. The drink? Well, surely you recognise the aroma of some of its components. They were sold to me at great cost some time ago by Monsieur Coultier, I swear the man is amongst the richest in London. The overriding flavour is nutmeg, Lizzie. Drink it all so that you may benefit from its calming medicinal qualities.' She took her time, but eventually emptied the glass.

'I must go out shortly, but I would like you to put on the clothes that I have laid out for you in your room, upstairs. I know that you did not sleep well last night, but I hope not from lack of comfort in your new surroundings. I assure you that upon my return, your life will take on new meaning.'

Katy Tyler turned her head as the mute driver opened the carriage door. He was an unfriendly looking man, who with furtive eyes, never once looked directly at her. His hands felt clammy as they took hers to assist her descent to the straw covered courtyard. It was early evening, and having been working since seven o'clock that morning she was very tired, but the prospect of a few more hours serving the handsome Mr Valletort helped to maintain her smile. She was slightly confused by her surroundings as she had expected that the soiree would be in a big house. Maybe this stable yard was purely an entrance for servants.

'Follow me, young lady, and I'll show you where everything is.' Valletort led the way, not into the domestic quarters, but into the stable block through the already part opened high double doors.

'I'm sure that this wasn't what you were expecting, but my soiree is somewhat fanciful, and a surprise for my lady guest. I wanted her to feel like a queen, and as I do not live in a palace, I thought that I would treat her as royalty in our own Garden of Eden. Clever don't you think?'

The girl looked around her at the bales of straw that had been laid out in a circle, in the fashion of a miniature arena. At one end, more bales had been stacked to form a raised dais, upon which had been placed a heavy chair, draped in green cloth, giving it the appearance of a throne. In the centre of the straw arena, four bales had been pushed together to create a crude table, over which had been thrown a large white cloth. On top of the bales creating the arena, flowers had been strewn, giving the whole tableaux the air of an ancient Greek play.

'Oh it's beautiful, Mr Valletort. It's like a dream, your lady will love it. Am I to serve at the straw table?' Valletort smiled at the girl.

'Just so, Katy, Just so. Now you will find in that empty stall an apron and cap, together with a flask of wine and two glasses. In a moment I will lead my guest through, and when I clap my hands I would like you to come out and enter the arena through this gap in the straw and set the wine on the table. Is that clear?' The

girl nodded and made her way into the clean vacant
horse stall. She put on the cap and apron, and sat on
the stool that had been provided, next to a second,
upon which lay a pewter tray holding the wine and
glasses. She could see the raised dais through a gap in
the wall of the wooden stall, and felt quite excited at
the prospect of being part of the surprise that was to
play out for Valletort's guest.

Lizzie was in an emotional turmoil. The heartbreak
she was feeling at the news of Thaddeus's death had in
itself put her into a subdued state, and now, the effects
of the nutmeg were adding to her state of confusion.
After Valletort had left on his errand to fetch the
chocolate girl, Lizzie, as requested and as if by way of
duty to this man who had declared himself her
protector, had gone up to her room. She now stood
motionless, looking amazed at the beautiful gown that
he had laid out for her on the bed. She stroked the rich
fabric, and told herself that this was her wedding dress,
which she had to put on as Thaddeus was waiting.

Moments later Lizzie stood before the tall faded
mirror, and knew that Thaddeus would be pleased. She
had never in her life worn such a fine dress, but had
seen similar on the grand ladies that attended the
upper chambers at the chocolate house. The tight
bodice, decorated with fine lace, accentuated her tiny
waist, and a heavily brocaded floor length skirt swept
out fully over her hips from beneath it. The bodice
neckline was trimmed with deep lace, cut low on the
shoulders to show off her long white neck, and puffed
lace sleeves stopped at her elbows, giving elegance to
her delicate forearms and wrists. She felt as if she were

floating, and as if every movement she made had been slowed down tenfold.

Valletort entered the room, but all she could see was the smiling face of Thaddeus as a string of plain white pearls were fastened around her smooth, soft neck. Valletort then gently placed and tied a white carnival half mask over her face, before laying a garland of yellow corn marigolds and blue cornflowers upon her head. He then gently led her by the hand down the stairs, out into the courtyard, and into the stables. Once inside, he helped her up onto the dais, and sat her carefully in the chair before clapping his hands.

All Lizzie's eyes could see in her intoxicated state was Thaddeus, standing before her as he took a glass of wine from a tray held by a nymph. Thaddeus and the nymph appeared to dance in front of her, a writhing slow dance, during which a snake wrapped itself around the nymph's wrists, prompting her to sing a high pitched song, the words of which Lizzie could not understand. She found herself standing with Thaddeus by the side of the straw table upon which the nymph now lay, as they both tried to free her from a flock of wild birds that covered her body. They both grabbed at the flapping birds, pulling them away until the nymph now free of them, lay naked.

Thaddeus was guiding Lizzie's hands to touch the nymph, urging her to comfort the girl by caressing her. She was aware that the birds were now covering her and Thaddeus, and they frantically began pulling them from each other. All three now lay naked on the straw table, free of the birds, kissing and touching each other at Thaddeus's direction. Lizzie touched his muscular back as he mounted the nymph, then, he was gone. In his place was Richard Valletort, his eyes raised in his head as he thrust himself, again and again into the naked nymph.

Lizzie's confused mind was being directed now by her base instincts. She was finding pleasure in the sensation of warm bodies against her skin, and she found her hands stroking hard muscle and probing soft pliant flesh. The singing beside her grew louder and louder as a serpent, as if charmed by the sound, coiled itself around the nymph's throat. She felt as if she was floating above the table and looking down, as Valletort, wielding a long knife appeared to hack into a sack of grain, the contents of which, instead of falling to the ground as white seeds, seemed to erupt, and then fall to the floor, twisting and turning like crimson ribbons.

Valletort, kneeling astride, thrust his hand into the sack, and pulled out a red rose, which having pulled apart, he began to feed to Lizzie as he consumed the rest. He then put into her hand a golden ball, which he made her place inside a red velvet lined casket, which had mysteriously appeared in place of the sack of grain. Her head was spinning, and the stable, now silent, was closing in and retreating as nausea eventually overwhelmed her, before she slid into welcome unconsciousness.

28 THE HUNTER

London Early June 1666

'Too little, too late, Cleaver. I'm not blaming you. We should have sent you over there much sooner, for now the damage is done. I received news yesterday that the English fleet, under my employer, the good General Monck, has lost ten ships in a four-day battle. Fortunately for us, De Ruyter, having broken our line many times, did not pursue us when we retreated. Had he done so our losses would be much greater. Can you believe, that having grounded the *Prince Royal*, Vice Admiral Ayscue surrendered? The man actually surrendered. We are of course claiming it as a victory for England, after all De Ruyter, by not pursuing us, in essence, did himself retreat. Anyway, the information you have given us is now confirmed to our cost, they outgun us, and can make good their losses far more quickly than can we.'

Thaddeus could hear the words being spoken by the General's aide, but he was not really listening; his mind was elsewhere. He had arrived back in England three days after Richard Valletort. Johan Evertsen, had, by knocking him unconscious, saved his life. And once he had arranged passage for Valletort that evening, he made the diplomatic decision to detain Thaddeus for two days before putting him onboard a slower vessel. This in his mind would demonstrate a continued loyalty to Valletort by giving him a head start, yet openly show his condemnation of the man, by allowing Thaddeus to sail to England to pursue him.

Once back in London, Thaddeus immediately made his way to the boot maker's shop, where he was devastated to learn from John and Martha, that Lizzie had disappeared. He knew immediately that Valletort had fulfiled his desire, and taken her. Yet not wishing to further distress her parents he did not tell them of Valletort's intentions.

The Generals aide and his two-man escort walked back towards their carriage, leaving Thaddeus and Captain Henderson alone on the quayside.

'I know it's no consolation, Cleaver, but you have done well. You have carried out all that was asked of you, and I can only imagine what you are now going through, knowing that your woman has been taken by this vile creature. Take some comfort from the fact that, as we have not discovered her body, then she is probably still alive. Unfortunately we have discovered the body of another poor wretch butchered in his twisted fashion, and we have identified her as another of the chocolate girls working at *Le Puits de Chocolat*. At least this time, we know who we are looking for. His admission to you in Amsterdam makes it easier for us to question those known to him. We will find him, Cleaver, rest assured.'

Thaddeus stood silent. He felt as if he had betrayed Lizzie by leaving. He had been her protector, yet his desire to be of use to his country had ultimately resulted in her being lost to him.

'I swear that I will hunt this evil bastard down, and when I find him, I will make no apology as to what I will do to him. With your permission sir, I will return now to the city to speak with all that have previously claimed this man a friend, and search under every roof that has ever given him shelter. I will find him sir, this plague upon our city, I will find him, and I will destroy him.'

Father Turnbull sat alongside Thaddeus in the front pew of the church of St Bride's. The two men stared fixedly ahead as they conversed.

'Thaddeus, I feel for you, I really do. I pray for Lizzie and the downfall of this animal, but in your place I would know not where to start. From what you say, the fox has gone to ground.' It was now late July, and Thaddeus had not been idle in his pursuit of Valletort.

'My starting point, Father has been to track down and arrest all that were known to associate with this man. I have interrogated them at length, including the Adamites Carlisle and Harper, and even Coultier, the French fantasy monger from the chocolate house. It seems that Valletort is known to everyone, yet remains a mystery to all. No one has ever been to his home, or knows even where that may be. As a man of high fashion and influence, he has successfully managed to create a wealthy powerful persona without one piece of substance to collaborate it. They do all, however, make mention of a servant, a carriage driver. No one has heard his name, but some suspect that he is a mute. Does that bring anyone to mind?'

'Not immediately, but I will check the parish records. If he is of local birth, some note may have been made in them of his infirmity. I will ask also of those working here at the church, most, unlike me, have been brought up in this neighbourhood. From what you say, Valletort has taken Lizzie, not to harm her, but for her to share his delusion of longevity and ultimate power. If this is true, then possibly, she may be observed out in his company should they be so bold as to walk abroad, unless he has her incarcerated.' Thaddeus turned to look at the priest.

'Lizzie would not comply willingly with this man's demands. She has a strong spirit and would defy him, which is my concern. If she were not easy to coerce, then at what point would he resort to harming her. Coultier reluctantly divulged, that he had sold his secret dream recipe, and its ingredients to Valletort. I fear that if he applies this to Lizzie, then she may not be able to help herself, and bend to his will. Father, I am afraid that this man will take her to the deepest depths of depravity, and should we manage to rescue her, she may not return as the woman we have known.' As Father Turnbull struggled to find words of reassurance, the heavy doors of the church noisily swung open, causing both men to turn their heads towards the stream of bright light now illuminating the isle.

'Mr Cleaver, Mr Cleaver sir. There's been another one.' The watchman screwed up his eyes to compensate for the comparative gloom of the church interior, and stood silhouetted in the doorway. Thaddeus rose from the pew, ashen faced and feeling nauseous, his heart pounding in his chest as he walked towards him.

'Do you know her? Who is she, man?'

'Its not your lady sir, but she is from where she works, someone knows this one as Katy Tyler from the chocolate house at Bishopsgate.' Thaddeus grabbed the back of a pew to support himself as the surge of relief made him feel unsteady on his feet.

'Where was she found?'

'Lower Thames Street sir. Just dumped in the road like the others. We've taken her to the watch house. Shall we get old Mary to look her over?'

'Yes, I'll follow you back there shortly.' The watchman turned on his heels and was gone, leaving the church to descend once again into its ethereal shadows as the doors gently slid shut behind him. Father Turnbull stood up and placed a hand upon Thaddeus's shoulder.

'Don't feel guilty about the joy that you feel at the news that someone else has the burden of grieving for this poor soul. Go to her, Thaddeus, and see if in death her body can speak to you, and maybe whisper through its condition, the whereabouts of Richard Valletort, and more importantly your good Lizzie.'

'Tell me, Mary, what have you found?' The old woman sat down upon a hard wooden chair, still wiping her hands on a grimy cloth as Thaddeus handed her a mug of gin.

'Same as all the others, Mr Cleaver. No different. The poor soul was taken advantage of and then robbed of her heart, only to have it replaced by an apple. When will it stop, Mr Cleaver?'

I don't know, Mary, but we must find something, anything at all that can lead us to this man.' The girl's body lay uncovered on a rough table in the watch house. Her eyes stared up at the ceiling unseeing, and one arm hung loosely from the table, pointing towards the floor. Thaddeus took the now stiffening limb, and brought it up to lay it by her side. As he did so he noticed that the dead girl's hand was bunched into a fist, as if clutching something. He forced her fingers apart, and there, in the palm of her hand, lay a small piece of straw.

'Look at this, Mary, tell me what you see?' The old woman stood up and made her way around the table to stand with Thaddeus, and gaze down at the girls now open palm.

'Straw, Mr Cleaver, it's just a piece of straw.'

'Would you agree, Mary, that this girl probably closed this hand as she was near to death, and therefore at the place of her murder?' The old woman looked up at him quizzically.

'I don't understand what you're getting at, Mr Cleaver.'

'I think, Mary, that this piece of straw comes from the place where the girl was murdered, and not from the place where she was found. If so, Mary, where would you find straw?' The old woman stroked her chin and looked again at the girl's hand.

'Animals, Mr Cleaver? Places that have animals?'

'Yes, Mary, animals, and I am thinking more specifically horses. It has been said that Valletort has been regularly seen with a carriage driver. This girl's body, and those of the others that we have found, appear to have been dropped onto the street from a height of a few feet or so. What if then, having been murdered in a stables, they were pushed from a carriage?'

'But you can't know that for sure, Mr Cleaver.'

'Not for sure, Mary, but it is a possibility, and I would rather be looking somewhere than just waiting around for the next body to appear. We need to be looking for stables.'

'And just how many stables do you think there are in London then, Cleaver?' Captain Henderson having entered the room stood by the door, shaking his head at the prospect of visiting every stable and carriage yard in the city.

'I know, sir, that we don't have the men, but a thought just occurred to me. There must be fewer feed merchants in the city than stables, and we know that a mute often drives the carriage that Valletort uses. We could start by visiting the merchants, and see if they know of such a man. Its better than doing nothing sir.'

'Three weeks, Cleaver. You have until the middle of August. This warm summer is making the criminal classes either lazy or content, so at present we are not overburdened with thievery. After that if you have made no progress, the magistrates will need to know why, as the people are starting to shake once more in their beds and talk again of the devil killer. Just get him Thaddeus, just get him.'

29 UNEARTHED

London – Mid August 1666.

'Eat my dear, eat.' Lizzie turned her head away sharply as Richard Valletort thrust a partially devoured heart towards her tightened lips. Her gown was blood splattered from the carnage that he had just reaped, and the smell of warm human flesh pervaded her nostrils as she tried not to vomit. This innocent victim had been taken from near a chocolate house close to London Bridge whilst on her way home from work. Valletort's grisly tally had grown since his return from Holland as he endevoured to coerce Lizzie into becoming his consort.

'In time, Lizzie, you will come to understand the gift that I bestow on you. You will appreciate me for giving you a lifespan known to no other woman. As others grow old, their beauty fading, you, Lizzie, will remain as you are now, perfect. You will grow in terms of knowledge, experience, and ultimately power. Together we will have it all. We will see the game reset every sixty or seventy years, new players, new challenges and fresh excitement. But best of all, Lizzie, the game will be played to our rules, yours and mine alone. But you must eat girl. You must join me in the ritual that makes our future possible. We must do this to achieve Adam's span.'

With eyes closed and head spinning Lizzie Jephson parted her lips at the touch of the warm offering. She felt Valletort's hand stroking her hair as her teeth bit into the human offal, and giving herself up to his diabolical influence she began to devour the heart, immediately realising that she would now be forever lost.

For some weeks Thaddeus, and a small group of his fellow watchmen, had been systematically visiting feed merchants on a list acquired from the guild of mercers. It was a slow laborious task, but one that he still believed would be quicker and more effective than visiting every stable and carriage yard in the city. As he rode into Tile Lane he could see straight away three carts being loaded with straw for delivery to various stables around London. Dismounting, he led his horse slowly towards the merchant's yard and made his way towards a raised deck upon which stood a stocky balding man in his mid fifties who was wearing, over his lace shirt and breeches, a course calico bibbed apron. The man stood behind a paper strewn rostrum like a preacher, but instead of evangelising, he barked out instructions to the men below, who with pitchforks, heaved large bales of straw up onto the waiting carts.

'Thirsty work on a day like today I'm thinking.' Thaddeus spoke in a friendly tone as he looked up at the man, but he did not appear in the mood for small talk.

'If you are buying straw I'm listening.' The man did not look up from his paperwork as he replied to Thaddeus, and then looked right past him as he continued to bellow orders to the loaders.

'I'm here on Magistrates business, so I'll be obliged if you would get down here and give me your full attention.' The man looked down at Thaddeus, gave a loud sniff and descended the four wooden steps to stand in front of him, brushing small pieces of thresh from his sleeves as he did so.

'So what do you want?'

'Information. I'm looking for a purchaser of straw, possibly for a stable or carriage yard.' The man began to smirk.

'You're in luck, I've got hundreds of 'em, take your pick.' Thaddeus was finding it hard to resist the temptation to punch the man.

'This one's special, he's a mute, drives a carriage for a gentleman. Ring any bells?'

'A mute you say. There is one. Don't know his name though, as he can't tell me, see.' The man began to laugh at his own joke. Thaddeus grabbed the man by the throat and pulled his face close to his own.

'I'm not a patient man, so unless you want to share his affliction, tell me where he can be found. Now.'

'All right, all right, just having a little joke. I think I know who you're after. He always pays in cash after miming out what he wants. I told you it was your lucky day, that's his cart on the end. He's gone into *The Crown* for a drink whilst we load it up.' Thaddeus looked towards the inn as he let go of the man's throat. ' We're nearly done. He should be out in a few minutes if you want a word with him. Mind you it will only be one way won't it.' Thaddeus shot the man a steely look, which made the merchant involuntarily take a step backwards.

'I don't want to talk to him; I need to follow him. So I will wait across the street for him to take his cart. Don't tip him off or I'll get you closed down. Do you understand?' The man sheepishly nodded as Thaddeus led his horse back up and across to the other side of the street where he stood patting its nose, patiently waiting for the mute to emerge.

Within a few minutes a grim sullen looking man, dressed as if he were in service, walked out into the street. He made his way across to the feed yard and began roughly signing to the merchant who, having had coins counted out into his hand, gestured towards the loaded cart. The merchant then looked across and gave a small nod to Thaddeus, who by now had been joined by two other members of the watch. The mute whipped up the carthorse and the loaded vehicle began to trundle along the cobbles, now being followed discreetly, at a distance, by the three men.

After a journey of some fifteen minutes or so, the cart pulled up outside a pair of large wooden gates. The mute jumped down from the cart and pulled them open, before proceeding to drive it through into a stable yard. One of the watchmen's horses was becoming skittish, and as the mute began to close the gates it reared and whinnied causing him to look in the direction of the noise, and in so doing observe the three riders. Immediately the gates were slammed shut and bolted, leaving Thaddeus to consider his next course of action. All access to the premises lay beyond those gates, therefore as far as he could tell, if he was in there, Valletort could not leave other than through this entrance.

Thaddeus rode his horse close up to the gates, and then proceeded to climb up onto the saddle, allowing him height enough to grab the top of one of them with both hands. He heaved himself up onto its edge, and then swinging his body over, dropped down the other side into the stable yard, where he unfastened the bolts allowing the two watchmen to join him. The noise of a door being flung open caused the three men to look to their left, where emerging from the stables, the mute began running towards the living quarters. Turning as he ran, he raised a pistol and fired at the watchman, dropping one of them to the ground mortally wounded. His companion returned fire, and hitting a doorframe, showered the mute with splinters as he ran into the house.

Thaddeus and the watchman gave chase. Once inside they could hear the man's footsteps on the landing at the top of the stairs. Although the mute would not have had enough time to reload his pistol, they had to be mindful that Valletort could also be in the house, and most likely armed, therefore they took great caution in climbing the stairs. As they neared the top, a heavy wooden chair came hurtling over the landing balustrade, bouncing off the wall of the staircase and knocking the watchman back down the stairs. The mute's face appeared over the balustrade followed by a heavy sword swishing through the air, narrowly missing Thaddeus's head. As he stepped back to avoid the blade, he stumbled over broken debris from the chair, his body twisting and falling backwards against the stair rail, which he managed to grab to save himself. The mute had begun to descend the stairs after him as Thaddeus aimed his pistol and fired. The man buckled at the knees clutching his stomach, before pitching forward and falling past Thaddeus onto the stone flagged floor below next to the dazed watchman.

Helping the watchman to his feet, he could see that the mute was dead. The man's actions had at least validated the fact that this was Valletort's hiding place, but where was he? They searched the house and found evidence of the fact that he had been living there. They also found a coif cap and apron that could have belonged to Lizzie. Thaddeus's stomach was now churning. He was so close to finding her, and all he wanted to do was hold her safely in his arms again, yet it appeared that Valletort had somehow made good his escape. He walked across the yard to the stable block, closely followed by the limping watchman. Inside his heart fell as he saw the straw arena, and at its centre the blood soaked bales forming a sacrificial table. The watchman stood propping himself up in the doorframe as Thaddeus searched each of the horse stalls, looking for the smallest sign that Lizzie was still alive. He fought back the tears as he walked towards the open door to stand beside his comrade.

'We were too late. But where in God's name has he run to? The cart is still here, as are the carriages in the yard, and none had horses within their traces. We would have heard him surely had he ridden out of the gates. Maybe he wasn't here to start with. I feel now that my only hope of finding Lizzie has gone forever.'

Richard Valletort held his hand tightly over Lizzie's mouth as he looked up at the trap door in the horse stall. The mute had served him well. He had closed the wooden hatch and covered the floor of the stall with fresh straw before the watchmen had come through the gates. Lizzie had stopped struggling now; she lay on the floor next to Valletort frozen by the horror of her most recent experiences. A small shaft of light coming down through the cracks at the door's edges, illuminated a band across the open, dead eyes of the mutilated chocolate girl, hastily thrown down into the small cellar, just before they themselves climbed down into it. Valletort could hear Thaddeus walking above them. He could hear him moving from stall to stall, and he was strangely excited by the prospect that at any moment he could be exposed, and would have to fight for his life. They lay in silence, yet not still. Every so often Lizzie's body would tense as a wave of activity flowed over her. Valletort himself could feel the sensation of something picking and pulling at his clothes. He felt life pulsing over his feet and along his legs. Occasionally it was as if he was being stroked, then it would stop momentarily, only to begin again. Then there were the tiny sounds, scurrying, sliding, scratching, and the recognisable squeaking... of rats.

Time passed slowly as Valletort and Lizzie lay entombed beneath the stable floor. At what point would it be safe for him to emerge and then effect an escape from the livery yard. He could occasionally hear voices above, and having heard pistol shots, he could only assume that the mute and maybe others were dead or injured. Possibly therefore bodies would need to be taken away. He imagined that Thaddeus would search the house, and that this would take time, but how long? He decided that he would wait at least until nightfall, the coming of which he would be able to gauge through the cracks in the trap door.

Although cooler than the atmosphere above, the air within the small dark cellar had now become stale and fetid. This was mainly due to the bloating corpse of the dead girl that Valletort was now regretting hiding in there with them. Lizzie had not spoken a word since being forced into the hiding place, and he now felt it safe to release his hold on her. Having let her go and shifting from the fixed position that his body had held for hours, he began to experience the aches and pains brought about by their confinement. He ventured up the wooden ladder, and cautiously raised the trap door, just enough to enable him to view the stable at floor level. Feeling confident that the watchmen had gone, he raised it fully and stepped up into the straw covered stall. The yard was devoid of life, save for the horse still within the traces of the hay cart. This would be their method of escape, but to where? Society by now would know of his crimes, and having no true friends or family there was no one that would readily take him in. The watch would surely have alerted all hostelries as to his presence, which meant that the obvious solution was to seek an unattended bolt hole somewhere, a bolt hole that would be the last place that anyone would ever think of when looking for them.

30 THE NEW RIVER

London –31st August 1666

The cart trundled noisily along the pitted road out of the city towards Saddlers Wells. Valletort had pulled off all but two bales of straw to lighten the vehicle, and had wrapped Lizzie in a blanket. She now sat beside him on the drivers seat looking blankly out onto the road ahead. He had had little time to gather much by way of belongings, a small hidden cache of coin, a few clothes wrapped in a sheet, and the mute's coarse cloak, which he now wore in an attempt to disguise himself. The pair attracted little attention at this early hour of the morning as trade and farm vehicles of this type were a common sight.

Very soon he could see the reservoir ponds at New River Head, and he drove the cart towards the manned pump house at its centre. He had visited the site before, as at certain times of the year it had become fashionable to walk there. The pump house door was unlocked, and leaving Lizzie on the cart he entered the keeper's quarters, surprising the man at his breakfast. Despite looking somewhat dishevelled from his time in the cellar, it was still obvious that Valletort was a gentleman, and the man rose from his table wiping his mouth with the back of his hand.

'You startled me, sir. How can I help you?' Valletort stood by the open door gesturing out towards the ponds.

'My carriage has broken a wheel, throwing me from it and injuring my driver. Can you help?' The man touched his forehead as he walked towards the door to see. As he approached, Valletort stepped in towards him and thrust a knife deep, up under the man's ribcage. Automatically his hand reached out and grabbed Valletort's shoulder, his expression seeming to question why as he fell to the floor. Having brought Lizzie inside, he wrapped and tied the man in the blanket that she had been wearing, before dragging him out and sliding his body into the reservoir.

This would be their sanctuary, it had food and a bed and no one passing would bother knocking on the door. The man he had killed was no more than a caretaker, and he wouldn't be missed for some time, giving Valletort time to think upon his future plans. He considered speaking with the King and concocting a story that mutual enemies had plotted against him, naming him for these crimes; by doing this, maybe he could obtain royal protection. However, he knew that to obtain an audience would involve dealing with others that would be quick to expose him before he could put his case. In the meantime he hoped that being out of the city would be enough to evade Thaddeus.

He sat beside Lizzie on the keeper's untidy bed, and held her right hand between his.

'I had hoped that in time you would have come to relish the life that I could give to you. Sadly you are not Lydia Fitz-Herbert, you have neither the appetite, passion or vision to appreciate its merits. You have beauty, Lizzie, that I will grant you, and in truth I took you in part to toy with Cleaver, but I will not give up on you just yet.' Lizzie had retreated more and more into herself with each tableau of horror that this deranged man had lain before her. She had rarely spoken during the past few days, and was fast losing focus on any aspects of normality that she could cling to.

'I have decided, Lizzie, that tomorrow, I will bring about the slow death of all that hunt me. I will bring an end to their already brief lives so that when they are gone, I can re-invent myself. I will put upon London such sickness and misery that its inhabitants will not give a moment's thought as to my existence, and when eventually the torment does subside, any vague memory that any survivors may have of my deeds, will be replaced by the images of the tortured faces of those that have died. You see, Lizzie, we are in a special place. From this reservoir, as if via thousands of wooden veins, water flows to every heart in London. At a stroke I have the power through one simple act to kill a city. But for now I must sleep, I have become uncommonly tired.'

Thaddeus stood transfixed by the open trap door. Looking into the cellar he could see by the light from his lantern the grey face of the dead chocolate girl, her lifeless eyes wide open as if looking back up at him. Once again a feeling of relief flowed over him; it was not Lizzie. He had returned early that morning to the livery yard to hunt for any small clue that may have given away the location of Richard Valletort. On entering the yard he was shocked to see that the hay cart had gone, and where it had stood, in disarray, lay hastily thrown hay bales. Walking into the stable his eyes were immediately drawn to the empty stall, and seeing the open trap door he realised that the man he hunted had been here beneath his feet all of the time, probably with Lizzie.

A few hours later, men from the watch reported back from every city gate, that most had that morning, had horse drawn carts pass through them. This of course was an everyday occurrence. Assuming that he had left the city, Thaddeus was still none the wiser as to which direction Valletort may have taken. On the other hand, had he remained within the city walls, where now would he seek refuge? Thaddeus now stood before the assembled watchmen.

'I want every inn, whorehouse and church searched. Any place that can offer a man, possibly with a woman, sanctuary, I want it taken apart. Cellars, lofts, any space that can hide a man, I want them scoured inch by inch. As you know Valletort made good his escape on a hay cart. Search the city, and any such vehicles found in yards or on the street, I want someone to claim ownership for it. If none come forward then I want everyone in the area interrogated as to who may have been seen near it, and their current whereabouts. Is all that understood?' The men acknowledged his orders and hurriedly left the watch house to carry them out. He realised that he was acting now in desperation, but activity was the only thing that could combat the gut churning anxiety that he was feeling, knowing that Lizzie was still in the hands of this man.

Richard Valletort had slept the rest of that day and right through to the following morning with Lizzie, slumped and still dazed, in a chair beside the bed on which he lay. It was a restless sleep, and when he finally awoke around 6:00am, he vomited over the side of the bed. Standing up he felt slightly unsteady on his feet, and his skin was clammy. Without speaking to Lizzie he opened the door of the pump house and stood deeply breathing the cool morning air. This seemed to clear the haziness in his head. Picking up a heavy sabre belonging to the caretaker he walked around to the back of the pump house to where the cart and its now un-harnessed horse were standing, and proceeded to mount the saddleless creature.

In a nearby field a herd of cows stood almost motionless, until they caught sight and sound of Valletort galloping towards them, whooping and waving the sabre above his head. The startled animals began to move as one as he herded them back towards the now open gate and onto the road next to the reservoir. From his mounted position he struck their flanks with the flat of the blade, pushing the frightened animals closer and closer to the water's edge where one by one, he slashed at them like a cavalryman on the battlefield, forcing them into the reservoir where systematically they were butchered. The bellowing cries of the terrified creatures filled the air as he opened up long bleeding tears in their bodies, spilling their organs like bucket slops into the cold water as he continued to hack off pieces of the animals heads as some, still living, floundered, splashing noisily in their death throes.

Valletort knew that it would not take long for the morning chill to give way to yet another blisteringly hot day, hastening the decay and putrification of the animal carcasses. Later he would investigate how to turn the pumps on, and by doing so, send this catalyst for disease flowing down the wooden pipes into the homes, shops, taverns, and breweries of the city of London.

Back inside the pump house he stood at the small table, head bowed, knuckles pressing into its scrubbed wooden surface. His exertions had released endorphins into his system masking temporarily the malaise that had fallen upon him when he first awoke. He ran his fingers through his tousled black hair and straightening them, ran his palm slowly down to the nape of his neck. As his hand followed around the contour of his jaw line, his thumb came to rest on a small lump. In panic he rushed to the keeper's washstand and hastily poured water from the jug into the large washing bowl. Lowering his face towards the water he looked at his reflection as he ran his fingers across his neck finally coming to rest at the small black bubo developing there. Even though he had spent much of the previous year outside of the city he had seen enough victims to be sure in his mind that this was without question the plague, but how? The city was now plague free and he knew none that currently bore signs of the disease, so how could he have fallen victim to this? He, Richard Valletort, the man who was to become all powerful and live nine hundred and thirty years. Had all of his research and rituals been in vain? It was not within his destiny that he should die like this.

He knew that there had been talk of many remedies, therefore it was obvious that one of these would save him. This was just a trivial annoyance in the scheme of things, but he knew that he had to act quickly. The city was some two miles away, and within it there was an apothecary that he had heard of, one that attended the rich and persons of influence. It was to him that Valletort must now go for a solution to his malady. But why waste the journey, this man of medicine would surely also be able to furnish him with strong toxins to add to the waters of the reservoir to guarantee their potency to crush his enemies.

Having waited for the cover of darkness, the horse was re-harnessed to the cart, and the compliant Lizzie, now wrapped in the keeper's old cloak, was made to sit by his side as he took the reins once again to begin the journey from the relevant peace and calm of Saddlers Wells into the late evening clamour of the city. They had no difficulty entering through the city gate, and drove unchallenged to Blackfriars where the apothecary practised. The smell of the river, saturated into the warm night air filled their nostrils, as music and raucous laughter from the alehouses did similarly their ears. Valletort, looking out for the sign of the apothecary, guided the cart along the dry dusty street, narrowly avoiding the staggering drunkards that would occasionally spill out into his path.

The carthorse was reined in underneath the guild sign of the pestle and mortar. The practitioner's shop stood in darkness, as due to the hour it was now closed and locked. Valletort looked up at the building for signs of life. Seeing none, he pulled Lizzie behind him into the alley beside the shop. It was narrow and dark, but a shaft of light emitting from a propped open doorway gave him hope of entry. Reaching the side door he cautiously pushed it further open until inside, he could see a young man standing upon a small step ladder, apparently taking count of stock, ferreting amongst the bottles and jars upon a high shelf.

Hearing the door open the youth turned sharply, almost losing his balance on the ladder, and missing his footing, he slid unceremoniously to the ground.

'Pray, sir, we are closed.' Embarrassed by his ungainly descent he stood flicking at imaginary dust on his shirtsleeves as he looked upon the intruders.

'But your door is open, I have forced no entry young man.' Valletort's superiority of rank and age flustered the youth.

'It is open for the heat, sir, or should I say, because of it. The nights have been unbearably hot of late, don't you think, sir?' Valletort grew impatient.

'Enough of this chit chat, I assume from your lack of years that you are not the apothecary.'

'No, sir, I am apprenticed to him. My master takes a late supper upstairs in his chambers.'

'Well go fetch him, boy; I have an urgent need of his services that has no respect for the hour. What are you waiting for? Off you go.'

The young man blushed as he nodded, and left through a door making his way hurriedly and noisily up a flight of stairs. There was a few moments silence, before much slower and heavier feet could be heard making the descent. The door re-opened and the elderly apothecary, looking angry at being disturbed, entered the room, followed closely by the anxious apprentice.

'What is your business, sir, that you drag me from my supper? As you have been told, we are closed.' Letting go of Lizzie's hand Valletort stepped up closely to the old man.

'My business is that of life. Or should I say, my life.' Pulling aside the neck of his shirt he turned his head slightly inviting the apothecary to view the bubo upon his skin. As he saw it the old man instinctively raised the palm of his hand to cover his nose and mouth.

'You have the plague, sir. Get away from us immediately; you must leave now.' Valletort grabbed the sleeve of the man's nightshirt.

'I am fully aware of my affliction, sir, hence the reason for my visit. I want you to cure me of it. That is what you do isn't it, or are you just a charlatan?' The old man grew visibly more agitated, and clawed away Valletort's hand. He then reached to his side, and opening a drawer in the large dresser, upon which his medicinal wares were displayed, he pulled out a long dagger, which he brandished menacingly at Valletort. Despite his weakened state, It was easy for the more youthful man, to deflect the old apothecary's hand away, and pulling the weapon from his grasp, spin the man around and hold its blade against his throat. At the sight of this, the young apprentice pushed his way past Lizzie and ran out into the alley and off down the street.

The apothecary ran his tongue over his dry lips and swallowed hard, as the touch of the cold blade against his skin froze him like a statue under Valletort's grip.

'Let us be calm, young man. There is no guaranteed cure for the plague. Some have been tried and failed, and others have been purely speculated upon.' Valletort wiped his free hand over the old man's forehead and slowly down the side of his face.

'Think harder, old man, as now you too have been touched by death; that is, unless you can furnish us both with a remedy from your vast stock of pills and potions.' The apothecary thought for a moment, his eyes darting from side to side in their sockets as if taking in the labels on the coloured jars, bottles and boxes neatly stacked on the shelves around the room.

'There is one possible solution. I have not practiced it myself but it is a theory put about by the most learned men in my profession. I do believe that it has been tried, but I know not to what success.' Valletort pressed the blade harder against the man's neck.

'Well don't waste time, what is it, man?'

'Mercury, sir. Mercury. As you may know, it has been proved beneficial against the pox. Therefore there are those that have theorised that because of its toxicity, it may well destroy the bad humours in the body that are caused by the plague.'

'And how should this be administered? Are we to drink it?' The old man gently placed his fingers on the blade of the knife and delicately began to pull the blade away from his skin.

'The substance is to be applied to the body, all over. Not an easy process for, as I'm sure you know, mercury is a liquid metal. It must be rolled over the skin; but to allow it to be absorbed, the body must be heated to a very high temperature opening the pores of the skin to their maximum.' Valletort pulled the man's head around to face him.

'How so?'

'Roasting, sir, your body must be subjected to the extremes of heat found only in an oven. Obviously not to death, but for as long as humanly possible, it is the only solution that I know.' Valletort pushed the old man away from him, and still clutching the dagger stood with his head bowed, one hand stroking his forehead. After a few moments he turned to the apothecary who had by now seated himself uncomfortably on the low stepladder.

'Do you have mercury? And, if so, how would you suggest I go about subjecting myself to being roasted?'

'Yes, sir, I have mercury in abundance, in that bottle, there. And as for roasting, you would need to locate a large oven, such as possibly a kiln in a brick makers yard. There are a few located somewhere in the city, and obviously you are used to gaining entry to premises closed to you.' Valletort ignored the slight, and instead questioned the man further.

'I firmly believe that I am not destined to die from this disease. So, for when my cure is accomplished, I need further assistance from you. Poison, sir, I need poison. Such that would not lose its potency when placed in say, a river, but would still be strong enough to kill all that drink from it. Can you concoct such a potion for me?' The apothecary looked aghast.

'Why would you need such a thing, there is evil in the very thought of it. No, sir, I will not.' The sound of a woman's voice made the old man turn his head towards the door where until now, Lizzie had stood in silence. She spoke, not directly at the man, but as if to an unseen object ahead of her on the floor that seemed to hold her gaze.

'It would be better that you should take your own life than furnish this devil with the means to destroy the city. I would pluck out my own eyes if it would erase the images of what this man has done in his madness.' A blow from the back of Valletort's hand knocked her to the floor.

'Uncork your bottles and mix me the potion I seek, old man. And don't try to trick me as I will try it first upon the girl, she has outlived her purpose.'

31 RETRIBUTION

London – 2nd September 1666

Thaddeus sat by the half open window in the watch house. It had just passed midnight and the stifling heat in the room foretold of yet another hot dry day to come. There had been no rain for weeks, and the night watch were being kept busy trying to keep the peace, as the heavy atmosphere was making the population irritable and brawls were frequently breaking out in taverns and on the streets, causing much concern to the city's magistrates. Father Turnbull, unable to sleep for the heat had joined Thaddeus, and as the two men enjoyed the remains of a jug of ale, Thaddeus's attention was drawn through the window to a young man that he could see running at full speed towards them. The door burst open and the young man ran inside, stopping breathless in front of the two men. He bent double to catch his breath, raising a hand to beg the men's pardon whilst he did so.

'Sir, you must come at once, my master is in grave danger.' The words were interspersed with panting as he struggled to speak.

'Catch your breath, lad. Here, have a sip of this.' Thaddeus handed him his half full mug of ale from which the young man took a long swig before coughing profusely. 'Now take your time. What endangers your master?'

'A man, sir. A gentleman. With a lady. He comes into the apothecary's shop and says he has the plague. Then he holds a knife against my master's throat, after which I know not what as I ran out into the street and came straight here to raise the alarm, sir. You must come at once.'

At the mention of a gentleman and a lady Thaddeus looked across at Father Turnbull who had already risen to his feet, and the three men proceeded to run out into the yard. Thaddeus hoisted the youth up onto Father Turnbull's already saddled horse and helped the cleric up behind him, before throwing a bridle over the head of his own mount and pulling himself up onto its unsaddled back. It was a short distance to Blackfriars, and the men were soon running up the alleyway alongside the shop to the still open doorway.

On entering the shop Thaddeus almost tripped over a hooded figure lying motionless on the floor. A surge of relief passed through his body as, lifting it to a sitting position he realised that it was Lizzie. She was alive. She stared towards him blankly, not making direct eye contact. Father Turnbull entering the shop behind him knelt down beside them both and took Lizzie's face in his hands. He looked into her dim eyes and at her expressionless face.

'Thaddeus, it is as you feared, I believe her mind has gone.' Thaddeus felt as if he had been kicked in the chest, and his throat tightened with emotion.

The sound of exploding glass rose up from a cellar, the door to which, now open, was beside the door to the upper chambers. He made his way halfway down the stairs into the apothecary's storeroom to see Richard Valletort and the old man standing beside a large smashed bottle, the contents of which now lay seeping between the cellar flagstones. The two men looked up in surprise at Thaddeus, the face of the old man showing relief and that of Valletort, hatred.

Drawing a pistol from beneath his cloak, Valletort pushed the apothecary to the ground, and taking aim fired. The shot hit Thaddeus in the thigh, bringing him tumbling down the stairs to lie in agony on the wet flagstones. Brandishing the discharged pistol, Valletort stepped over his fallen adversary and unsteadily climbed the stairs back up into the shop, where grabbing the large bottle of mercury, he forced his way past Father Turnbull and the terrified apprentice.

'Give me that broom'. Father Turnbull turned to see Thaddeus standing slumped in the cellar doorway, bleeding heavily from his leg wound. Without arguing he handed over the long handled besom, which Thaddeus proceed to use to support himself out into the alley in pursuit of Valletort. He could see the man ahead of him climbing up into the saddle of Father Turnbull's mount. The pain in Thaddeus's leg was excruciating as he hobbled towards him, trying in vain to pull him from the horse, only to feel the man's boot thud into his chest, knocking him to the ground.

Valletort, keeping the river to his right, rode at speed along upper Thames Street, peering into the darkness, trying in desperation to seek out the sign of a brick maker. If he were to survive he had to medicate himself as directed by the apothecary, as bizarre as the method seemed. It was his only hope as his strength was failing.

Within less than a mile he saw faint lights from a group of black and white wooden tiled houses occupied by citizens not yet within their beds. Turning left at these, he came into a street within which he was drawn immediately to a half lit timber framed shop. From it emanated the glorious smell of baking bread.

This would be his salvation. He slid exhausted from the horse and began to beat heavily upon the shop's closed door. Within moments a stout man wearing an apron streaked with flour opened it.

'In God's name, sir, what is it that you want this time of night? My family are abed, as will I be shortly after damping down my oven.' The man backed up into the shop as Valletort brandished the unloaded pistol.

'It is indeed your oven that I require. You must stoke the fire beneath it and bring it back to a good heat.' The baker looked afraid at the sight of the pistol and the manic expression on the night caller's face.

'What is it that I am to bake, sir, that requires it to be carried out at pistol point? Poached game, contraband of some description? Tell me that I may prepare my oven best.'

'It is me, sir. I need you to bake me.' The baker looked at Valletort open mouthed.

'I have no time for your questions, just clear out the oven so that I may slip inside it. Do not close me in, for I will be in there for the briefest of time. Just long enough for my skin to heat up enough to absorb this medication. Now find me a sheet, sir within which I may wrap myself.' The baker stepped into the back of the shop followed by Valletort. The man pulled from a pile of newly washed garments that were piled on the floor a rough linen sheet, and he held it out to the madman that stood before him. Valletort kicked off his shoes, undid his shirt and let fall his breeches, standing there looking ridiculous in just his hose. These he removed as he began the difficult task of rubbing his body from top to bottom with the ever-moving droplets of liquid metal.

Having completed this task to his satisfaction, he herded the baker back into the shop, and opening the warming oven door, he clumsily spread out the linen sheet within it, before, with the aid of a chair, he climbed up into it to be himself engulfed by its claustrophobic black confines.

The oven was already uncomfortably warm as the bemused baker, still fearing being shot, stoked up the fire beneath it. Valletort was covered in perspiration from both the fever he was experiencing and the oven's increasing heat. Within a few minutes the heat was almost unbearable. The linen sheet was beginning to turn brown and his flesh was searing where his shoulders and elbows touched the oven's sides. Valletort began to scream as the pain from the intense heat wracked his body. He began to shuffle his body feet first in agony towards the still open oven door, but the linen had now begun to adhere to his roasting flesh. As his upper thighs rested on the bottom edge of the oven doorway, the sheet burst into flames, engulfing his upper torso and setting his hair alight. Now, standing outside of the oven, he frantically pulled at the flaming material as pieces of it floated to the ground, setting alight the sawdust covering the shop floor.

Thaddeus had by now reined in his horse some twenty five yards or so up from the baker's shop, which was now spewing smoke from its door and windows. He had managed to mount his horse despite his leg wound and follow Valletort, at some distance, into this narrow street. Its houses, with their overhanging stories were now illuminated and animated by dancing shadows, as the flames now flickered through the roof of the burning building.

The shop door crashed open as the body of Richard Valletort, totally engulfed in flames, fell out onto the street. His screams mingled with the cracking sound of the burning timbers and the crashing of falling debris from inside the building.

Thaddeus dragged himself as close as he could to the burning body, and raising his pistol, fired his single shot into what he made out to be the man's head. The body fell to the ground like a stone, and the air had become filled with the sickening smell of burning flesh. Richard Valletort was now dead. A painful end, such as that he had inflicted upon his innocent victims.

The fire had now spread from the baker's shop, and the baker having escaped across the rooftop into the adjacent building, was endeavouring to muster help in trying to unsuccessfully get the fire under control. Thaddeus knew that he had to summon the watch to help with this task, but where exactly was he. He had followed Valletort blindly from Blackfriars into the very heart of the city. With one arm around his horse's neck to support himself, he limped his way to the corner of the street, where up on the side of a house was secured the street sign. Through gaps in the smoke, illuminated by the inferno behind him, Thaddeus Cleaver read the two words painted there. *'Pudding Lane.'*

AUTHOR'S NOTE

Pudding Lane

The city of London has been scene to many notable historic events, and even today in schools in the UK children are taught the facts surrounding the *Great Fire of London*. For fourteen years I performed theatre in education in Primary Schools around the country and the *Great Fire of London* was by far the most booked show.

Whilst researching the period and looking for interesting facts to impart to the young audience, I became fascinated by the times. It was inevitable then, that when considering a backdrop for my first novel that I should choose the period around the Great Fire.

History tells us that the *Great Fire of London* started in Mr Thomas Faryner's baker's shop in *Pudding Lane* on the 3rd of September 1666, probably due to embers falling from his oven onto a straw covered floor. The summer had seen a drought, and according to the diarist Samuel Pepys, a strong wind spread the flames very quickly, engulfing the mile by a mile and a half area that was then the *City of London*, and burning for five days.

The city was saved by the creation of fire breaks, with houses eventually being blown up with gunpowder to create the open spaces that would inhibit the spread of the flames. As a consequence of the fire, 13,200 houses were destroyed, making homeless over 100,000 people. Conflicting records show that miraculously, the death toll was only somewhere between 5 to 9 people. Taking into account that only the names of the rich were recorded in the bills of mortality, the death count was probably, in fact, much higher.

I decided to fictionalise the cause of the fire in *The Plague Hunter* and realise that many readers outside of the UK may have little or no knowledge of the significance of *Pudding Lane* in UK history.

I have written *The Plague Hunter* with an adult audience in mind as it contains mature themes. I hope that you enjoy the book and that it may inspire you to delve further into the fascinating period of UK history that is bracketed by the *Plague* and the *Great Fire of London*.

ABOUT THE AUTHOR

Having had a successful sales career in the telecommunications and IT industry, Bob Sanderson changed horses at the age of fifty two to become as he would say, 'Amongst other things,' a professional actor, musician, voice artist and video producer. He found himself writing scripts for business films as well as performing historical educational theatre. It was at this time that he became fascinated with the time period around the *Great Fire of London*, and having a creative mind, he chose this period in which to set *The Plague Hunter*, his first adult novel. Bob defines himself as a multi platform creative, moving between acting, producing, writing and playing music.

Printed in Great Britain
by Amazon